T0356363

# AN
# UNQUIET
# PEACE

Books by Shaina Steinberg

UNDER THE PAPER MOON

AN UNQUIET PEACE

Published by Kensington Publishing Corp.

# AN UNQUIET PEACE

### SHAINA STEINBERG

KENSINGTON
PUBLISHING CORP.
kensingtonbooks.com

KENSINGTON BOOKS are published by

Kensington Publishing Corp.
900 Third Ave.
New York, NY 10022

All Kensington titles, imprints, and distributed lines are available at special quantity discounts for bulk purchases for sales promotion, premiums, fund-raising, educational, or institutional use. Special book excerpts or customized printings can also be created to fit specific needs. For details, write or phone the office of the Kensington Special Sales Manager: Attn. Special Sales Department, Kensington Publishing Corp., 900 Third Ave., New York, NY 10022. Phone: 1-800-221-2647.

KENSINGTON and the K with book logo Reg. U.S. Pat. & TM Off.

Library of Congress Control Number: 2024951040

ISBN: 978-1-4967-4782-2
First Kensington Hardcover Edition: May 2025

ISBN: 978-1-4967-4783-9 (ebook)

10 9 8 7 6 5 4 3 2 1

Printed in the United States of America

The authorized representative in the EU for product safety and compliance
is eucomply OU, Parnu mnt 139b-14, Apt 123
Tallinn, Berlin 11317, hello@eucompliancepartner.com

In memory of my parents—

Michael Steinberg, who taught me to dream

and

Lynn Steinberg, who made those dreams possible.

# AN
# UNQUIET
# PEACE

# Chapter 1

*Los Angeles, 1948*

A simple truth of detective work is that stakeouts are profoundly boring. Nick Gallagher had trailed a man to an imposing mansion in Brentwood. Three hours later, Nick was still outside in his car with the windows rolled down. The ocean was four miles away and he caught a faint hint of salt in the air. Sometimes he wondered if he judged all locations by their distance to the water. There were worse measurements. Nick glanced impatiently at the door again. After spending years as a spy in the OSS, fighting with the French Resistance, and bringing down the Nazis, Nick felt wildly overqualified for the task of catching cheating husbands. He had no doubt his client's instincts about her husband's fidelity were correct. Several well-dressed men entered and left while Nick watched the door, which made him believe his quarry was visiting high-end prostitutes. Twisting his watch, Nick glanced down at the time and swore. He was late. Evelyn was going to kill him.

The Biltmore Hotel occupied a prime location in downtown Los Angeles across from Pershing Square. With fifteen hundred rooms, the interior was designed by the same man who worked on the White House and the Vatican. It was meant to impress and succeeded admirably. The last time Nick was here, he was thirteen. His best friend, Hildegard, thought this was the perfect place for Nick to learn how to pick pockets. Hildy was wearing a pale blue dress she liberated from a woman whose house she cleaned. Meanwhile, Nick's shirt and pants were stolen from an obliging clothesline. They were still damp, but they were also nicer than anything Nick had ever worn. He and Hildy looked like guests, so long as no one saw their shoes. Nick's were bursting at the seams, which was the impetus for this particular field trip.

The key to stealing in an upscale location, Hildy told him, was acting like they belonged. That meant no looking at security guards. No glancing toward the staff for approval. No fear of inconveniencing anyone. They simply had to move with the confidence of a person who had never been unwelcome. It was a concept Nick struggled to understand at the time but would prove invaluable during the war. Nick played a rebellious youngster and Hildy the frustrated older sister. They ran around the lobby, ricocheting off wealthy guests, each gathering more wallets, watches, and bracelets. The coup de grâce was when Hildy finally chased Nick outside. They each picked up a suitcase from the bellboy's cart and carried it down the street.

After pawning their ill-gotten gains, they ate well that night, treating themselves to steak before buying Nick a good pair of boots from a secondhand shop. Hildy, ever practical, insisted he purchase them two sizes too large so he would have room to grow. She even bought him a new pair of socks. That memory of a full stomach and comfortable feet stayed with him for years as one of the happiest days of his childhood.

Now, standing in the ballroom of the Biltmore as three hundred people swirled around him, drinking champagne,

Nick still felt like the boy pretending to belong. The difference was, he currently wore a tuxedo whose cost would have fed his family for months. This was not a place he ever imagined being welcome. Then again, he never imagined finding a woman like Evelyn Bishop. They met during the war, when she walked into his office at the OSS and announced herself to be the newest member of his team. At the time, he believed love was just something written on a greeting card. Now he knew better.

Across the room, Evelyn wore a sleek silver dress that drew the light. Her dark hair reflected the illumination of the chandeliers and her green eyes did not miss a thing. More than her clothes or even her beauty, it was her confidence that made her stand out. Nick always described her as inevitable, as if the world had spent the past thousand years waiting for her arrival. Nick watched her, a smile on his face. It was impossible not to feel joy in her presence, even when she was incandescently angry at him . . . a state that happened more often than he'd like to admit. If he was being fully honest, eighty-seven percent of the time it was his own fault. Like now.

Spotting Nick, Evelyn raised her wrist and tapped the place where a sapphire bracelet replaced her usual watch. Nick would go to the ends of the earth for Evelyn. He would fight Nazis and Communists and even spiders for her, but he was not wading into the morass that was Los Angeles high society. With a wave and a smile, Nick turned away and headed toward the bar, steadfastly avoiding Evelyn's glare.

"Scotch, please," he asked the bartender, who set a heavy-bottomed crystal glass in front of him.

"You should know better than to leave a man behind," said a deep voice from over his shoulder.

Nick turned to see Carl Santos, the third member of their team from the OSS and Nick's closest friend. Carl was a tall man with broad shoulders, dark hair, and an intimidating presence that served him well in the FBI. He rarely smiled, but when he did, it lit up his face. His innate kindness and intelligence shone through his eyes.

"Evelyn's tough. She'll be okay," Nick replied. "Besides, you're pretty much the only other person I know here."

"Isn't this your engagement party?" Carl asked.

"Yes, but no."

Nick pointed out a slender woman in her late fifties, dressed in diamonds and Dior. Some people looked slightly ridiculous in designer dresses, as if the opulence of the fabric was meant to be a substitute for their personality. In this case, however, the dress seemed appropriate, almost like a soldier in a uniform.

"Evelyn's aunt," Nick said. "Taffy came from Boston specifically to plan the wedding."

"Taffy?" Carl asked.

"Well, it's actually Mrs. William Winslow Foster III, nee Tabitha Gardiner, descendent of the *Mayflower* and a daughter of the American Revolution. She's staying with us."

"How's that going?"

"When she arrived last week, she handed me her luggage, thinking I was the butler."

"Evelyn has a butler?"

"No, which was her second issue."

Carl laughed and looked over Nick's shoulder to see Evelyn's eyes boring holes into Nick's back.

"You really can't feel Evie glaring at you?" Carl asked.

"Oh, I can feel it," Nick replied. "I'm just choosing to ignore it."

"You are a brave and stupid man."

"I'm going to kill him," Evelyn said under her breath, before turning back to a short man with gray hair who had yet to notice her boredom as he monologued at her.

"And that's why you should feel so proud!" he said, catching her off guard. "It's such an accomplishment!"

"Finding someone to marry me or running one of the largest companies in the country?" she asked.

He chuckled but did not answer. There was an awkward silence Evelyn could not be bothered to fill. Her Aunt Taffy swooped in, knowing instinctively where she was needed most. She had what Evelyn thought of as her society smile plastered firmly in place. It was warm but did not invite confidences.

"Arnold," Taffy crooned sympathetically to the man. "I'm so sorry about your neck. How did you injure it?"

"My neck?" he asked with a frown.

"I assumed that's why you're staring straight at my niece's chest, instead of her face."

Arnold coughed uncomfortably and made his escape.

"You amaze me." Evelyn laughed at her aunt. "If I'd said that, you'd have rapped my knuckles for being impertinent."

"Well, you're no longer seventeen, dear. Never hesitate to demand the respect you deserve," Taffy said, wrapping her arm around Evelyn's waist. "Are you having fun?"

"You know, when you suggested a dinner to celebrate my engagement, I was thinking ten people at home. This is . . ."

"What's appropriate for the new president of Bishop Aeronautics," Taffy insisted.

"I can't believe you pulled this together in just a few weeks," Evelyn said in awe.

"I used to do it all the time for William's business," Taffy replied, referencing her late husband. "Think what fun we'll have planning the actual wedding."

Evelyn bit her lip as Taffy drifted off to find the photographer. She had never been a girl who dreamed of that one magical day. In fact, marriage was not a state to which she aspired, having always had enough money to render it unnecessary. Instead, the thought of being legally attached to someone frightened her in ways she could not acknowledge. Only her love and faith in Nick made her consider this particular institution. In the distance, Carl made his way through the crowd with a glass of Scotch.

"You're my hero," Evelyn said, taking a long pull of the drink.

"How are you surviving?" Carl asked.

"There are folks asking who really runs Bishop Aeronautics, because, of course, a woman can't do it. There was the lady who insisted I did have time to join the board of her charity. Then there are those who ask me for favors because they think we're friends."

"And you're not?"

"I have seven friends."

"Am I one of them?" Carl asked.

"Obviously," Evelyn replied.

"Is Nick?"

"Not currently," Evelyn said, glaring at Nick, who turned around with a jaunty wave. Then she softened, slightly. "This really isn't his kind of thing."

"Not yours either, so far as I can tell."

"Yeah, well, I was raised with it. I've perfected the art of saying absolutely nothing and being found a brilliant conversationalist. It's a useful skill."

"Don't forget the fake smile."

"It is not fake. I am profoundly interested in your take on cattle futures or your favorite place to summer."

"I didn't know 'summer' was a verb."

"Oh yes. As is 'winter.'"

"How did I go my entire life without this knowledge?"

"Peasant," Evelyn teased.

She slid her arm through Carl's and led him across the room to Nick, who stood alone at the bar.

"I know, I know. I was late," Nick started. "Which is awful. And I'm sorry, but in my defense . . . I have no defense. I just didn't want to come."

"You only think you're roguishly charming," Evelyn replied tartly.

A flashbulb went off nearby, and Evelyn turned to see a photographer for the *Los Angeles Times* being shepherded over by Taffy.

"I missed the happy couple earlier," he said. "Can I get a photo for the paper?"

"Is it really necessary?" Evelyn asked.

"It is," Taffy insisted. "Your engagement isn't official until it's been announced."

The photographer gathered Evelyn and Nick together.

"Might as well look like we like each other," Nick said, putting his arm around Evelyn.

She turned toward him. The wry smile she had worn all night faded and a real grin took its place. There was a flash and their image was forever burned onto silver nitrate.

# Chapter 2

In the kitchen the next morning, with a fresh cup of coffee, Evelyn unfolded the *Los Angeles Times* to see news of her engagement on the front page, just below an update on the Berlin airlift. It was four months since the Soviets blockaded the land routes into Berlin and the US was struggling to fly enough food into the city on a daily basis. There was a certain irony in using US bombers to keep their former enemies alive.

Nick entered through the French doors that led to the pool house and gave Evelyn a kiss. Ever since Taffy's arrival, Nick pretended to live there to keep up appearances. Evelyn knew it was silly. She was a grown woman. However, Taffy was like a second mother and she had a very strong sense of propriety. Evelyn did not want to disappoint her. Nick poured himself a cup of coffee. Evelyn held up the picture on the front page.

"So much for anonymity," she said.

"You gave that up the moment you took over Bishop Aeronautics," Nick replied. "If I remember correctly, there was quite a large picture in the paper then, too."

"Yeah, but now you're here with me," Evelyn said,

knowing that Nick often needed to blend into a crowd to follow his subjects.

"I'm a man in a suit. People will forget my face before their paper hits the trash bin."

"Well, I think you're pretty unforgettable," Evelyn said. "Assuming you show up . . ."

"Sorry about that," Nick replied. "I lost track of time during the stakeout. Though why I'm still on this case is anyone's guess."

"Don't think you'll get results?"

"Pretty sure the husband is patronizing high-end prostitutes. It's unlikely they'll be canoodling in public anytime soon and the wife wants photographic proof," Nick said. "Though, from what I've heard, this place also bills itself as a gentleman's club. He could be in there sipping tea and playing backgammon. I keep trying to end the case, but my client insists on a few more days. Then a few more."

"Is she looking to have her fears confirmed or denied? Figure out what result she wants, then try to give it to her."

"Is she angry or scared?" Taffy asked as she entered the room and kissed Evelyn on the head. It was such a maternal gesture that it made Nick smile. He had always known Evelyn as a complete adult. He sometimes forgot she was once a child.

"I don't know," Nick replied.

"Ask about her divorce settlement," Taffy said bluntly. "Her feelings might depend on how much she'll get if the marriage ends."

"What kind of woman stays with a man just for the money?" Evelyn asked.

"It's easy to judge when you've never been poor," Taffy chided.

Considering Taffy was born into wealth that had only increased with her marriage, Nick was impressed with her matter-of-fact assessment of the situation. Changing the topic, Evelyn showed Taffy the *LA Times.*

"Made the front page."

"Well, the marriage of the heir to Bishop Aeronautics is big news."

"Not heir. President," Evelyn corrected.

"President," Taffy amended.

"Speaking of which, I'm late for my first meeting," Evelyn said, gathering up her things. She gave Nick a quick kiss and headed out the door.

There was an awkward moment when neither Nick nor Taffy knew what to say. The only thing they had in common was a love of Evelyn. Taffy poured herself a cup of coffee, which she sipped silently. Usually, Nick appreciated someone who did not feel a need to fill the void, but right now he felt uncomfortable. Though he would never admit it, he was a bit intimidated by Taffy.

"That was a great party, last night," Nick said. "Thank you for putting it together."

"I'm glad you enjoyed it," Taffy said. "I wasn't sure."

"Oh, um. It's, uh. I'm just . . ." Nick stammered.

Taffy raised her eyebrow, not offering to end his flailing. The corner of her mouth twitched in a way that was so reminiscent of Evelyn that he stopped speaking and shrugged.

"I've never been to something that formal before," Nick finally confessed.

"The tux was a bit much?" Taffy asked.

"No, it was . . ." Nick started. "Rented. The tux was rented."

Taffy laughed.

"Two points for honesty. We'll have to get you one of your own. Or are you going to wear white tie and tails to the wedding?"

"I hadn't thought that far ahead."

"You and Evelyn have been engaged for six months. Surely you've done some planning."

"Evelyn's been so busy with work," Nick said, feeling the need to defend their lack of action. "With everything going on in Berlin, there's a huge demand for more planes. Plus, she's working on getting the permits for the factory expansion. She has a lot on her plate."

"A woman's wedding is the most important day in her life," Taffy insisted.

"Well, sure," Nick said. He was not convinced Evelyn would agree with that statement, but he dare not argue with Taffy.

"We'll start by touring venues," Taffy said.

"What if we did something small at home with close friends?" Nick asked.

Taffy considered that for a moment. She looked around the kitchen, then went to the French doors and threw them open. She walked onto the patio and surveyed the backyard.

"In California, you don't have to worry as much about weather. We should be all right with tents on the lawn. We'll have to improve the landscaping, but if we do a spring wedding, there's plenty of time. The only issue is that we'll have to cap the guest list at two hundred people."

"Sorry, did you say two hundred?" Nick asked.

"Yes. Then again, having this be exclusive adds to the allure."

"We were thinking around twenty."

"Then you weren't thinking about Bishop Aeronautics. Evelyn's business contacts may not be close personal friends, but they're not people she should snub. Why do you think there were so many people last night?"

"I . . . I never considered it."

"I spent years managing our social calendar to help my

husband's status and grow his company. It was a good partnership," Taffy said. "No one expects you to take on that role, but you do need to accept that this is part of marrying into the Bishop family. Now, show me around the house, so I can see what we're working with."

Nick trailed behind as Taffy marched between the rooms. She stopped at the library, which Evelyn's father Logan had used as his home office. There were bookshelves lining the wall, filled with everything from Herodotus to the latest Agatha Christie.

"You should consider this for your study," Taffy said.

"Oh no," Nick protested. "It's Logan's."

"Logan is gone," Taffy said crisply. Her tone left no doubt as to her feelings about her former brother-in-law.

Nine months before, while investigating a murder, Evelyn discovered her father had committed treason in an effort to keep his son Matthew safe in a German POW camp. Matthew's capture was Evelyn's reason for joining the OSS. Unfortunately, he died in her arms during a rescue attempt. Having seen the war firsthand, Evelyn was conflicted about her father's actions. She loathed what he had done, but she also understood it. Logan loved his children fiercely and they returned the sentiment. During the war, his name had never been far from Evelyn's lips. Now Nick couldn't remember the last time she spoke it.

"Mostly, Evie uses it," Nick said.

"Then we'll have to find somewhere else for you," Taffy insisted. "Everyone needs their own space, and in a house this size there's no reason not to take over a room or two."

"Oh, I . . . I couldn't."

Taffy turned to face Nick.

"Do you really want to feel like a guest for the rest of your life? You need to figure out how to make this place your own."

Nick had never had a home. Not really. He just had places where he slept and kept his things. Until this moment, he had not realized he considered the Bishop mansion the same way. Yes, it was nicer than anywhere he had been before, but it was not his.

Taffy marched up the central staircase and threw open the door to Evelyn's parents' room. Nick had never been in here. The air was musty from having been trapped so long. Yet everything looked as though its inhabitants only left that morning. A man's hairbrush sat on the dresser, slightly askew, as if its owner would pick it up momentarily. A woman's makeup and perfume rested on a vanity table. In the bathroom a used toothbrush sat in the rack and a tube of toothpaste was dented in the middle. Taffy opened the door to the walk-in closet. The hangers were filled with women's dresses, twenty years out of style. Below them stood shoes, the leather cracked with age. Taffy turned to Nick.

"Why hasn't Evelyn moved into the master bedroom?"

"I doubt she ever thought about it."

Taffy turned on her heel and marched out of the room, down the hallway, to another room. On the wall was a poster for the movie *Wings*, with Clara Bow and Buddy Rogers. A well-worn baseball glove sat near a desk that still held term papers with the grades slowly fading from the top. A stretched-out sweater hung over the chair with a dog-eared copy of *The Sun Also Rises* on the nightstand. The bedsheets were yellow with age and the quilt had a fine layer of dust. It was a teenage boy's room, perfectly preserved for a man who would never return home.

"Oh, Evelyn," she said to herself.

Taffy met Nick's eyes and then she quietly closed the door.

# Chapter 3

As Evelyn walked up to the front door of Bishop Aeronautics, she saw Ruth, her secretary, waiting. Ruth had worked with Logan almost twenty years and now she was helping Evelyn adjust to her new responsibilities. To describe her as a battle-ax would be both accurate and considered a compliment. Though she was short, with trim gray hair, she was formidable. A single glance could reduce a person to silence. She kept track of everything happening at the factory and managed all the details, allowing Evelyn to focus on the bigger picture.

"Morning, Ruth," Evelyn said with a smile. It was still hard not to refer to her as Mrs. Sacks, as she had throughout her entire childhood.

Without preamble, Ruth launched into a recap of the previous day's production totals. They opened the door to the main factory floor. The hangar was large enough for six airplanes to be built at once. Between this space and the others on the Bishop campus, they were turning out new planes at a rate of five per month. Evelyn hoped to double that with an expansion of the current facilities. Aside from the fact that air travel was becoming more regular and affordable, the airlift in Berlin was at a critical stage. The US Army needed new planes faster than Evelyn could manufacture them.

"Any word from Lewis about a timeline for county approvals?" Evelyn asked.

Lewis Bryson was the vice president in charge of operations. He had been with Logan since 1928 and Evelyn had known him most of her life. To go from remembering her in pigtails to seeing her as his boss was a hard adjustment. Part of her wondered if he had expected to get the top job. If so, then he had never understood the value Logan placed on family.

"Lewis is Lewis," Ruth said with exasperation.

"How much was his expense account this month?" Evelyn asked.

"You don't want to know," Ruth replied. "He says all wining and dining of the officials is necessary."

"I suppose he's right," Evelyn agreed, visualizing Taffy's scolding visage urging her to go out more.

"Maybe, but he's also getting fat," Ruth replied.

Evelyn smothered a laugh as she met Ruth's eyes.

"Even if we got the approvals tomorrow, the new factory would still have to be built and we need to ramp up production now."

"You're thinking night shifts," Ruth guessed.

"Will you have Miles and William do an informal poll about whether people would be willing to take on night shifts at, I don't know, a thirty percent raise? Working those hours are brutal. I'd like to sweeten the deal enough to get good volunteers."

Ruth made a note in the steno pad she carried everywhere. They crossed the floor of the factory, greeting people as they went. Evelyn liked to make herself available to her employees. She stopped by a woman in thick gloves and goggles who was welding a part into place. The woman finished the task, then turned to Evelyn with a smile.

"How's your mom, Alice?" Evelyn asked.

"Good. The pneumonia is almost gone."

"I'm so glad to hear it," Evelyn said.

She stopped by a man to ask about his son, who had just left for college on the East Coast.

"He's doing great. It's just . . . too quiet at home," he said.

Evelyn noticed another man was missing from his usual position and asked Ruth about it.

"His wife went into labor last night. Two months early. Apparently, there were some complications."

"Are the mother and baby okay?"

"From what I've heard, but it looks like it's going to be a long recovery. The baby's in an incubator."

"Let's send some food to the hospital and make sure we take care of that bill."

Ruth made another note and they continued through the factory, eventually climbing the stairs to the office. It was almost nine months since Logan fled the country, but Evelyn still thought of this as his office. She wondered if it would ever feel natural to call it hers.

"Do you have anything from the engineers about the new guidance systems?" Evelyn asked as she sat behind her desk.

"They're hoping to have something for you by the end of the week."

"The fog in Berlin is getting worse—soon they'll have almost no visibility. They'll need to transport even more supplies into the city once you add coal for the winter."

"The army is notoriously slow adapters of new technology," Ruth warned.

"Necessity is the mother of invention," Evelyn replied wryly. "What else?"

"I'm leaving."

"Sorry, do you have a doctor's appointment?" Evelyn asked, twisting around her watch to find the time. "It must have slipped my mind."

"No, I mean I'm retiring."

"I don't understand."

"I know it's going to be an adjustment," Ruth began.

"You can't retire," Evelyn said. "You're what? Forty-two, forty-three?"

"My cold cream must really be working," Ruth replied. "I'm sixty-five."

"That's impossible."

"Would you like to see my driver's license?"

"I mean, I know you worked for Dad forever, but . . ."

"I was planning on leaving in the spring, then with everything that happened," Ruth trailed off. "I wanted to make sure you were settled."

"I'm not settled. This is still new and I have no idea what I'm doing."

"Yes, you do," Ruth said. "It just hasn't been long enough to become routine."

"Is this your way of saying you're bored?" Evelyn asked.

"I have loved every single day I spent at Bishop Aeronautics. I've felt appreciated and respected in a way few other professional women ever do," Ruth said. "But I have grandchildren I want to spoil and books I want to read and places I want to see. It's time."

Evelyn did not know what to say. For a brief moment, she wanted to burst into tears like a child being abandoned.

"When?" Evelyn asked finally.

"Not for a little while. I'll find someone to take my

place," Ruth promised. "Your father and I had a grand time building this place together. Supporting each other and growing old. You need that person to take the next step with you."

Evelyn understood the logic, but that did not mean she had to like it. She came around from behind her desk and wrapped Ruth in a hug. The older woman stood straight, embarrassed by Evelyn's outpouring of emotion.

"It'll be okay," Ruth said as she stepped out of the embrace. "I promise."

"I know," Evelyn said. "That was to say thank you."

Ruth nodded crisply, a small smile on her face.

"What's next?" Evelyn asked.

"General Gibson called for you."

"You mean General Hayworth?" Evelyn corrected. "Who we've been dealing with about Berlin?"

"No," Ruth insisted. "General Henry Gibson."

Shocked, Evelyn sat down. General Gibson was her commanding officer during the war. They had only spoken twice since V-E Day. The first was when she told him to go to hell after he offered her a job working as a translator in Washington, DC, instead of keeping her on as a spy. The second was when her father was discovered to be a traitor. Gibson testified on her behalf, convincing the tribunal of her patriotic service.

"Did he say why he was calling?" Evelyn asked.

"Just requested you call him back."

Ruth handed Evelyn a slip of paper with a phone number in Berlin. Evelyn stared at it for a long minute. Then she slipped it into the top drawer of her desk and looked back to Ruth.

"What's next?"

# Chapter 4

That evening found Nick parked, once again, outside the same house in Brentwood. Earlier in the day the wife stopped by his office for a progress report. Truthfully, Nick had little to show, explaining the difficulties in getting the photographs she desired. He did not want to waste his time or her money chasing something that might never happen.

"I need to get out," she said. "I can't do it anymore."

"Is he abusive? Does he hurt you? Drink too much?" Nick asked.

"That's a floor, not a ceiling," the woman chided. "Just because I don't have any bruises doesn't mean he's a good man. Can you imagine what it's like to spend your days trying to keep a house clean, do laundry, make dinner? Only to do it again tomorrow? And tomorrow? And tomorrow?"

Nick shook his head. He had never really considered it.

"Then my charming husband comes home and points out everything I did wrong. No appreciation. No gratitude. No recognition of the fact that I, too, have been working all day. Instead, he demands dinner, then complains about my cooking. Demands a drink, but chides me for having one, too. Criticizes my figure, the way I dress, how I do my hair. Do you know what it's like to never feel good enough? I can't do it anymore. I won't survive."

So, she needed proof of adultery to force a divorce, seeing her husband was perfectly content with their arrangement. At least now, Nick felt a sense of purpose in the monotony of staking out this house. Several men entered the building. They were well-dressed, often wearing business suits. Their shoes were professionally shined and looked like they cost more than most peoples' rent. A few of the men glanced at Nick as he sat in his car. He waved and held up his camera, at which point they often turned and hurried back to their cars. Others pulled their hats low and rushed up the front stairs. The bouncer, a large black man with a shaved head, ushered them inside. Dressed in an expensive suit, he looked more like he was on his way to the opera than working security. After a half an hour, and two other men turning away, the bouncer decided to have a chat. With a polite smile, he approached Nick's car.

"Good evening," the bouncer said. "My name's Gregory."

"Pleasure to meet you," Nick said, leaning out the window to shake his hand.

"I'd appreciate it if you'd park your car somewhere else. You're making some of our guests nervous."

"Having a party?"

"Every day on this earth is cause for celebration."

"That's certainly an optimistic way of looking at life," Nick replied. "But I'm not moving my car."

"Perhaps I can make you reconsider."

"Was that a threat? Are you going to call the cops?"

"Now why would I do that?" Gregory asked. "You're

parked legally. As far as I can tell, you're not intoxicated, nor are you disturbing the peace."

"Just your guests."

"Exactly. I'd be happy to pay you for the effort of moving your car."

"What's to stop me from coming back tomorrow?" Nick asked.

"All the nearby parking spots might be filled for the next few days or weeks or months. Whatever it takes for you to lose interest."

"While that's a tempting offer, I'm here on a job." Nick handed Gregory his card.

"Private investigator. I'm assuming you're interested in one of our guests. I'd be happy to double your fee and save you the inconvenience of staking out the front door."

"And save you the inconvenience of finding two dozen cars."

"That, too."

"It's clear you are very good at your job, and I respect that," Nick started. "But I also try to be good at my job. It's a matter of principle."

"So, I can't convince you to leave?"

"Afraid not."

"Then why don't you come in and join us for a drink? On the house."

Nick stared at Gregory in surprise.

"Once you see that we are nothing but an upscale gentleman's club, you'll realize your investigation might be more fruitful elsewhere."

"That's a very kind offer," Nick said. He rolled up his window, locked his car, and pocketed the keys. Then he followed Gregory across the street.

"How long have you worked here?" Nick asked.

"Ever since I got home from the war. I'm a night owl, so I don't mind the hours."

They walked up the front stairs and Gregory held the door open. Inside, the floors were a rich cherry wood, polished to a high shine. The room was a large, open space, running from one side of the house to the other. The walls were painted in various shades of blue with yellow accents. Thick rugs covered the floor and leather armchairs dotted the room. Several men were drinking whiskey and reading the paper. Others sat at the poker tables. Various women walked between the tables, checking on patrons, sometimes sitting down for a chat. They were all attractive, running the gamut from early twenties to midfifties. There were all races, heights, and shapes. The one common denominator was that they looked like they were enjoying themselves.

Gregory led Nick to the bar, which stretched a quarter length of the room with rows upon rows of top-shelf liquor. Standing behind it was a young woman with her black hair in a high ponytail. She wore black slacks, a crisp white button-down shirt, with an open collar, under a pin-striped black vest and a loose black tie. Nick watched as she set a martini in front of an older man.

"Here you go, Derek. I just waved the vermouth over the top. Should be drier than the Sahara."

"You're the best, Julia," the man said, taking his drink.

Julia turned and offered Gregory a smile. Without his asking, she poured soda into a glass, added grenadine, and topped it with two cherries.

"To the manliest of men, the manliest of drinks." She laughed as she set down the glass.

"Don't knock it until you've tried it," Gregory said, sipping his Shirley Temple.

Then, nodding to Nick, Gregory said, "Julia, this is Nick Gallagher, private investigator and first-time guest."

"Welcome!" Julia said enthusiastically. "What can I get you?"

Her ponytail bobbed with her words and it made her look even younger than Nick initially thought. He guessed she was twenty-one, if a day. Despite that, she had the assurance of someone with a lot of life under her belt. Nick appreciated that in people.

"What do you recommend?" Nick asked.

"What do you usually drink?"

"Scotch."

"I've got you," Julia said, turning away. She dropped a sugar cube into a glass and added a few dashes of bitters. Carefully, she measured out the bourbon, then swirled the drink to dissolve the sugar. She added a large ice cube to the mix. Then, as a final flourish, she grabbed a fresh orange.

"Grown right in the backyard," she informed Nick as she peeled off a thin sliver of the rind. With a Zippo lighter, she ran the flame up and down, teasing out the oil. Then she flipped it around, igniting it with a flash and dropped the peel into the glass.

"Impressive," Nick said, taking a sip. It was one of the best drinks he had ever enjoyed. "You have real skill."

"I've got good teachers," Julia replied modestly.

Gregory set down his empty glass and Julia put it in a wash bin.

"Back to the grind. You let me know if he causes you any trouble," Gregory said.

"Aye, aye, Captain," Julia said with a jaunty salute.

Nick looked around the busy room. There was no sign of the husband he was following. Nick took a ten-dollar bill out of his wallet, slipped it and his business card to Julia.

"Do you know a man named Edward Gilsby?"

"Doesn't ring a bell," Julia said with a bright smile as she swept up both the card and the money.

"Brown hair, about my height. Kind of guy who looks perpetually disappointed in the world?"

"Nice description, but no. Sorry."

"Just for reference's sake, do you know that man's name?" Nick pointed to Derek, the man whom Julia had served a martini.

"Not a clue," Julia lied smoothly.

"Had a feeling that was going to be the answer," Nick said.

"Never hurts to ask," Julia replied.

"How long you been working here?"

"About seven months."

"You like it?"

"Very much so."

"Even with the, uh, extracurricular activities?" Nick asked.

"I don't know what you're referring to," Julia said as a woman in a short dress led a businessman past the bar and up the stairs.

"Why work here? Why not a club downtown?"

Julia laughed. Then, seeing Nick's face, she stopped.

"You're serious," she said, surprised. "There isn't a single club in the city that will hire me. For one, I'm a woman."

"I had noticed," Nick replied.

"I'll take that as a compliment. Second, my family's from Mexico."

"And you're saying this isn't the most open-minded, welcoming city in the world?" Nick asked sarcastically.

Julia snorted in derision.

"And third, everyone knows the score here. The owner's a woman. She treats us well and looks after us. You're not going to find some sleazy manager at the end of the shift hoping for a 'nightcap.' "

"So, it's a good place to work?"

"Best place I've ever been, and I've worked since I was twelve."

"That's about when I started, too," Nick said. He noticed a silver chain slip out of the top of her shirt. On it was a locket with an intricate filigree design. "Nice necklace."

Julia blushed slightly and tucked it back into her shirt.

"From your boyfriend?"

"I don't have a boyfriend," Julia said.

"Does anyone here?" Nick asked.

"Of course not."

"Even if they're married?"

"Especially then," Julia replied with a smile. "Don't you know? The world doesn't exist outside these doors. This is a place to escape your life."

"And if I'm not looking to escape?"

"Then you are a rare and lucky man," Julia said as she cleared away Nick's empty glass.

"Can I get you another?"

"No thanks," Nick said. "Time for me to head home. I'm suddenly missing it."

"Pleasure meeting you, Nick Gallagher," Julia said.

"And this from a woman who can't remember names."

"It will disappear from my mind by the time you reach the door," she promised.

"You'll stay with me a bit longer than that, Julia," Nick replied.

As he stepped down from the barstool, he felt someone's gaze. He turned to find a striking woman in her midthirties wearing a formfitting, low-cut dress, standing in a doorway, surveying the room. Red hair cascaded over her shoulders.

Though the color was masterful, Nick guessed it was artificial. She wore a fair bit of makeup, but it was well-applied. The apparent artifice was part of the appeal—a doll upon which any man could cast his own desires. Her eyes were a tawny brown that reminded Nick of a lioness. There was something irrepressibly familiar about her. Nick cocked his head sideways, trying to place her. She smiled, amused, and gave him a wink.

# Chapter 5

Evelyn loved the end of the workday when everyone had gone home. Looking across the silent floor with airplanes in various stages of completion, she marveled at the fact that this had all been built by her father. It was in these moments she felt closest to him. Sometimes, she spoke into the darkness, seeking his council. Every so often, she thought she heard his words echoing in her mind. With a sigh, she went back to her desk to look over the day's production reports. When she finished, she twisted her watch to check the time. It was late enough.

Pulling the slip of paper out of her desk, she dialed the number in Berlin. General Gibson was a gruff man who did not suffer fools gladly. He kept Evelyn, Nick, and Carl alive during the war by the sheer force of his will. It was his job to put them in dangerous situations, but they trusted him. Though they lost people, he never sent them on a suicide mission. Other teams were not so lucky.

"Gibson," barked the voice on the other end after the operator had connected them.

"And a lovely morning to you, too, General," Evelyn said.

"Do you know what time it is?" Gibson grumbled.

"Five a.m., by my calculations," Evelyn replied. "Don't tell me you haven't been up for at least an hour."

A low growl was the only response.

"One day, you're going to retire and sleep until noon every day," Evelyn joked.

"Six a.m. feels like an indulgence, but who knows? I hit forty years in the service next June, then I'm done."

"Impossible!"

"I have a strawberry farm right on the coast near Oxnard. My sons are running it now, but there's a little house in the corner of a field. Theresa and I have lived abroad long enough. We intend to sit on that porch swing, drink wine, and watch our grandkids grow up."

"Can I visit?" Evelyn asked.

"Only if you bring the good Scotch."

Evelyn laughed.

"I saw the papers," Gibson said. "You and Nick are finally making it official."

"Good God," Evelyn said. "They reported on it all the way over there? When did my personal life become newsworthy?"

"That is an excellent question," he replied. "Congratulations, by the way."

"Are you coming to the wedding?"

"Am I invited?"

"Obviously. You introduced us," Evelyn said.

"You mean I twisted Nick's arm until he agreed to lead a team?"

"Sounds nicer when I say it."

"What about your father?" Gibson asked. "Is he going to walk you down the aisle?"

"If I knew where he was, I'd report it to the FBI like a good, patriotic citizen."

They both knew she was lying. Evelyn would never turn

in her father. In fact, she was the one who helped him escape.

"Had to ask," Gibson replied.

"How's Germany treating you?" she said, changing topics.

"Why do you think I'm retiring? It's a fucking mess," he replied.

"Tell me about the airlift," Evelyn said.

"LeMay's throwing his weight around, bragging about winning the Pacific. Meanwhile, he has no fucking idea how to solve the problem.

"And of course you need more planes."

"Always."

"We're building them as fast as we can," Evelyn said. "But that's not why you're calling, and it certainly isn't to congratulate me on my engagement."

"Think back to 1942. One of your first missions with Gallagher."

"That feels like a thousand years ago."

"It was," Gibson replied dryly. "You were sent to get a scientist out of Berlin."

"Hans Adler," Evelyn said, pulling the name from her memory.

"His real name was Kurt Vogel. He was a chemist working on rocket fuel."

"It was a rough extraction," Evelyn remembered. "We chanced the train to Munich but ran into the SS outside Ingolstadt. Ended up going over the Pyrenees and got caught in the snow. Between the cold, the Vichy army, and Franco's troops, it was a nightmare. Carl finally met us in Bilbao and got us to Porto. From there to London."

"Do you remember Vogel's family?"

"They were traveling separately because the Gestapo was hunting him. The OSS thought they'd be safer taking a different route. We knew the mountains were always a possibility and his five-year-old daughter wouldn't have survived. Kurt talked about her the whole trip. He seemed like a doting father."

"He was."

"Was?"

"The other team came back ahead of you, but without Kurt's family."

"What happened?" Evelyn asked.

"Don't know. Their debrief was classified."

"Who was supposed to get them?"

"Don't know," Gibson repeated. "That was classified, too."

"Did they even try to get the family out? Or was it all for show?"

"I didn't run the mission," Gibson replied. "Always thought it was a mistake breaking up the family, but command insisted Vogel was the primary target."

"That poor man."

"It gets worse," Gibson said. "His family was Jewish."

Evelyn sat back in her chair. In her mind's eye, Evelyn could still see the little girl with her hair in braids, tied at the end with red ribbons. Kurt had knelt down and held his daughter tightly, as if imparting all his love to her. It was only Nick's insistence that they make their train that finally got Kurt to let her go. Kurt's wife bravely blinked back tears, promising to see him soon. Everyone believed it would be a temporary separation. Until that moment, Evelyn imagined them living all together somewhere in the States.

"We presumed the worst," Gibson said. "But he called us yesterday. He received a postcard from his wife post-marked Berlin."

"Is it real?" Evelyn asked.

"He seems to think it is."

"How did she know how to reach him?"

"She sent it to the former OSS headquarters and it got routed through there. He's working at the Jet Propulsion Laboratory, just north of Cal Tech."

"You want me to meet with him."

"He asked specifically for you. I know you're out of the service, but you're qualified, well-positioned, and familiar with the situation. Plus, if there's merit to his claim, you can use your position at Bishop Aeronautics to come to Berlin."

"Why didn't his wife come to an American base herself? What's with the postcard?"

"Our fear is that the Soviets are using her, or at least the idea of her, to lure Kurt back to Germany. He's one of the finest scientific minds, and the last thing we need is to have him working for Russia."

"You never make my life easy, do you?" Evelyn asked.

"Where would be the fun in that?" Gibson asked.

"Fine," Evelyn said. "I'll go tomorrow morning."

"Ten a.m., he's expecting you."

# Chapter 6

The next morning, Evelyn woke to the sun streaming through the window. Nick leaned over and kissed her. She wound her arms around him and pulled him close, enjoying the feeling of his skin against hers. Some days this quiet in the morning was the only time they had together.

"You got home late," Nick murmured, his fingers tracing the lines of her body.

"You'll never believe who called," Evelyn said, before filling Nick in on her conversation with General Gibson.

"I remember that mission," Nick responded. "It was brutal. He was a good man, though. Never complained, just did as we asked."

"The thought of his family kept him going."

"Listening to him tell stories was the first time I realized not all families were like mine," Nick said. "I mean, I knew that from a logical standpoint. People don't usually abandon their children, but I assumed behind closed doors, everyone was miserable in one way or another."

"Is that what made you realize you were a little in love with me?" Evelyn teased.

"By then, I was a lot in love," Nick said. "He made me

believe we could have a future. There was that one night in the crypt outside Lyon. I don't know. Something changed."

"I think those first few months, I was so focused on finding Matthew and learning how to survive behind enemy lines. I didn't have room for emotions," Evelyn confessed. "Though I did notice you were roguishly handsome."

"Trained investigator at work."

"That mission made me see I needed to live my life, rather than waiting for it to start. Who knew how much time we might have together?"

Evelyn kissed him. He teased down the strap of her nightgown and his lips moved lower. She leaned her head back, enjoying the moment, when she caught sight of the clock.

"Is that the time?"

"No," Nick murmured without looking up. "Time doesn't exist here."

"Well, it does at JPL."

"I can be quick," Nick said.

"Not too quick." Evelyn laughed.

He pulled her closer and began to show what he could accomplish in five minutes.

An hour later, Nick sat at his desk overlooking the pristine sidewalks of Rodeo Drive. They were swept daily, with trash cans every hundred feet to remind people of their civic duty to maintain the beauty of Beverly Hills. It was a far cry from his last office. There, the window was above an alley, with the smell of garbage drifting upward. All of his furniture came from secondhand shops or was scavenged from the street. In here there was a definite sense of intentionality. Probably because this place was recently Evelyn's. Painted pale blue, with dove-gray couches, Tiffany lamps, and muted Persian rugs, it exuded quiet money.

Nick sat behind the mahogany desk, contemplating putting his feet up on it. Despite Evelyn encouraging him to redo it in his own style, he had barely moved a book on the shelves. He was not sure whether his hesitance stemmed from the fact that the office reminded him of her, he liked the aesthetic, or he was too damned lazy to make the effort. Nick suspected it was a combination of all three. Unfortunately, the result of this inertia was that he felt guilty putting his shoes anywhere but the floor.

Settling down to work, Nick began writing notes about the previous night's investigation. He tallied up the hours and added it to the total he kept in a notebook. As he was finishing his notation, there was a knock on the door.

"Come in!" he called. The door opened, revealing the mysterious woman from last night. Her hair was pulled back demurely and she wore an understated pale pink dress that looked as though it had come straight off the runway in Paris. It accentuated her figure, but in a way that would not be inappropriate in church. Nick came around the desk.

"Nick Gallagher," he said, offering his hand.

"I know," the woman said. Her voice was rich and cultured, as though she had perfected it at one of the Seven Sisters. She looked around the office curiously. "I wouldn't have guessed this was your style."

"I'm sorry," Nick said, utterly confused. "Have we met?"

The woman laughed. It was low and sultry, carrying the intimacy of late-night conversations had in bed.

"Oh, yes," the woman said. "But it's been a while. We've both changed quite a bit."

Nick narrowed his eyes. It was not possible.

"Hildy Brecker?" he asked incredulously. The girl who had taken his twelve-year-old self under her wing had grown up to become the sophisticated woman in front of him.

"Helen now," she replied. "No one wanted to fuck a Hildegard."

Nick stared for a moment longer, then shook his head and hugged her. She wrapped her arms around him, and for a moment they were back to being the teenagers who relied upon each other to survive.

"Oh, Nicky," she said, her head buried in his shoulder. "I've missed you."

"I missed you, too."

Nick poured them both coffee and they sat on the couches facing each other. They talked of old acquaintances and forgotten misadventures. When Nick was fifteen, he lied about his age to get a job down at the docks, loading and unloading incoming vessels. He was fast, efficient, and paid a fraction of what he deserved. There was no point in complaining about it. It was during the Great Depression, and in the mornings, he passed a long line of men desperate for work to feed their families. Though it was miserable, backbreaking labor, Nick felt lucky to have a steady income.

Hildy, who was three years older, took a very different path. The first time her mother pimped her out, she was thirteen. It soon became a common enough occurrence that she fled down to the waterfront and found a basement room in the small house of a widow. Unheated, with a single light bulb hanging in the center, it was cold and dank. She slept on an old army cot, wrapped in several blankets she stole from linen bins in the backs of hotels. At the time, Nick thought Hildy survived by cleaning other people's homes, but when the husbands were alone, they expected services beyond dusting. Instead, she sold herself and kept all her profits. She was unsentimental about it, stating bluntly that it could be worse. At least Hildy had her own refuge. Many women did not. They were forced to sleep at their pimps' house and chained to radiators if they tried to flee. She told Nick all of this in a matter-of-fact voice, sounding slightly amused by the horror on his face. Life had given her a dark sense of humor. Without it, she would not have survived.

"How didn't I know?" Nick asked.

"When we met, you were too young to ask," she said. "Then we became friends, and you thought you understood my situation. I didn't have the heart to disabuse you of that notion."

"I'm so sorry," Nick said.

"We don't get to pick our lot in life." Helen shrugged. "We only get to choose what we do with it."

"You were always practical," Nick said.

"I've had to be."

"I guess we both did."

"No," Helen said with a smile. "There was a secret optimist under all your anger."

"When you and I . . ." Nick started, unsure how to phrase the question.

They had slept together exactly once, to celebrate Nick getting his job. Helen took his virginity. It was terribly awkward, yet also tender. She had always taken care of him, and this was just one more thing he needed to know. There were no romantic feelings, though Nick experienced the usual teenage longings for almost every girl his age. When it was over, Nick was grateful, but also understood nothing had changed between them.

"You were never an obligation," Helen said, saving him from his embarrassment. "We had fun."

His relief was so visible that Helen laughed.

"How did you get where you are?" Nick asked. "You came to say goodbye, then you were gone for good."

"As a kid, the pimps mostly ignored me," Helen said. "However, as I grew up, everyone wanted a piece of me.

They threatened me to join them, but I swore after my mother, I'd never let anyone else control my life. I knew I had to leave, but I had no idea how. One day, I was at the Beverly Hills Hotel. There was an elegant woman wearing a diamond bracelet. As I slipped it off, she grabbed my hand. Told me I had a choice. Either she could alert security or I could give up for the day and meet her for dinner in the restaurant. Somehow, she knew what I was without my having to say the words. Turned out, she had been in the same situation when she was my age. She offered to teach me everything I needed to know—how to dress, how to speak, how to carry myself, and why it was important to be well-informed. Certain types of men weren't just paying for a body, they were paying for an experience. She found me wealthy clients, who were very different from the men we grew up around. In exchange, I paid her back for my education and gave her twenty percent of my earnings. She wasn't a pimp. I always had the option to leave and I had the right to choose my own clients. Together, we built what you saw last night. When she retired a few years ago, I bought her out and kept it running."

"So, you recruit girls like you?"

"I find my employees from all kinds of places."

"How can you encourage other women to go into prostitution? It ruined your life."

"I got to see the *Mona Lisa* at the Louvre before the war. I've heard opera at La Scala and seen ballet at the Bolshoi. I own my own home as well as my club. I've invested enough to retire comfortably. To the world, I'm a very successful businesswoman. I wake up every morning free to do what I want. Does that sound like a ruined life?"

Nick had to admit that it sounded pretty good, yet it still bothered him.

"But you had to . . ."

"Sleep with men and shouldn't I be ashamed of myself? Maybe a puritanical God in will banish me to hell for all eternity. What do I care? No hell can be worse than how we grew up. We do what we have to do to survive. Then we do what we can to thrive. I won't apologize."

For a moment, that hung in the air between them. Then Nick shook his head.

"No, but I should," Nick said. "I was surprised by everything. I had a gut reaction and I'm sorry."

Helen looked at him sideways, startled by his easy capitulation.

"You actually mean that, don't you?" she asked.

Nick nodded. "I'm learning to admit when I'm being an ass."

"And I thought I'd seen everything," she said. Then she gestured around the office. "You've done pretty well for yourself, too."

"I inherited the office."

"From your fiancée?" Helen asked.

"How did you . . ."

"Even whores read the newspaper. Congratulations. She's really quite something."

There was an undertone of cynicism in her voice, which Nick ignored.

"That might be the understatement of the year," he said with a smile. "So, tell me why you're here. As much as I'd like to believe this is a social call, something tells me you do very little without a specific purpose."

"Fair," Helen conceded. "I run a gentleman's club. A place for men to relax and have a drink. For some of our clients, that's genuinely all that it is. However, for others, we offer private entertainment, at an additional cost."

"Of course," Nick said.

"I've worked very hard to make my establishment the best in the city. There's only one requirement I have for the women I employ. They have to love sex. If the women enjoy themselves, the men always leave satisfied. The women I hire are educated enough to carry on intelligent conversations, they are kind, they are friendly and outgoing. I make no distinction when it comes to race, size, or other factors. Everyone has different tastes."

Nick nodded encouragingly.

"Because of these standards my employees are not the type of women who usually go into this work. I have actresses, college students, but also housewives looking to earn some extra money or who are simply bored and need a hobby. I pay them well and do everything in my power to make sure they feel safe. I screen my clients very carefully and I do not tolerate violence, threats, or contact outside the house. That's why it's so distressing that one of my employees was attacked last night."

"At the club?" asked Nick.

"On her way home."

"By whom?"

"That's what I'd like you to find out. You chose a particularly opportune moment to stroll back into my life, Nick Gallagher."

"I'd love to help," Nick said. "But we have conflicting interests. I'm still following one of your members."

Helen reached into her purse, withdrew a manila envelope, and handed it to Nick. Inside were photographs of the cheating husband kissing a woman on a nondescript street.

"I'll start today," Nick said.

# Chapter 7

Evelyn pulled her hair back into a low chignon, then se-
lected a wine-colored suit from her closet. Though it
was entirely too warm to wear wool, Evelyn found that
she rarely garnered a man's respect without the shared dis-
comfort of unseasonable clothes. Downstairs, Taffy was
already in the kitchen, nursing a dry piece of toast and a
cup of coffee. Evelyn reached for the pot and found it
blessedly half full. She poured a cup, took a long sip, then
began to pack up her briefcase.

"You're not having breakfast?" Taffy asked.

"I'm already late," Evelyn replied.

"Well, you're about to be later. We need to talk about
the wedding. I'm setting up meetings with photographers,
florists, and other vendors. The caterer is coming tomorrow night."

"Arrange it with my secretary."

"You'll be there?"

"As long as you talk to Ruth," Evelyn promised. "I really have to go."

Evelyn gave Taffy a quick kiss on the cheek and headed
out the door.

*    *    *

There was no good way to get from Bel Air to the Jet Propulsion Laboratory, or JPL, as it was commonly known. While it was founded as part of Cal Tech in the 1930s, it was now one of the army's leading research centers. The location, at the northernmost edge of Pasadena, was chosen specifically because it was a dry riverbed and there was not too much to set on fire.

Evelyn drove up to the guard shack and handed over her driver's license. The MP on duty checked it against his list of approved visitors and waved her through. There were a series of low buildings that looked newly built. It felt less like an army facility than the campus of a small private college. Evelyn parked her car, entered a building, took the stairs to the second floor, and knocked on door 218.

"Enter," barked a voice with a faint German accent.

Evelyn walked in to find the man she had known as Hans Adler. Once, he had been tall and broad-shouldered, but now his body was hunched and rounded. His brown hair was streaked with gray. Where his eyes used to crinkle with laughter there were now dark circles caused by late nights. Dressed in slacks and a short-sleeved shirt, he was standing at a chalkboard, writing an equation. For a moment, Evelyn was forgotten as he scratched out chemical symbols. Studying his work, she realized he was creating a new type of jet fuel.

"You'll need a different injection system to handle the extra hydrogen," Evelyn suggested.

He stared at the board for another moment, then began writing a new equation. Evelyn picked up a piece of chalk and drew a rough sketch, doing the math to describe the physics that would help more planes break the sound barrier.

"Rather than design a new engine, you can swap out the throttle body," she said.

He stopped and looked at Evelyn. "Anna Schmidt."

It was Evelyn's code name during the war.

"Evelyn Bishop," she corrected.

He dusted the chalk dust from his hand and shook her hand.

"Kurt Vogel," he said. Then, turning back to the equation, "You understand this, yes?"

"Most of it. I have an engineering degree from UCLA. Plus, I'm pretty decent at building airplanes."

"I've never understood why Cal Tech doesn't accept women for their undergraduate studies. What a waste of human potential."

Evelyn looked at him sideways. "Most scientists don't agree with you."

"Most scientists are idiots. If you knew my wife, you'd understand. She's absolutely brilliant. Should have been a household name like Einstein."

"It's a shame she never had the chance."

"Perhaps then she would've been rescued instead of me. Do you know what happened to my family?" Kurt asked.

"Until yesterday, I assumed your wife and daughter were living with you in America."

"They never arrived. I reached London, expecting to find them, but no one knew their fate. Can you imagine what it was like, every day hoping? Every day hearing nothing?"

"My brother was a POW," Evelyn said. "It's torture."

"So, you know," Kurt said. His breath caught in his throat and came out in a ragged sigh. "It's too hot in here. Let us take a walk."

Without waiting for Evelyn's agreement, he opened the office door and headed down the hall. Evelyn hurried to catch up to his long stride. Kurt led Evelyn to the outdoor lunch canteen. It was a shack that housed a small kitchen, with a U-shaped counter and a few stools. Kurt ordered two bottles of Coca-Cola, popped the tops, and handed one to Evelyn.

"How do you like JPL?" Evelyn asked Kurt as they walked in search of a shaded bench.

"The science and technology are among the best in the world. I find the Americans irreverent, but they get their work done. Somehow all the joking opens up something in their minds. I don't understand, but I've come to appreciate it."

"I heard Wernher von Braun joined the team," Evelyn said, naming the scientist who helped design the German V-2 rockets.

"The man is a Nazi. He should have been hanged." Kurt spat into the dirt.

"Even if he can help against the Russians?"

"The Russians didn't threaten my wife and daughter," Kurt replied bitterly. "Von Braun worked for a regime that murdered millions of people. He pleads ignorance, but slave labor was used in his factories. The man may be brilliant, but he has no soul."

"Is that why you wanted out of Berlin? You didn't believe in the Nazi cause?"

"I believed in science, and Germany was the most advanced in my field. I stayed and pretended not to know what was happening. My wife begged me to leave in 1935 when the Nuremberg Laws went into effect. She pleaded again after Kristallnacht. I always said no. For all that I valued her brilliance, I was too selfish to leave my work and too foolish to listen to her when it came to anti-Semitism. I never saw the point in religion, so I acted like it didn't matter. Hannah grew up with the small insults and the larger violence. She felt the hatred I couldn't bother to recognize.

"It all came to a head when our daughter Sophie was

born. My wife couldn't go to the hospital. She had to give birth at home with a Jewish midwife. The next year, they made us add Sara to Sophie's name, so the world could identify her as *other*. I'm ashamed to say I only saw Hannah's struggle when it began to affect me."

"That's true of a lot of people," Evelyn replied.

"Someone, probably von Braun, put my name on a list of valuable scientists. For a while, it kept us safe. My wife and daughter were not deported, but they were also not free to leave our apartment. Sophie was growing up without sunlight. Hannah flourished no better. We were living on borrowed time."

"That's when you reached out to the United States?" Evelyn asked.

"October 1941."

"It took a year to put together a plan?" Evelyn asked in surprise. She knew how quickly the OSS could move when it was motivated.

"They didn't realize my value until they, too, began trying to build a rocket. Then they couldn't extract me fast enough."

"Whose idea was it to separate your family?" Evelyn asked.

"I thought it was yours," Kurt said in surprise.

"I was given orders, not options."

"They told me going separately would be safer," Kurt said. "I was desperate to get them out of Germany. By then, it was next to impossible. When I arrived in England, they were nowhere to be found. I was frantic. I wanted to go back, but of course, that could never happen. The days turned into weeks, into months, into years. Every morning I thought, 'Maybe today they'll be found.' Every night the disappointment almost destroyed me. After the war ended, I searched for answers but came up with nothing."

"I'm so sorry," Evelyn said. She wanted to reach out and comfort Kurt, but sensed her touch would not be welcome. Though he was still the same person she remembered from their harrowing trip, there was a new reserve in him. Part of it was anger and sorrow, but there was something else she could not name.

Kurt pulled a postcard out of his pocket and handed it to Evelyn. One side was addressed to the UNRRA, United Nations Relief and Rehabilitation Administration, with a postmark from the French sector of Berlin. The other side was written in German:

My Beloved Kurt, I am trying, once again, to reach you. I heard rumors from Herr Neubert's niece that you are alive. Please find us so we may be reunited. All my love, Hannah.

Evelyn studied it for a minute before handing it back to Kurt.

"Do you think it's her?" Evelyn asked.

"I don't know," he said, his voice anguished. "I thought I had made my peace with my family's absence. I was wrong. How do I cope with the guilt of leaving them behind? Or the fear they will never forgive me? And if this isn't them, then please, find me answers. I never got to mourn them properly, because that felt like giving up hope. I can't live with the uncertainty anymore."

"I will," Evelyn promised.

She was returning to Berlin.

# Chapter 8

Nick slid into a booth in a dark corner of the Formosa Café. Though not large, the restaurant had many small, interconnected rooms, which gave it a mazelike quality. With red walls and low lighting, it was easy to disappear into the shadows. Helen sat opposite Nick, beside a woman wearing large sunglasses and a scarf wrapped around her head.

"This is Ilene," Helen said.

The woman curled into herself, her arms wrapped tightly around her torso and her shoulders hunched. She nodded in Nick's direction without making eye contact. He thought he recognized her from Helen's club, but her confidence was replaced by fear. Instead of clothes designed to be noticed, she wore a black sweater over a gray skirt.

"You can trust Nick," Helen said.

Ilene finally looked up, and Nick got the impression he was being assessed. After a moment, she took off the glasses and scarf. Her pale skin was marred by a constellation of dark bruises across her right jaw and surrounding her right eye. A cut on the left side of her face was neatly bandaged. Nick suspected the bruises extended to places he could not see.

"You're very brave for speaking with me," Nick said. "I've taken this kind of beating and I know the only thing you want to do is stay in bed and drink whiskey for a week."

Ilene cracked a small smile.

"And I'm a person who does this professionally. It's a job hazard. This never should have happened to you. It isn't your fault."

"Thank you," she said softly. "I think I needed to hear that."

"Can you tell me about it?" Nick asked again.

Ilene looked to Helen, who nodded and took her hand.

"Usually, I catch a ride with a few of the other girls. However, I was working late last night."

"Is that unusual?" Nick asked.

Ilene shrugged.

"Sometimes we have clients who want a little more time, or regulars who stay after hours."

"On those nights, Gregory gets the girls a cab and they bill the fare back to us," Helen explained. "We have a standing arrangement with the taxi company, for them and for patrons who've had too much to drink."

"Smart," Nick replied. "Keeps your employees safe and avoids the police scrutiny that comes from a car accident."

"It was a normal night," Ilene said. "I waited inside until the taxi arrived."

"Anyone see you leave?" Nick asked.

"I don't know. We use the side entrance to come and go."

"It maintains the illusion," Helen said.

"And gives us a bit of privacy. We change into street clothes. It's funny. I've seen one or two clients outside of the club and I don't think they recognize me without the costume."

"What do you do other than work for Helen?" Nick asked.

"Well, I'm an actress," Ilene said. "I'm also getting my teaching degree. I know the odds of becoming the next Ava Gardner, but if I didn't try, I'd regret it for the rest of my life."

"Good to have options," Nick replied.

"Sometimes, when I'm at work, it feels like I'm playing a game. It's fun, but it's not part of real life. I don't want it to be part of real life."

Tears sprang to Ilene's eyes, and Nick handed her a clean handkerchief from his pocket. She dabbed at her eyes.

"It'd be one thing if it happened outside the club, but he followed me home. He knows where I live! I had to go inside to my parents, who are already horrified because they think I'm a cocktail waitress. My mother was crying. My father was swearing revenge, and the whole time I have to pretend like I'm not really hurt."

"Why?" Nick asked.

"Because they would have called the police," she replied, as if it was obvious. "I don't want to make it worse."

"Worse how?" Nick asked. "Was the man angry? Did he threaten you in other ways?"

"No. That's what made it so scary. It was methodical. Told me he was just sending a message."

"Which was?"

"He said Helen knew what he wanted and he was tired of waiting."

"And do you?" Nick asked.

"Know what he wants? No," Helen replied.

"What else can you tell me about him?"

Ilene shook her head.

"He's a lefty," Nick said, studying the pattern of bruises. "What did he look like? His general build? How tall was he?"

"He'll kill me," Ilene whispered.

"I'll keep you out of it," Nick promised.

"I don't know his name," Ilene said quietly. "But I've seen him around. He's that mob guy who used to come on Tuesdays."

"Dark hair? Medium height, medium build, perpetual sneer?" Helen asked.

Ilene nodded.

"Joey Gallo," Helen said.

"One of Mickey Cohen's crew?" Nick asked.

"I pay the cops. Pay the mob," Helen said. "Never had a problem before."

"Any chance they could have raised your rates?" Nick said.

"No," Helen replied. "In the past, they've been very forthright, and I pay them. Cohen isn't someone you haggle with."

"And you're sure you don't know what he wants?" Nick asked Helen again.

She shook her head no. Nick could not tell whether it was the truth. He had known Helen for a long time, but the woman before him was far different from the girl of his childhood.

"All right," Nick said. "Let me see what I can do."

# Chapter 9

Nick often found the less someone was liked, the easier it was to locate them. It took Nick under five minutes to learn that Joey Gallo's usual hangout was the Brown Derby. True to its name, the restaurant was a round, brown-domed building shaped to look like a hat. At the top of the dome was a neon sign, also in the shape of a hat. Apparently, redundancy was key. Inside, the walls were decorated with photos of famous faces. Beneath them, leather booths lined the room.

Nick entered and refused the hostess's offer to find him a table.

"I'm here to see Joey Gallo."

"Oh," the hostess replied.

"Not your favorite?" Nick asked.

"We value all our patrons at the Brown Derby," she said in an official voice devoid of emotion. "Are you a friend?"

"I doubt he'll be happy to see me."

The hostess stepped back with a smile and ushered Nick inside.

"Have at it. Last table on the left."

Gallo was sitting in a corner booth, flanked by several men in their twenties. They were all dressed in flashy suits, drinking cocktails. Beside them were girls, still in their late teens, possessing the jaded wariness that comes from growing up too quickly. Even if Nick had not judged Gallo by his willingness to beat up women, he would have disliked him on instinct alone. Hair thinning, with a paunch that stretched the buttons of his shirt, Gallo lounged against the banquette as if he owned it. His loud voice traveled the length of the restaurant and he was oblivious to the frequent glares nearby diners shot his way. His speech was littered with curse words meant to display toughness, but to Nick, they simply evidenced a lack of vocabulary. These men were a dime a dozen, yet they always thought themselves unique.

Nick steeled himself and approached the table. A waitress was dropping off another round and received a sharp smack on the ass. She lurched forward, spilling the remainder of the drink she had just cleared.

"Fucking watch yourself!" Gallo snapped at her. "Do you have any idea how much this suit cost? It's more than you're fucking worth."

The waitress gritted her teeth, wiped up the spill, and turned away.

"Aren't you going to apologize?" another man at the table asked.

"Sorry," she said.

"I don't think she's sorry, do you?" the man asked his companions. "You can do better than that."

The waitress started to walk away, but the man jumped up and grabbed her arm.

"I said you owe us a better apology."

Gallo laughed at his friend's antics, enjoying the woman's distress.

"I'm very sorry for spilling the drink," she said with a false smile.

"Another round of drinks, hon," Gallo said. "Make sure they're on the house."

The woman fled as Nick arrived at the table.

"Are you Joey Gallo?" Nick asked.

"Who's asking?" Gallo's sidekick asked.

"I am," Nick said. "Obviously. The words came out of my mouth . . . or did they not? Was that whole thing in my head, because that would be very bizarre. I guess it's possible I'm having this whole conversation to myself and I'm just standing in front of you wearing a strange expression on my face. Is that what's happening? Tell me if that's what's happening. Or more specifically, don't say anything, because you won't have heard anything."

"The fuck are you?" Gallo asked.

"See? That is a less obvious question, for which I thank you. My name is Nick Gallagher."

"That supposed to mean something?" Gallo said.

"I suppose it meant something to my mother when she gave it to me. Then again, she might've been drunk and picked it out of the phone book."

"Got a wise guy here," said another man at the table.

"And what do we do with wise guys?" Gallo asked.

"We show 'em out, Joey," said a third guy.

"So, you are Joey," Nick said. "Glad we cleared that up."

Gallo nodded at one of the men, who got up from the table and rushed Nick. He was big but not fast. Nick stepped out of the way, giving him a shove that tumbled him into another table.

"Sorry about that," Nick said to the diners. Then, pointing toward Gallo, "Your meal's on this guy."

Gallo nodded at another man, who came out swinging. Nick ducked under three or four punches.

"Wouldn't this be better handled outside?" Nick asked, still evading the attack. "There are nice people here who are just trying to have a good time."

The man swung again and Nick came up from below, catching the man under the chin and knocking him backward. For a moment, the man shook his head, then came toward Nick again. With a sigh, Nick released three quick jabs into the man's stomach. He curled over in pain and Nick hit him again, knocking him to the ground. The last man stood uncertainly in front of the table. He looked to Gallo, who nodded his chin toward Nick. He put up his hands and danced back and forth a few times. Nick watched him, judging correctly that his boxer's stance was all for show. Considering Mickey Cohen was once a fighter of some renown, Nick thought he would have trained his men better. After a moment of bouncing from foot to foot, Gallo got restless and gave him a small push toward Nick. The man stumbled forward and Nick, more on instinct than aggression, hit him with a right cross. The man went down harder than anyone should from that kind of impact. He lay preternaturally still, and Nick realized he was faking the whole thing.

The girls scattered, leaving Gallo alone in the booth.

"All I wanted was a conversation," Nick said. "Now, you've made a mess of this place. I'm not sure they'll let you back in."

"You're the one causing trouble," Gallo said, hauling himself out of the booth.

"Yes, but they don't know me. And frankly, I don't really care if they ban me. There are plenty of restaurants in Los Angeles. You, on the other hand . . . It hurts to be kicked out of your usual haunt."

Nick glanced around the room at the shell-shocked diners and waitresses The corners of the hostess's mouth ticked up slightly as she surveyed the wreckage.

"There's a rumor going around that you beat up a young woman last night," Nick said.

"She's a fucking whore."

"I honestly didn't think you'd cop to it so quickly," Nick said.

"Never said I touched her."

"It was implied. You seemed to know quite clearly who I was talking about. Besides, I know you did it. You know you did it. Let's just skip to the part where you tell me it was a mistake and it's never going to happen again."

"Go to hell," Gallo said.

Behind Nick, Gallo's men got to their feet. They were shaky and less interested in proving their manhood.

"That was not the answer I was looking for. To refresh your memory, the words were, 'It was a mistake. It's never going to happen again.' "

Gallo pulled a switchblade from his pocket and slashed toward Nick, catching his sleeve.

"Do you know how much I hate shopping?" Nick asked. "Now I have to buy a new shirt."

Gallo nodded toward his men. One of them came toward Nick, who grabbed his arm and kicked out his knee. The man went to the ground with an agonized cry. Not waiting for anyone else, Nick charged Gallo, grabbing his hand and twisting it back until he dropped the knife. Continuing the pressure, he brought Gallo to his knees.

"Say it," Nick demanded.

Gallo gasped in pain.

"Say it."

"Do you have any idea who I work for?" Gallo asked.

"I do, but I don't think you're going to go to Mickey Cohen. Something tells me this was freelance."

Gallo's silence confirmed Nick's assumption. Nick bent back Gallo's hand, further driving him down until his cheek rested against the floor. Kneeling on his back, Nick brought his mouth close to Gallo's ear and whispered, "Say it or I'll break your hand."

After a long moment, Gallo finally whispered the words. "It was a mistake. It's never going to happen again."

"Thank you," Nick said. "If I have to return and have this conversation again, it will be significantly less pleasant."

Nick reached into Gallo's pocket and withdrew his wallet. Opening it, he took out a stack of cash. Releasing Gallo's hand, Nick stood up. Gallo sprung to his feet.

"I'll kill you. I'll fucking kill you."

Nick looked at him as if he were not worth the bother of an argument. Walking over to the waitress, he handed her the money.

"A well-deserved tip," Nick said.

She smiled slightly and tucked the bills into her pocket. As Nick passed the hostess on his way out, she leaned close to him flirtatiously. "You ever want to come back, drinks are on me."

"Thanks," Nick said. "But I prefer drinking at home."

# Chapter 10

Carl decanted the wine as Evelyn carried over plates. As always, Nick had cooked. That night's meal was pasta puttanesca with fresh garlic bread from the Italian bakery hidden away on Little Santa Monica. Evelyn set the table with brightly colored cotton place mats and napkins. She would have set out juice glasses, but Carl insisted proper stemware was worth the effort. Nick carried the steaming bowl to the table and dished out dinner. Carl poured the wine and Evelyn got Nick a Scotch from the sideboard. They sat down and Carl held up his glass.

"*Ojalá vivas todos los días de tu vida!*"

May you live all the days of your life. It was something his father always said, and Carl had turned into a tradition during the war. Back then, it was a reminder to seize every moment. Now, it spoke of the close bond they shared from having been through so much together. Evelyn and Nick touched their glasses to Carl's, then they all drank. Evelyn looked at the wine, noticing its dark ruby color and the streaks it made as she swirled it in her glass.

"French?" she asked.

"Italian," Carl said. "A nice Sangiovese from Tuscany."

Evelyn took another drink and sighed in happiness. Then, passing her glass to Nick, "Here, try this."

He took an obligatory sip and nodded.

"Good. Really good."

"You can't tell the difference, can you?" Evelyn asked.

Nick shook his head. Despite her and Carl's efforts, he had never developed a taste for wine. "Bad grape juice with a terrible hangover" is how he described it.

"We keep trying to civilize you," Carl said. "But it's an uphill battle."

"I'll never understand how you learned about all this," Nick said. "We always drank Scotch."

"Which has its own place and time," Carl said. "But wine is for friends and food. At least that's what my grandmother always said."

Nick grated some Parmesan cheese over the pasta and they all dug in.

"Incredible, as always," Evelyn said. "Between the two of you, I'll never go hungry or thirsty."

"You should get a cook," Taffy said as she swirled into the room, rustling her taffeta evening dress.

"They would be bored," Evelyn said. "Or even worse, insulted. Can you imagine how often they'd prepare dinner only to be told that we're both stuck at work? Plus, it's a waste of food. Bread and cheese is a perfectly acceptable dinner."

"No, it's not," Taffy and Nick said in unison. They looked at each other, surprised for a moment at being of the same mind.

"You've had bread and cheese for dinner plenty of times," Evelyn said to Nick.

"When it was the only option. And I never called it dinner. It was food."

"What's the difference between dinner and food?" Evelyn asked.

"Style," Carl said.

Evelyn laughed. Nick matched her smile and, as always, she felt her heart flutter.

"You should come tonight," Taffy said to Evelyn. "Kitty Worthington Walsh was one of your mother's closest friends."

"Mom tolerated her. Barely," Evelyn said.

"Well, it would be good for your business to socialize more," Taffy said.

She had a point, but Evelyn was loathe to concede it.

"Small talk is torture," she replied.

Taffy sniffed in disapproval, then swept out of the room. Once they heard the front door slam, Carl looked from Nick to Evelyn.

"How long is she staying?"

"That is a very good question," Nick replied.

"I don't know." Evelyn sighed. "She showed up two weeks ahead of our engagement party with six trunks. She means well, but . . . my mom's family has very strict ideas about comportment."

"Comportment?" Nick asked.

"Etiquette, appropriate ways of behaving. How one displays oneself to the world. It's a shame, because when I was a kid, she was so much fun."

"When you were a kid, she wasn't trying to turn you into someone else," Nick retorted.

"True." Evelyn sighed. "You should have seen her and my mother together. They found all kinds of crazy things for us to do, like dressing up in fabulous costumes and going to high tea. Once Matthew went as a pirate king and I was a cockatoo, with real feathers. Another time Taffy planned a scavenger hunt through Beverly Hills that ended with ice cream sundaes. I miss that woman."

"Then that's who should be planning your wedding," Carl said.

"If only. We could have dragons and unicorns."

"I'm on board with a dragon. Or a unicorn. Or any other mythical creature you choose, but we need to sit down and figure out what we want," Nick said. "Before Taffy plans the wedding *she* wants."

"It's just going to be a party filled with people I barely know," Evelyn said.

"And the person you're planning on spending the rest of your life with," Nick insisted.

"Yes, but every wedding is the same. Bride walks in a puffy white dress that looks wildly uncomfortable. And, of course, she must wear heels underneath. I mean, why? No one's going to see them. They say some words in front of a man from a religion neither of us believe in and then there's a reception with passed appetizers and a five-course meal. Meanwhile, everyone's just waiting for the cake to be cut so they can go home and sleep off their hangover."

"Wow," Carl said softly, glancing toward Nick.

"That's really how you envision this once-in-a-lifetime event of us joining our lives together?" Nick asked sardonically.

"Don't be like that. You know I love you," Evelyn replied. "Isn't that enough?"

Frustrated, Nick turned to Carl, who held up his hands, refusing to referee.

"This is why I'm not married," he said.

"Well, that and the fact that you never date," Evelyn teased.

"I like my life," Carl insisted. "Just the way it is."

"I get that a wedding isn't something you dreamed about as a kid, but it still has meaning," Nick said, trying hard to keep the hurt out of his voice. "Don't know about you, but I'm only planning on doing this once."

"Nick Gallagher," Evelyn replied playfully. "If it wasn't for you, I wouldn't even consider getting married that many times."

Nick shook his head. Evelyn kissed him. He was still frowning. She kissed him again and again, until he finally threw up his hands.

"Enough!" He couldn't help laughing with her.

Evelyn turned to Carl and asked him about work.

"Sometimes, it feels like a wild-goose chase," he said of the FBI. "They have me looking into Frank Malina."

"The cofounder of JPL?" Evelyn asked. "I was there earlier today."

"Yeah, he did some labor organizing when he was a grad student and attended a few meetings for the Communist Party of America."

"That's it?" Nick asked.

"As far as I can tell," Carl said. "It's not just him. It's actors, writers, and directors. A lot of people dabbled in the CPUSA because it was trendy or because of civil rights or they were trying to get laid. Shouldn't haunt them for the rest of their lives. Even the true believers . . . If they're not passing information on to the Russians or trying to sabotage people at home, how is that being a traitor to the country?"

"Don't let J. Edgar Hoover hear you say that," Nick replied. "You'll be out of a job."

"I read about that interview with Elizabeth Berkley," Evelyn said of a Russian spy. "Didn't she name a lot of names?"

"Even some who worked on the Manhattan Project," Carl confirmed. "The question is, how can you trust someone who's willing to say anything to save their own skin? It turns into a carousel of blame with people's lives held hostage until they point the finger at someone else. Bet you could get them to name Santa Claus."

"He is a man who gives out toys willy-nilly to both rich and poor children," Evelyn said. "He spies on you to know when you're sleeping or awake. He checks in to see if you're bad or good. He's clearly Stalin in disguise."

"There are legitimate spies out there," Carl said. "But it takes time to build a case. This kind of testimony isn't real evidence."

"Do you want to go back to the LAPD?" Nick asked.

"No. I don't know." Carl sighed. "At least I felt like I was doing something. There's a finality in closing cases and arresting the bad guy."

"Why did you leave?" Evelyn asked. "Captain Wharton liked you. You were moving up in the ranks. . . ."

"Wharton's a good man," Carl said. "But I was never going to fit in. Do you have any idea how exhausting it is when every day's a battle? Not just witnessing the worst of people, but the fact that I could never really trust the other guys. At best, someone would say something ignorant or hateful. At worst, I worried about being out there on my own when the shit hit the fan."

"Is it better at the FBI?" Nick asked.

"Not really getting to do a ton of fieldwork, so . . ." Carl trailed off. "I don't know why I thought it would be different."

"Because it should be," Evelyn said.

"If only you ran the world," Carl replied.

"Doughnuts would be healthy," Nick said.

"And strudel," Evelyn added. "Speaking of which, I'm going to Germany the day after tomorrow to see if I can find Kurt Vogel's wife and daughter."

"That mission was years ago," Nick said.

"True, but I feel for him. It's bad enough to lose your family, but to not have any answers . . . ? If you simply disappeared, I don't know how I'd survive. Even if I managed to put one foot in front of the other, there'd be a hole in my heart where you belong. It wouldn't beat properly."

"Mine either," Nick replied as he took her hand and lay it over his heart. "That's why you must promise to be careful. Berlin isn't exactly the safest place in the world."

"Are you worried I'll get myself into trouble?" Evelyn teased.

"Always," Nick and Carl answered in unison.

# Chapter 11

Nick was in his office, doing the daily crossword puzzle. He had picked up the habit during the war, when he was bored, and now it was his daily indulgence. In fact, he often bought the newspaper just for the game . . . and maybe Dick Tracy on the last page. He was three quarters of the way through and stuck on a particularly difficult seven-letter clue. The phone rang and Nick looked up in annoyance.

"Nick Gallagher," he answered.

"You have to come over," a panicked voice said.

"Helen?" Nick guessed.

"Who the hell else would it be?"

Nick could think of a number of people, but it did not seem like the time to mention it.

"What's wrong?"

"Another girl was attacked last night. I just picked her up from the hospital. That animal broke her leg."

"Give me ten minutes," Nick said.

It only took nine to reach Helen's club. By the time Nick had parked, Gregory had the door open. Unlike his usual polished self, he had a five-o'clock shadow and his eyes were bloodshot.

"Rough night?" Nick asked.

"Rough couple of mornings. It's my job to protect these women," he said, his voice cracking.

They walked through the empty main room. It seemed smaller when not filled with people. They proceeded through a door to Helen's office in back. It was well-appointed, with a dark leather couch studded with brass rivets. There was a heavy oak desk in the center with client chairs across from it. Several bookcases lined the room, stocked with leather tomes whose spines had never been cracked. Velvet curtains shrouded the windows and a dark blue carpet pulled everything together. It was a room that gave the impression of a very successful businessperson.

A young woman lay on the couch with her leg in a cast. Bruises riddled her face and arms, and Nick winced in sympathy. He pulled up a chair beside her, held out his hand, and introduced himself.

"Rosa Hernandez," she replied.

"I'm so sorry this happened to you," Nick said. "I'm going to do everything in my power to make it stop."

"Didn't you try that already?" Rosa snapped. "I heard what happened to Ilene."

Before he could respond, the door burst open and Julia, the club's bartender, rushed to Rosa. Dressed in a skirt, sweater, and loafers, she looked like a schoolgirl. Yet she still had a commanding confidence. She knelt down beside the couch and spoke to Rosa in rapid Spanish. That language had never been one of Nick's specialties; then again, very few were. He didn't need to hear the exact words to understand the concern in Julia's voice. Rosa's grew louder, angrier, while Julia's was calm and reassuring. She held Rosa's hand, repeating over and over again that she was not alone. She was safe now. Finally, Rosa started crying and Julia held her, like a child. When Rosa eventually dried her eyes, she began to tell them her story.

It was the same as Ilene's assault, but hers was more brutal. Rather than just using his fists, Gallo brought a crowbar and broke her leg. He left her on the sidewalk for hours, in agony, unable to walk until a milkman found her and called an ambulance. It was one of the longest nights of her life.

This time, Gallo was more specific, demanding photos and promising to keep coming back until he got what he wanted. Even if that meant hurting a hundred girls. Even if it ruined Helen's business.

"How could you let this happen?" Rosa asked Helen.

"The man who did this is a monster," Julia said softly, brushing back Rosa's hair. "And I've yet to find a way to guard against those."

"You're welcome to recover here," Helen offered.

Rosa laughed humorlessly. "I'm going home."

"All right, I'll come by later with food, supplies, whatever you need. Don't worry about anything. I'll cover your expenses for as long as you . . ."

"The only expense you can cover is a train ticket to El Paso," Rosa said.

"But school," Julia insisted. "You've worked so hard and we only have one more semester."

"I'll finish in Texas," Rosa replied.

"Come stay with my family," Julia offered. "You'll be safe there. We'll take care of you. You can finish college and . . ."

"It's time to put this part of my life behind me. You understand, don't you?"

Julia sighed, unconvinced but also knowing that arguing was pointless.

"I'll help you pack."

Rosa reached for her crutches, but Gregory swept her up in his arms and carried her outside. Julia hung back for a moment.

"You need to fix this," Julia said sharply to Helen. "There's more than you're telling us or Nick."

Nick was flattered she remembered his name.

"I don't know—" Helen began.

"Of course you do," Julia said matter-of-factly. Her tone was not unkind, but Helen looked startled to be challenged. "It won't just be Rosa who leaves. It will be all your other employees. It's one thing keeping a secret from our families when work is good. It's another trying to explain away a black eye or a broken bone. And that's not even the worst of it. Do you think Rosa and Ilene will ever feel safe again? Would you?"

Helen didn't answer. Julia let that sink in, then followed after Rosa.

"Are you ready to tell me what's going on?" Nick asked. "I can't work with one hand tied behind my back. I need the truth."

Helen still hesitated.

"I'll send you my final bill," Nick said as he turned away.

He made it to the door before she called out, "Wait! Wait!"

Nick turned back.

"I don't trust people," Helen began. "Especially men. You'd be surprised how quickly they can turn on you. One moment you're their everything and the next you're cowering in a corner with a broken nose."

"You're involved with Gallo?" Nick asked, surprised.

"Oh hell no. I'm involved with my clients. I do my best to screen them, and we have no tolerance for inappropriate behavior. Sometimes, however, they step out of line. At which point, I remind them of their manners."

"Spit it out."

"I take pictures of every single man who comes through my establishment. They don't know about it, of course, but I have photos of several prominent individuals in compromising positions. Cops, politicians, judges, even the Mafia."

"And Gallo knows about it?"

"Does he strike you as especially well-behaved? He tried to get certain services for free. When I refused, he threatened to tell Mickey Cohen I stiffed him. I showed him a picture of himself in a less than flattering position. Later, he returned, telling me that if there were pictures of him, there were probably a lot more. If it ever got out that I have these photos . . . ?"

"Your business is ruined," Nick finished.

"As are the lives of my employees. Their faces are visible. These are respectable young women. Some are mothers. Some college students. There's even been a few who started with me before making it big in Hollywood. All of that would come crashing down."

"I might know a way to get him to stop," Nick said, thinking. "Let me talk to Evelyn."

"Your socialite has contacts in the Mafia?"

"You don't know Evie," Nick replied with a smile.

"Well, I applaud you for landing her," Helen said. "She's one of the richest women in the country. Hell, in the world."

"It's not like that," Nick insisted.

"Uh-huh," Helen said sarcastically. "A boy who grew up dirt poor and you have no interest in her money. Don't get me wrong, marrying for love is exactly the right line to take, but everyone sees through it."

"I'd marry Evelyn if she were penniless," Nick insisted. "I'd marry her if it meant living in a dirt hut in a field. . . . I'd marry her if it meant going back to where we started."

"It's very convincing," Helen said. "If I didn't know better, I'd almost believe you."

"We're done here," Nick said, standing up.

"Don't get all prickly," Helen said. "I'm on your side. Just remember my club when you start to get bored."

Nick stalked out. In his car, he looked down and saw his hand trembling. With effort, he uncurled his fingers and released his fist. He could not remember the last time he was this angry. He knew how his and Evelyn's relationship looked from the outside. Somehow, though, it had never bothered him until now.

# Chapter 12

Evelyn had a habit of talking to people before she was actually in the room with them. It was something she picked up from her father and it drove Ruth crazy.

"Your flight's at noon," Ruth called, answering Evelyn's mumbled question from her office. "And if you want anything else, you can come here and talk to me like a civilized person."

Chastened, Evelyn came out to Ruth's desk.

"Apologies. Before I leave for Germany, will you please compile a list of our current expenses? Break it down by quarter, and per plane. I'll need all the information on our future projects, as well as the latest report from Hank. Call down and see where he is with the new radar technology for the fog. Ask him if there are ways to drop the weight of the planes themselves so they can carry more freight. Also—"

"Would you like me to call your chief engineer and ask him to come up?"

"Oh, no," Evelyn replied. "He has a new puppy and hasn't slept in a week. Cranky barely begins to describe him. I'd better go find him myself. I'm hoping to come back from Berlin with another five million in orders."

"Five million dollars?" gasped a young woman in the corner.

Evelyn looked to Ruth questioningly.

"This is Betsy," Ruth said. "A candidate for your new assistant."

The woman stepped forward to shake Evelyn's hand. She had a wide smile and radiated an eager, cheerful energy. She wore a bright pink sundress and her hair was curled into perfect ringlets.

"It's so nice to meet you, Mrs. Bishop."

"Miss Bishop," Evelyn corrected. Then, looking to Ruth, "This isn't the best time—"

"You'll put it off forever if you have the chance. You're meeting four people today. This is happening."

Evelyn sighed, then led Betsy into her office. Almost every surface was covered with papers and Evelyn cleared away a few stacks from a guest chair, then motioned to Betsy.

"Please," Evelyn said.

Betsy sat down on the edge of the chair, delicately crossing her ankles. Evelyn noticed she had impeccable posture.

"Tell me about yourself," Evelyn began.

"I'm pretty typical. I grew up in Pasadena with my parents and two older sisters. Straight A student in high school, and I tutored other kids for pocket money."

"Anything else? What do you do in your free time?"

"I love to go to the pictures, and sometimes my family will head down to the beach on the weekend."

"It's a long drive from Pasadena to here. Will that commute be a problem?"

Betsy's eyes widened. "I hadn't thought about it."

"What other jobs have you held?" Evelyn asked.

"Recently, I worked for the president of the Tournament of Roses."

"In what capacity?"

Betsy hesitated for a moment before admitting, "Rose Queen."

"I see," Evelyn said. "Saying no is a big part of this job. How would you deal with someone I didn't want to see?"

Betsy thought for a moment, then said, "I'm sure we can find a way for everyone to get along."

Evelyn stood up. "Thank you so much for coming."

"Okay, then," Betsy said brightly as she left the office.

Ruth appeared in the doorway. Evelyn just raised her eyebrows.

"She wasn't that . . . buoyant when I met her."

"She's barely out of high school."

"But she had a good attitude, which is important," Ruth said. Then, seeing Evelyn's expression, she promised, "The next one has more experience."

An hour later, Evelyn was buried in expense projections for the factory expansion. There was a knock on the door.

"One moment," she said without looking up. With a red pen, she circled a few numbers, then made a quick calculation on the margin.

"I have an appointment," a man's voice said.

Evelyn ignored him.

"Why don't you take a seat?" Ruth suggested.

"I'm fine standing."

Evelyn felt his presence in the doorway as she continued working. After a minute, she heard the man turn to Ruth and say, "My appointment was at two p.m."

"Miss Bishop will see you when she is able."

Evelyn heard footsteps pacing.

"Ruth!" she called without looking up. "Door, please."

Ruth pulled the door shut. Even through the wood, Evelyn heard the man's protest. Fifteen minutes later, she finished her review and jotted down a few notes. She carried the documents outside to Ruth.

"Will you please turn this into something legible for

Lewis to look over before we speak to the contractors next week?"

Ruth took the documents and stood up.

"This is Jared Longrove."

"It's two seventeen," he said by way of greeting.

Evelyn twisted her watch and glanced at the time.

"So it is."

"As I was walking through the factory, I noted several places where I think you can improve. For one—"

"I'm going to stop you right there," Evelyn said, turning to Ruth.

"Overcorrection from this morning," Ruth said.

Evelyn nodded and headed back into her office. Jared started to follow but was greeted with a door closed in his face.

"But I'm not finished," he said, offended.

"Yes, you are," Ruth replied firmly.

"You're making a huge mistake," he called through the door. "I'll be running a company one day. You have no idea what you're giving up."

The next applicant seemed good on paper and she certainly had confidence, but when Evelyn asked about her career goals, the woman looked shocked.

"I'm going to have children, once I meet the right man," she said. "Fingers crossed he's here!"

"Have you considered working at a bank?" Evelyn suggested. "I think you'll find more of the type of men you're looking for."

"Oooh! That's a great idea. Plus, I can sneak a look at their finances to make sure they can support a family," the girl enthused.

The last interview was toward the end of the day. Evelyn was finishing the last of her work when there was a knock at the door. Beside Ruth stood an attractive woman who wore pants but no makeup. Her hair was brushed back into a low ponytail and she looked like she couldn't be a day over seventeen.

"I'm Willa," she said, extending her hand as she approached Evelyn.

Ruth nodded encouragingly before closing the door.

"Please, sit down," Evelyn said, motioning to a chair. Willa sat and crossed her legs at the knee. There was an eager anticipation about her.

"Tell me about yourself," Evelyn said.

"My dad died when I was a baby, so I was raised by my mom. She fancied herself an actress, and we moved from one gig to the next. Maybe not the most conventional upbringing, but there was always a roof over our heads and food on the table."

"Let me guess, you want to follow in her footsteps?"

"The insecurity that comes with that kind of life . . . ? No thank you. I moved to Los Angeles because we'd been living in Fresno for the last two years of high school and UCLA offered me in-state tuition and a scholarship."

"I went there, too," Evelyn replied. "Several years before your time, though."

"Don't be so certain," Willa said with a smile. "I'm older than I look."

"Graduated?" Evelyn asked, and when Willa nodded, she asked what she studied.

"Double major. Engineering and chemistry," Willa replied.

For the next twenty minutes, they happily discussed professors and classes they once had in common. It was an easy conversation and, to her surprise, Evelyn found herself enjoying it.

"So, tell me," Evelyn finally said, returning to the topic at hand. "Why do you want to be a secretary?"

Willa hesitated, debating with herself.

"I don't," she said eventually. "I want to go back to

school and get my PhD, then put that to use making something that will change the world. Right now, no one's hiring female engineers or chemists. This job would allow me to save up some money. If I keep my ear to the ground, I can learn a lot about how to design airplanes. Plus, I've heard this is a good place to work."

Evelyn picked up her phone and dialed a number.

"Hank," she said once she had her chief engineer on the phone. "I'm sending down someone you can use. Talk to her and see if you agree."

When she hung up, Evelyn turned to Willa.

"Here's the deal. You're going to go speak with the head of our design team. If he likes you, you'll start full-time in his department. We're expanding our production of jet engines, so we can use all the help we can get. After six months, if you still want to attend UCLA, the company will pay for your PhD while you continue your work here."

"What?" Willa asked, stunned.

"I believe in investing in people. The hope is that after you have your degree, you'll want to stay and use your newfound knowledge."

"What?" Willa asked again.

"Large companies do this for men all the time. I happen to think women bring a different point of view, which is valuable when creating something both men and women will use."

For a moment, Willa sat there, stunned. Finally, words came back to her.

"Thank you," she said. "You won't regret it."

"I don't think I will," Evelyn said with a smile.

She stood and escorted Willa to the door. Ruth looked up eagerly as they exited. One of the engineers was sitting in the waiting area of Evelyn's office. He stood when Willa approached.

"Let me take you down," he said. "It's right this way."

He led her down the stairs towards the engineering department. Willa followed, her eyes still wide with excitement and disbelief.

"You two were in there for a long time," Ruth prompted. "It went well?"

"Great. She's a real find. I offered her a job."

"Fantastic!"

"In design and engineering."

Ruth deflated. "You're kidding me."

"She would have been wasted as my secretary," Evelyn said. "You're brilliant and the most amazing person I've ever met. Don't ever think I take you for granted. I'm just saying that everyone has different talents, and if you're trying to shove one person into a role that doesn't fit, it's not going to go well."

"Fine." Ruth sighed.

"Cheer up. It's just the first day. I'm sure we'll have many, many more days of my rejecting people."

"Something to look forward to," Ruth replied sarcastically as she picked up her bag to leave. Then, relenting slightly, she turned back. "Take care of yourself in Germany. I don't want to break in a new boss."

# Chapter 13

Evelyn sat in her old office on Rodeo Drive, curled up on the couch with her feet tucked underneath her. Technically, this was Nick's now, but seeing he had yet to change anything, she felt no guilt about using it to meet up with her friends, Colette Palmer and Lily Shen. In Evelyn's previous life as a private investigator, she had helped both women. Their relationships started with gratitude but quickly became rooted in common interests. All three of them owned their own businesses and loved that responsibility and sense of purpose.

Lily, who was born in Arcadia, of Chinese descent, was telling them about a particularly odious woman who had come to her store. When she saw Lily, she immediately began speaking loudly in broken English, asking for someone native. At which point, Lily replied in French that she spoke three languages perfectly well, then switched to English to tell the customer that while this land had originally belonged to the Tongva people, unfortunately, she did not employ anyone with that background.

"It's all about the pleasant smile," Lily explained. "You appear totally unruffled, even though you've just pointed out that they don't have the sense God gave a bumblebee."

"Please tell me she fled in shame," Colette said.

"No, then she asked to speak with the manager. I, again, had to disappoint her by telling her the manager did not work that day, but the owner did. The woman then demanded to speak with the owner. I wish I could properly describe her face when I told her this was my store. That's when it really started to go downhill."

"Oh, no," Evelyn said.

"It was pretty bad. The kind of stuff that would have destroyed me as a teenager, but after everything I've been through. . . ." Lily shrugged. "It's a lot harder to hurt me."

Colette reached over and squeezed Lily's hand in support.

"Who was this?" Evelyn asked. When Lily told her, Evelyn shuddered in dislike. "Oh, yes. I know her. As my grandmother used to say, money can't buy class."

"Ironically, she learned about my store during your engagement party because I dressed so many of the people there."

"Then I'm doubly sorry," Evelyn replied. "Aunt Taffy sent the invitations."

"You didn't look over the guest list?" Colette asked.

"The party didn't really register until Taffy showed up on my doorstep to do the final preparations." Evelyn shrugged. "If Ruth doesn't remind me, it's like it doesn't exist."

"How's the hunt for a new secretary?" Colette asked.

"If the first day of interviews is any indication, I expect Ruth to be a hundred and seven before I find her replacement."

"I can make some inquiries," Colette offered.

"Actually, what would be incredibly helpful is telling me how to navigate the permit system at city hall," Evelyn said. "I know you had to do it when you began the overhaul at the factory."

"It helped that George started the process before he died," Colette said. "Plus, Sean had connections."

"That's the thing, though," Evelyn said. "My father applied ages ago. Then, when the company changed hands, we had to start all over again. Lewis, my VP in charge of operations, is supposed to know everyone . . . and yet. We can't get any forward momentum."

"Alan Hunsaker," Colette said with authority.

"Alan Hunsaker?"

"He has a tiny office down in the basement of a nondescript building on Figueroa. He has no official title. Most people don't even know he exists, but he's the person who decides which permits get seen and when. He knows everyone and can shepherd things through quickly. After I saw him, it only took a few weeks."

"How did you find him?"

"One day Sean and I had a bunch of meetings at city hall. We were shunted from one office to the next without getting any answers. My favorite was the guy who told me I was running the company into the ground and ruining my husband's legacy."

Colette trailed off with a wave of her hand, but Evelyn knew better. The accusation stung.

"And . . . ?" Lily prompted.

"Sean practically had to carry me out of there I was yelling so much."

"At least it was probably in French," Evelyn offered.

"I got my point across," Colette said. "After that, both Sean and I decided the rest of the meetings would go more smoothly without me. I went outside to wait and a half hour later, I saw the man's secretary on her way to lunch. I bought her a meal and we gossiped over impossible men. At the end, she gave me Mr. Hunsaker's information."

"Secretaries know everything," Lily said.

"How much was the bribe?" Evelyn asked.

"Surprisingly, I didn't have to give him one. I went in prepared, but he's the type of civil servant who really cares about the city. I told him what I was trying to do and why. He found my application, looked it over, asked me some questions about whether I would have the same number of employees after the conversion. I told him that I expected to hire even more, but that I was keeping everyone on the payroll, even while the factory was closed. That seemed to impress him. He put it in a specific pile and that was that."

"Now I just have to find the time to go see him," Evelyn replied.

"Give me the paperwork and I'll pay him another visit," Colette offered.

"You are amazing," Evelyn said gratefully.

"As are both of you," Colette said, raising her glass. "To finding each other."

Evelyn and Lily raised their glasses to hers, then they all drank.

"Speaking of finding friends," Evelyn began. "Colette, after the war, you looked for people from your hometown, right?"

Colette nodded. She was French and her late husband moved heaven and earth to help her escape in 1943.

"Not just my family, but . . . but everyone who was rounded up by the Nazis," she said quietly.

"Was it hard to find out what happened to them?" Evelyn asked.

"No. My mother was still in the same place. Nothing much had changed, though my sister got married and moved to Reims."

"And everyone else?"

"Most of those deported ended up in Auschwitz. Very few survived."

"What about those who did?"

"Some went to Israel. Others returned home. For those

who wanted to come to the US, I sponsored their visas and offered them work."

"How did you locate them?" Evelyn asked.

"I reached out to the Red Cross," Colette said. "Their files from the displaced persons camps are pretty detailed. They include everything from 1938 onward, including records from the concentration camps."

"So, all it took was a request?" Evelyn asked again.

"Yes, but I also have resources."

"So does the US Army," Evelyn said.

"Something bothering you about this trip to Berlin?" Lily asked.

"There's a lot that doesn't add up," Evelyn replied. "I just don't understand how Kurt Vogel's family could disappear without a trace."

# Chapter 14

Evelyn came home to find Nick and Taffy sitting at the dining room table. Scattered around them were the remains of what seemed to be a five-course meal. Nick looked bemused, but Taffy was furious.

"Where the hell have you been?" Taffy demanded.

"I was at wo—" Evelyn broke off, seeing Nick shaking his head. "Work, before I met up with a . . . client. You always say I need to socialize more."

"Do you have any idea how many times I called your office?" Taffy asked. "No one answered."

"Everyone goes home at five thirty."

"It wasn't until six that I realized you weren't coming."

"Coming to . . . ? What's going on here?" Evelyn asked.

"The caterer. He made samples for the wedding. But no, you couldn't be bothered."

"Did you schedule it with Ruth?" Evelyn asked.

"I told *you*," Taffy insisted. "I'm not about to reach out to a stranger just to put things on your calendar. Especially something this important."

For a moment, Evelyn wondered if Taffy had the same reservations about reaching out to secretaries when it was her husband's schedule.

"Ruth manages my entire life. If you don't tell her, it doesn't happen."

"It's true," Nick interjected. "I have to set up date nights through Ruth."

"This is your wedding!" Taffy admonished. "It should be at the top of your list."

"Why?" Evelyn asked, genuinely curious. "Why is this more important than improving safety standards on our Continental 700? Or getting better air mileage from our new jet engine? Or improving radar technology to land planes in Berlin?"

"This is the biggest day of your life!"

"Why?" Evelyn asked again. She was not intending to be difficult, but it seemed like a lot of pressure to have this specific moment go down in the annals of personal history as being the most significant. "I mean, the day I took over Bishop was pretty important. So was the day the war ended."

"This is yours and Nick's. No one else's."

"So, we're not having a guest list of two hundred people?" Evelyn asked.

"I swear, Evelyn. Sometimes you're so deliberately obtuse I have to remind myself you're twenty-eight, not eight. This battle of wills wasn't charming then and it's certainly not charming now."

With that, Taffy stormed upstairs. Evelyn sat down across from Nick, feeling slightly chagrined. Partially because of Taffy's anger, but mostly for leaving Nick alone.

"Sorry I missed it," Evelyn said. "I'm even sorrier for leaving you alone with Taffy."

"Oh, it's all right," Nick replied. "She was so angry at you that she forgot I'm not good enough to marry her niece."

"She doesn't think that," Evelyn said.

"She thought I was the butler."

"If you had known their butler, you'd know that was a compliment. He was like family."

Nick was unconvinced. Instead, he held up a small crab cake.

"Try this."

Evelyn bit into it and her eyes lit up.

"It's really good!"

"Even better when it's hot," Nick replied. There was a teasing note to his voice, but underlying it was a justified grievance. "I know this isn't your idea of fun, but planning our wedding is important."

"What if, and here me out, we don't get married?"

Nick stared at her for a long moment. A variety of emotions, from anger to confusion to sadness.

"There was this time when I asked you," Nick began. "I distinctly remember it because I was down on one knee. You made me say the words. Then you said something back. Started with a 'y' and ended with an 'es.' What was that again?"

"We know what we mean to each other," she said. "Why get the government or religion involved? Isn't this enough?"

Nick sat back in his chair, trying not to take her words personally.

"Marriage is different. It's more. I love you, Ev—"

"And I love you!"

"My whole family abandoned me when I was twelve. I just came home one day and they were gone," Nick said. "I want someone who's legally required to stay."

Evelyn did not know what to say. Nick pushed a plate toward her. "I'm guessing there wasn't much food at your 'client' dinner."

"No food," Evelyn admitted. "But a fair amount of whiskey."

"Leave any for me?"

"I'll buy you a new bottle."

As Evelyn scavenged through the leftovers of what was, in fact, a five-course meal, she told him about her day. He, in turn, told her about his, conveniently leaving out his argument with Helen. There did not seem a point.

"I need you to do something for me," Nick said at the end.

"I feel like I owe you, after tonight," Evelyn replied.

"Can you arrange a meeting with a certain well-connected gentleman?"

Evelyn raised her eyebrows but went to get her address book.

# Chapter 15

Norman Roth was at his usual table at Canter's Deli, working on the crossword. Sitting in gray slacks and a light blue, short-sleeved shirt, he could have been any man in his forties. To the casual observer, he looked engrossed in his puzzle, but Evelyn doubted he missed anything that happened in this restaurant. Despite his easy posture, one arm leaning on the table, the other twirling a pencil, he possessed an undercurrent of tension.

Norman looked up as Evelyn and Nick slid into the booth across from him.

"It was a pleasant surprise to hear from you, Miss Bishop."

"I appreciate your taking the time to meet with us," Evelyn said.

"I was curious what the head of Bishop Aeronautics could possibly want from me."

It was a not-so-subtle reminder that favors granted required favors in return.

"Actually, I asked to meet you," Nick said. "Evelyn was kind enough to reach out, seeing you two have a better relationship."

"This keeps getting more interesting," Norman replied.

"I think we have a mutual problem," Nick began.

Norman's eyes narrowed. "I've never been a fan of people telling me about my problems."

"Well, I didn't know how to politely say, 'one of your men is going behind your back and fucking up your business.'"

A small smile turned up the corner of Norman's mouth. "Go on."

"Joey Gallo," Nick said. "Used to pick up your cut from Helen Brecker's club."

Norman gave no sign of knowing the name.

"Last couple of days, he's been following her employees home and beating them up," Nick said. "One even had to go to the hospital. If he kills the next woman, the cops will definitely be involved. I don't know that much about your world, but the situation doesn't seem ideal."

"Why did Gallo go after the girls?" Norman asked.

Nick explained about the blackmail photos.

"Those pictures could be very valuable," Norman mused.

"Those pictures only exist because no one knows about them. Would you patronize an establishment that took snapshots of your bare ass? More to the point, you and your associates have a stake in the club. If Gallo keeps this up, Helen's never going to be able to retain her employees. The club will go under and so will a source of income."

"Hypothetically," Norman began. "If such an arrangement existed, it would not be a substantial part of our revenue."

"Perhaps not," Nick said. "But letting Gallo continue his harassment makes it seem like you can't control your people. It would also send a very clear signal to other businesses that your word cannot be trusted. If Miss Brecker's club is under attack and you do nothing to stop it, why should anyone have faith in your arrangement?"

"Gallo's been a member of Mickey's crew for a long

time," Norman said. "Sometimes Mickey admires initiative. If Miss Brecker's business were to fail but we receive those photographs, I believe Mickey would consider it a worthwhile exchange."

"Have you met Helen Brecker?" Nick asked.

"Can't say I've had the pleasure," Norman said.

"I've known her since I was twelve. Almost all fear has been beaten out of her. Literally. Trust me when I tell you that she'd sooner burn her place to the ground than give it up to someone who threatened her," Nick warned. "She'd do everything in her power to ruin that person. Probably wouldn't be successful, but she'd inflict some pain."

Norman thought for a long moment. "I'll take this matter under consideration."

"Thank you."

"I hear congratulations are in order," Norman said. "I saw news of your engagement in the papers."

"I can't believe it's that big of a deal." Evelyn sighed. "I wouldn't have bothered with an announcement, but my Aunt Taffy swept in with the party."

"Mickey and I were disappointed not to receive invitations."

"Taffy made the guest list," Evelyn replied. "I'm pretty sure she went down the social register and chose the first three hundred names."

"Even so, I expect we'll be included in the nuptials."

"Um . . . uh," Nick started, not really knowing what to say.

"See?" Evelyn said to Nick. "This is the problem with getting married. All people want to discuss is the wedding."

With that, Evelyn stood, thanked Norman for his time, and headed out of the deli.

# Chapter 16

Evelyn thought about flying herself to Germany, but the trip took over twenty-four hours on a good day. Instead, she caught an army transport, with stops in Massachusetts, Newfoundland, and the Azores. When they finally touched down at Rhein-Main Air Base, near Frankfurt, Evelyn gratefully stepped off the plane, stretching her sore muscles. She was tired, cranky, and desperate for a stiff drink. Despite finding enough space to lie down and sleep for part of the flight, army transports were not built for comfort.

The scene that greeted her on the ground was controlled chaos. Rhein-Main was one of three bases from which the airlift operated. It was stretched far beyond its original capacity. Planes, both C-47s and C-54s, were lined up nose to tail, with departures every three minutes. Housing for the influx of American servicemen consisted of tents and tar paper shacks. These structures looked like they could barely withstand a strong wind. Evelyn hated to guess what would happen once winter arrived. For a moment she just looked around. She had forgotten the intensity of a major military operation.

"Evelyn!"

She turned at the sound of her name to see David Bernstein striding toward her. The last time she saw him was shortly after the end of the war. They had served together in the OSS, alongside Nick and Carl. David joined the team in 1944 at age twenty-one. Fresh faced and excited, he replaced their friend who had been killed. At first, they were not sure whether his innocent enthusiasm would prove an asset or whether it would grate on their nerves. By that point, Evelyn, Nick, and Carl were two years into working together and they had formed a bond that went beyond family. David's eagerness was tempered by empathy and humility. He worked hard and watched their backs. Never pushing for greater familiarity than they were willing to give, his innate kindness made him impossible not to love.

While Carl, Nick, and Evelyn returned to Los Angeles after the war, David elected to stay in the army and serve under General Gibson. Evelyn had kept in touch, yet she was still surprised to see him. They were not far apart in age, but he was so innocent when they met that Evelyn often thought of him as a much, much younger brother. Now here he was, a grown man who walked with confidence and commanded respect simply through his bearing.

"Captain Bernstein," she said, snapping off a smart salute.

"Stop," he replied, embarrassed.

"Army life suits you."

"President of Bishop Aeronautics suits you."

"Tell that to the bags under my eyes."

David scrutinized her. "Nope. Stunning as ever."

"When did you become such a smooth talker?" Evelyn asked.

"When I discovered there are women out there. Who like me," he replied. "It was a revelation. Let me tell you."

"You have a sweetheart?"

"Listen to you," he replied. "You've become a yenta."

Evelyn laughed. "Then let this shiksa remind you that you are a mensch. Don't turn into a shegetz just because the uniform buys you good will."

"I'd never take advantage of a situation. Besides, I'm looking for what you and Nick have," he said. "Until then, it's nice to have fun, so long as everyone's on the same page."

"Tell me everything," Evelyn said as she slid her arm through his.

David glanced down at his watch.

"We have just enough time to grab some grub before we catch our flight into Berlin."

The food in the mess hall was just as bad as their meals during the war. Rationing was still in effect and few things that were prepared for the masses could truly be called high quality. David brought Evelyn up to speed on the situation. The roads and rails through the Soviet section of Germany had been blockaded since June 24. Those first weeks were rocky. No Westerners thought the Soviets would keep it up and no Soviets thought that the Allies were prepared to do what it would take to supply Berlin. At first the airlift was a haphazard mess, with planes racing one another to Tempelhof Airport, only to find themselves circling the airport until they had permission to land. There were no set schedules, so pilots were dragged out of bed just minutes before their flight. No one was getting enough sleep and they still were not bringing in enough food to keep people above starvation levels. Meanwhile, the reserve supplies in Berlin were dwindling.

"Those were the warm months," Evelyn added. "What about coal?"

"That's the question," David said. "I used to hope the blockade would end any day, but then the Russians sprang the trap. After waiting for everyone to get good and panicked, they're offering plenty of food and coal in their sector. All you have to do is turn over your ration card."

"And officially become part of the Soviet machine."

"Very few people took them up on the offer," David said. "Most are holding out for the Americans. They want free elections. They want their chosen candidates."

"The Russians were not known as benevolent conquerors, either," Evelyn said.

When the Soviet Army took Berlin, there was mass rape and indiscriminate killing. Women had to make impossible choices just to get the food and supplies they needed to survive. It was not something people spoke about, but Evelyn imagined it was impossible to forget when the USSR asked for loyalty.

"There's that, too," David conceded. "General William Tunner recently joined the effort and he's been doing a good job getting everything organized."

"I don't think I know him," Evelyn said.

"He served in the Pacific, flying ten million pounds a day from a base in India to Kunming in the Yunnan Province."

"That's one of the hardest flight routes in the world," Evelyn said, stunned.

"If anyone can keep Berlin alive over the winter, it's him. His nickname is 'Willie the Whip,' and he's proud of his reputation for being tough as nails."

"Can you get me a meeting?" Evelyn asked. "I'd love to know what he needs in planes."

"Good to see you haven't changed," David said with a laugh.

He led Evelyn out to the tarmac. Standing next to a beat-up old Skymaster was a crew of three bleary-eyed men. They snapped off a salute to David.

"How many is this?" David asked.

"Second of three runs for the day," the pilot answered.

Evelyn looked at the plane. Out of habit, she ran her hand over the battered steel shell, inspecting it with her trained eye.

"Ma'am, we should get going," the copilot said.

Evelyn offered a smile but continued her inspection. The copilot started toward her, but David shook his head.

"It's her thing."

"There was a rumor during the war," the navigator began. "Of a spy who refused to step on a plane until she knew it was airworthy. Every single one of her crew made it home."

David inclined his head toward Evelyn and they watched her with rapt attention. Since the beginning of the airlift, several planes had crashed, killing everyone aboard. Considering how many runs they made every day, it was not a thought to dwell on, but every bit of luck was welcome.

"Your rudder flaps will need replacing after another twenty flights and your tires are a shambles," Evelyn said. "They'll get you there and back, but when you're done for the day, insist they be replaced. The mechanics will tell you they can get another week out of them, but that's wishful thinking."

Evelyn turned to climb the stairs, but the pilot stopped her.

"How do you know so much about this plane?"

"Because my father built it. Want me to show you how to *really* fly it?" she asked with a glint in her eye.

"A court-martial isn't my idea of a good time," the pilot replied.

The crew led Evelyn and David towards the nose of the plane where they found seats. The pilot in the cramped cockpit flipped the switches, turning on the plane's four engines. The propellers began to spin, spitting smoke into the air. The plane taxied to the runway, then began to pick up speed. It was not nearly as much as they needed. The throttle was all the way down, but they were quickly running out of room. For a person who was rarely nervous in a plane, Evelyn grasped the bottom of her seat with white knuckles. Finally, at the very end of the runway, Evelyn felt the wheels leave the ground and breathed a sigh of relief.

"Each plane is carrying exactly nineteen thousand five hundred pounds of food and supplies," the pilot said. He explained that for the first half hour, they were flying over Allied territory, directed by Morse code beacons. The steady beep was reassuring as it faded into the background. Once they crossed into Soviet territory, however, the sound stopped. All that could be heard was the wind against the exterior of the plane. The silence was haunting, not revealing whether the plane was inside one of the prescribed air corridors. Veering too far in one direction was cause to be shot down. Instead, the pilot relied on visual landmarks. Though they flew around the clock, the darkness of night made it difficult, and fog made it next to impossible. Everyone from the top general to the lowliest private crossed their fingers and prayed that winter's scourge would hold off as long as possible.

As they neared Berlin, Evelyn looked out the window and gasped at the destruction. Buildings were crumbled precariously and the streets looked almost impassable. It was more than three years since the war ended, but the city was still a bombed-out shell of its former self. It seemed uninhabitable, yet she knew it housed more than two million residents. Seeing it from above reinforced everything she had been told about the struggle to survive.

The approach at Tempelhof was harrowing. There was a tall apartment building to one side and a four-hundred-foot brewery smokestack on the other. The pilots had to avoid both, then descend sharply into the airport. The runways were held together by the rocks and tar local women poured into the cracks after every landing. The plane slammed down onto the runway, jarring Evelyn. The pilot pulled up on the flaps while breaking hard. They finally slowed to a taxi and followed a jeep over to the unloading zone. Before they were out of their seats, the workers had the belly of the plane open and were pulling out the cargo.

Evelyn unbuckled herself, then looked to the crew.

"Forget what I said about your rudders and tires. Get them changed now."

The crew headed toward the snack truck to get some food and coffee. David led Evelyn to a jeep and drove them to a stately administration building. Somehow, it had managed to escape the worst of the bombing. The stairs leading to the entrance were freshly poured concrete and the offices were furnished with leather chairs and couches. Velvet drapes covered newly installed windows and the polished oak desks were scrounged from the rubble. David led Evelyn through the opulent lobby to the space in the back where the army did its actual work. General Gibson was engrossed in a report when David knocked on his open door.

"What?" he barked.

"Is that any way to greet your favorite former spy?" Evelyn asked.

General Gibson looked up, his eyes taking a moment to focus.

"Is that any way to greet your former commanding officer?" he asked.

Evelyn laughed and Gibson broke into a smile. He came around the desk and gave her a hug.

"Thanks for coming, Evie."

"It's always good to see you, General. I'm thrilled to have a chance to see the airlift up close."

"You're already plotting to convince General Clay to buy your planes, aren't you?" Gibson asked.

"More than planes, you're in desperate need of parts to hold the ones you've got together," Evelyn said. "But yes, I'm going to swing by DC on my way home."

General Gibson shook his head fondly, then turned to the task at hand.

"When Kurt Vogel arrived in London, his case was taken over by a different section of the military. Someone else was supposed to handle the family reunion and get them settled in the States. Like you, I only just discovered they never arrived."

"How did you get pulled into this? Shouldn't it be the people who initially went to Berlin? Or his handlers in the US?"

"He asked for us specifically. Perhaps we're the only ones he knew," General Gibson said. "He put his trust in the US Army and we failed him. This seems like the least we can do."

"But I'm no longer army," Evelyn said. "Don't get me wrong. I'm happy to help; I just don't think I'm the obvious choice."

"Which is what makes you perfect," David said. "As far as anyone's concerned, you're trying to find out what happened to the family of an old friend. This is unconnected with your work during the war and you know nothing of his past."

"It doesn't add up," Evelyn said. "The war's been over for three years. Why did his wife wait so long to reach out to Kurt? Why couldn't he find her in the displaced persons camp? Why didn't she just come to American HQ? And the bigger question, why am I here, acting like a spy, when you have the entire army at your disposal?"

"I don't, actually," General Gibson said. "This is an unofficial mission. When Kurt's request first came in, we were ordered to leave it alone."

"Why?" Evelyn asked.

"That's an excellent question," David replied.

"It's almost like someone doesn't want us finding out what really happened," General Gibson said.

Evelyn was officially intrigued.

# Chapter 17

Nick sat in his office, reviewing a few files. Helen's perfume announced her long before she opened the door. She wore the latest Paris fashion and her makeup was impeccable.

"I just love that little boutique downstairs," she said by way of greeting as she swept into the office. "You're going to have to move because I've spent too much money already."

"What are you doing here?" Nick asked, his voice cold.

"You're not still mad at me?"

"For assuming my marriage is a scam? Why would that upset me?"

"It's a good question," Helen said. "My opinion's never mattered before."

"Your opinion's always mattered," Nick replied, softening. Then he motioned to the percolator in the corner. "Coffee?"

"How long has it been sitting there?"

"Long enough that I'd advise you to say no."

A small smile cracked her lips.

"I came to thank you," Helen said. "There haven't been any more attacks in the past few days. My employees are starting to feel safe again. Gregory no longer wants to hunt down Gallo. Life is almost back to normal."

"Glad I could help."

"Do you mind if I keep you on retainer?" Helen asked. "In case Mickey decides Gallo's initiative was a good one. Or if there's other trouble?"

"I'll always help you," Nick said. "We've been through too much for you to doubt that."

Helen pulled her checkbook out of her bag.

"How much do I owe you?"

Nick waved his hand. "Consider it a favor for an old friend."

"I like to pay my debts," Helen replied.

"If anyone's indebted, it's me. You taught me how to survive."

"I think we did quite a bit better than that," Helen said. "I'm sorry for what I said about Evelyn. You're right, I don't know her. She just seems like one of those people we used to hate."

"It's easy to hate people you don't know."

"It's easy to hate people who have everything," Helen replied. "Besides, I never would have guessed getting married was something you wanted."

"I never thought I was allowed to want it," Nick said. "Growing up, all we saw was the fighting, the yelling, the . . . the leaving. There was no way I was going to spend my life like that."

"Everyone fights."

"There's a difference. Before Evelyn, I didn't know it was possible to disagree without crockery flying."

"And now . . . ?" Helen asked.

"Nothing's perfect," Nick said. "But it's damned near close."

For so long, Nick's life had been a list of things he did

not want. Now, for the first time, he allowed himself to contemplate the things he did. It felt safe to ask for them, believing they were no longer impossible.

"If you're happy, I'm happy," Helen said.

"I am," Nick confirmed.

Nick returned to Evelyn's house at the end of the day to find no one home. He always thought the place was a bit too big and too empty when she was not there. Almost like a museum after dark. Despite her insistence that he make himself comfortable, he still worried about accidentally breaking some ancient artifact or dragging mud onto a priceless rug. The one place he felt comfortable was the kitchen. Perhaps because it was the one place Evelyn had never made her own. Cooking, beyond the basics, always seemed like a luxury to Nick, both in the time involved and the cost of ingredients. Here in Evelyn's kitchen, though, he liked experimenting. During the war, they had mostly survived on rations, but sometimes people invited them into their homes. For the first time, Nick tasted escargot, rich with butter and garlic. He discovered brie, Camembert, and all the cheeses France had to offer. He tasted fresh pasta made with tomatoes grown in backyard gardens. The difference between those savory bites and the scraps he had known as a child turned food into something beyond mere sustenance. When made right, it could feel like love.

Nick was rolling out the dough for gnocchi when Taffy entered the kitchen. He wore an apron and his hands were covered in flour.

"Hungry?" he asked.

"Starving, actually," she replied.

"Give me twenty minutes and we'll have dinner," he said.

\* \* \*

Nick and Taffy sat across from each other at the kitchen table. She had unerringly pulled a bottle of Chianti from the wine cellar and Nick had his usual Scotch. Taffy took a bite of the pasta and her eyes widened in surprise.

"Goodness! I haven't tasted anything like this since I was in Venice on my honeymoon."

"I'll take that as a compliment," Nick said.

"As well you should. It's incredible."

For a few minutes, they sat in companionable silence, preoccupied by dinner. When Nick stood up to get them seconds, Taffy refilled their drinks.

"You're like my husband," she said as Nick sat back down. "I tried for years to get him to drink wine, but he knew what he liked and could not be dissuaded."

"A man after my own heart."

Taffy lost her husband during the war. Her sorrow and loneliness were compounded by the fact that it was a quiet death, caused by a heart condition. Everyone around her was grieving the surprising, unendurable pain of losing their sons in battle. She did not feel as if she could speak of her heartache. Wives often buried their husbands, but parents should never outlive their children.

"He was a good man," Taffy said. "Rather straightforward. Took over the family business from his father and his grandfather before him. He stewarded it safely over troubled times and doubled its size. When I sold it after William's death, I was so proud of everything he'd done."

"You didn't have anyone to pass it on to?"

"No," Taffy replied. "We tried to have children for years, but . . ."

Nick saw the sadness in her eyes and wished he had not asked.

"Do you want kids?" Taffy asked.

"I want Evelyn," Nick said. "It's up to her."

"But if it was up to you?"

"Yes."

"Someone to pass down the family name?" Taffy asked.

"No," Nick said. "They can be Bishops for all I care. This . . . this is going to sound selfish."

"Having children is fundamentally selfish," Taffy replied. "No one asks to come into this world."

"It's a way to fix my childhood," Nick said.

"That's too big a thing for anyone to carry."

"I want them to have everything I never did," Nick clarified. "It's not about stuff, it's about two parents who love them more than anything. It's about spending time with them so they feel safe and secure. That's part of what drew me to Evelyn. She knows, beyond a shadow of a doubt, that she's worthy of love. Of course she's right. But she believes it, somewhere deep down that can never be taken away. I want to instill that in a kid."

"Maybe see if you can instill it in yourself?" Taffy asked. "A child's love is a powerful thing. It's all-consuming."

"And pure."

"When Evelyn was a little girl, I tried to visit every year. The highlight of my trip was always that first moment when Evie saw me. She'd run across the room and throw herself into my arms. I wonder when we lose faith that our love will be welcomed unconditionally."

"Some of us never had it."

"My parents were not especially affectionate," Taffy said. "They provided for us, but I always felt like they were more worried about stains on clothes than returning our hugs. It took me a long time to get used to that with Evelyn and Matthew. They ran all over the place, getting dirty as could be. One time I showed up and Anna was up to her knees in mud. Her dress was ruined and she had a look of such joy on her face. I was so jealous of her ability to be present and open herself up to them. She was a wonderful mother."

"I wish I'd had the chance to meet her."

"She'd have liked you," Taffy said. "Anna wasn't a person to put up with bullshit. Plus, you remind me of Logan."

Nick raised his eyebrows questioningly.

"I mean that as a compliment, even after everything. He worked hard and loved his family beyond measure. He was independent and strong-willed but always put my sister first. I see that same thing with you and Evelyn."

"Thank you," he said, touched. "You know I love Evelyn more than anything in the world."

"I do," Taffy replied. "Which is why I hope you'll sign this."

She stood up, went to her purse, withdrew an envelope, and handed it to Nick. It was a prenuptial agreement.

"I know Evelyn trusts you, but someone has to look out for her interests."

Nick flipped through the pages. It was a generous offer, with a hundred thousand deposited into his account on their wedding day and up to a million-dollar settlement depending on the length of their marriage.

"I don't want the money," he said.

"You might, one day."

"If I'm ever stupid enough to lose Evelyn, then nothing else matters."

"Don't let finances get in the way. Your marriage is always going to be uneven. You might be fine with run-down shoes and a watch that can't keep time, but slowly, you're going to want more. It might not be a lot, just enough to feel like the world recognizes you as Evelyn's equal. Don't let it be a burden and cause resentment."

"I'm marrying Evelyn because I love her. I don't want or need anything else."

"What about her?"

Nick frowned.

"Love isn't always enough to get two people through rough patches . . . and you've already had a pretty big one."

"That was . . ."

"Right, special circumstances. I understand," Taffy replied. "But it's always special circumstances when life falls apart. You say that Evelyn's the only thing you care about, so sign the papers. Protect her from what might be the worst version of you."

Nick contemplated that for a moment. He knew that deep down inside of him there was a core of anger he had never been able to extinguish. Most of the time it was under control. Most of the time it was well-hidden. Yet he also understood Taffy's words. Losing Evelyn would shatter him. How could he be certain he would never unleash all those pent up emotions? Taking the pen, Nick signed the papers and handed them back to Taffy.

"I never want to see this again."

"Let's both hope you never have to," Taffy said.

# Chapter 18

Evelyn sat beside David as he drove through the streets toward the Vogels' former home in the Dahlem district of Berlin. Before the war, Kurt and his wife, Hannah, lived in an upper-middle class section of Berlin and settled into the life of young academics. Hannah had her degree in physics, but she never got to use it after the Nuremberg Race Laws were enacted. Hating the attention that came from being forced to wear a Star of David and fearful of what might happen to her and their daughter, Sophie, on the streets, she largely stayed inside. She turned their home into a beautiful refuge, complete with murals on the walls and lush furnishings she embroidered by hand.

Evelyn did not know what to expect as they exited the car outside the Vogels' apartment. Like everything in the city, the façade had bomb damage and was blackened from the rampant fires during the war, but the building looked structurally sound. They went inside to what was once a grand foyer. The marble floor was stained and cracked. In the center of winding stairs stood an intricate wrought-iron elevator. Evelyn doubted it had been used in years, considering electricity was spotty at best.

As they walked up the stairs, Evelyn heard quiet rustling

and could almost feel people staring at her through the peepholes in the doors. It made the building feel haunted and ghostly, especially knowing the prison it became for Kurt's family. They reached the top floor, and Evelyn knocked on the door of Kurt's former apartment. There was no answer. She listened at the keyhole.

"They're inside," she said to David.

He stepped up and pounded his fist against the wood. "US Army. Open up."

After a long moment, the door cracked open and a woman's face peered out. Though she was middle-aged, her face was weathered and wary. She looked between Evelyn and David.

"What do you want?" she snapped in German.

"Information about the people who used to live here," Evelyn replied. "Kurt, Hannah, and Sophie Vogel."

"I don't know anything."

The woman went to close the door, but David stuck his foot in the crack and pushed it open further. Over her shoulder, they saw remnants of Hannah's murals on the wall. There was sparse furniture and few personal belongings. Most of it was probably sold off for food or used as firewood. The polished floors that once held colorful rugs were now bare. The shelves built into the wall were empty of books and pictures.

"I remember this place," Evelyn said. "I remember them."

"This is my home now. If anyone comes and tries to take it, I'll kill them."

"Even if they're the original owners?" Evelyn asked. "Do you have any sympathy for them?"

"No one has sympathy for me. They're probably rich Jews who fled somewhere better."

"Or maybe you're the one who turned them into the Gestapo?" Evelyn asked coldly.

"How dare you?" the woman screeched. "I was never a

Nazi. We're the real victims here. The Jews run America and Britain. They're the ones who forced us to go to war. In fact, I'll bet you're a dirty Jew looking for revenge, but you won't get it. I have rights, you know!"

David glanced toward Evelyn, who was seething with rage.

"Thank you for your time," David said, stepping back so the woman could slam the door.

"That awful—" Evelyn fumed, unable to find words.

"It's funny," David said. "In the three years I've been here, I've never met anyone who will admit to being a Nazi. Somehow the entire population of Germany was held hostage by an ideology none of them believed in."

"It's unbearable," Evelyn said. "How do you do it?"

"Like this," David said as he pulled out a notepad and wrote down the building's address and the number of the apartment. "That was a large space for just one family when so many others are homeless. I'm willing to bet the resettlement committee will be happy to reappropriate this apartment for a deserving family. Seeing Kurt Vogel is still the official owner, as far as I know, it won't be a problem, unless he wishes to return to Berlin."

"You make bureaucracy work for you."

"If I let it get to me, I'd never draw a sober breath," David admitted. "Let's talk to the other neighbors."

They turned and walked across the hall to another door. They heard the sounds of children playing and a baby crying. At their knock, everything fell silent. An older woman with a cautious expression looked out. Evelyn put on her most disarming smile. It worked on many occasions, but not this one.

"Yes?" the woman asked warily.

Evelyn explained that she was trying to find out what happened to the Vogel family. Having learned from the last experience, she started with the news that Kurt was happily ensconced in America and was not looking for money or to return. He just wanted to know about his wife and child.

The woman's countenance softened, but she shook her head. "I wish I could help, but I never met them. We were assigned this apartment after ours was destroyed in 1943." Then, glancing toward David, she added, "There's fifteen of us here. My three adult children and their families."

"I'm glad you all found shelter together," he said. Then he reached into his pocket and pulled out a chocolate bar. "For your grandchildren."

The woman's eyes widened as she took the chocolate.

"You might want to try Apartment 2B," she said. "I think they've been here the longest."

Thanking the woman, Evelyn and David headed downstairs. They easily found 2B at the front of the building. Evelyn knocked, and again she was greeted uncertainly. This time, it was a man with thick white hair and a round face.

"How can I help you?" he asked.

Evelyn began explaining about Kurt Vogel. As she spoke, the man began to smile. Before she could ask about Kurt's wife and daughter, he threw open the door and ushered them inside, introducing himself as Bertrand.

"Marie!" he called out. "Americans are here. They're looking for Hannah and Sophie!"

An older woman shuffled out from the kitchen. Her hair was pinned back in a careful twist. Her clothes were worn but clearly of good quality. The few holes were carefully darned and her shoes shined.

"Can you tell us what happened to them?" Marie asked.

"We were hoping you might know," Evelyn said.

Marie's face fell and Bertrand covered her hand with his.

"They lived here eight years," he said. "They became like family to us. Marie would babysit Sophie when Hannah ran errands."

"Or when she needed a break," Marie said. "Sophie was the perfect child, but every mother needs a moment to herself."

"Kurt worked a lot," Bertrand said. "He did something for the government."

"He should have taken Hannah out of the country long before Sophie came," Marie insisted. "Anyone paying attention could see what was coming."

"But that's the thing," Bertrand said. "He wasn't paying attention. There was a moment back in 1939 when we hadn't seen Hannah or Sophie for a while. I thought Kurt had finally gotten them to safety, but then I saw Hannah throwing away the trash at four a.m. She kept odd hours to avoid most people. The year before, a group of men attacked her when she was with Sophie. She recovered physically, but it broke her heart for her daughter to witness such violence. After that, she was terrified of going outside."

"They stayed in their apartment from then on. This building had some fervent Nazis, and Hannah would not let Sophie play in the halls," Marie said. "I began going upstairs, bringing cakes and cookies when our ration cards would allow. We should have done more."

"We did what we could," Bertrand said.

Marie turned to Evelyn and David with a pleading look. "We would have hidden them, but everyone knew of our friendship."

"After they disappeared, we were the first place the Nazis looked," Bertrand added. "Tore the whole place apart."

Marie started crying.

"Can you tell us what happened?" Evelyn asked.

"We don't really know," Marie said. "We were drinking

our morning coffee when we heard the trucks outside, and the boots on the stairs. By that time, we knew enough to bolt the door and pray they were not here for us."

"The whole building was surrounded," Bertrand continued. "We watched from the windows, but the Gestapo came out empty-handed. That's when they searched the rest of the apartments."

"Do you know where Hannah or Sophie might have gone? Someone who would have taken them in?"

Marie shook her head. "All I know is that Hannah would have done anything to keep her daughter safe. She loved that girl with her whole heart. So did Kurt. I can't believe he would just abandon his family."

"He didn't," Evelyn said. "He thought they were right behind him. Something went wrong and I'm trying to figure out what."

"When you do," Bertrand said, "will you please let us know?"

"Of course."

"We pray for them every day," Marie added.

With that David and Evelyn left, knowing little more than when they had arrived. As they stepped out onto the street, they heard a soft voice call out, "Americans!"

They turned to see a woman in a threadbare dress with a cloth wrapped around her hair. She stood in the basement entrance to the building.

"You are looking for Hannah Vogel?" she asked in Polish-accented German. "I was there the day she and her daughter left. They went out a back stairwell few people knew about. Two men were with them."

"What happened then?" Evelyn asked.

"The Americans said they knew a place to go," the woman said. "I can still remember where."

She looked between Evelyn and David, waiting. After a moment, David pulled out his wallet and handed her some

Reichsmarks. The woman remained silent and David handed over a few more.

"The Americans knew of a safe house in Wittenau. I think they said Lieberoser Strasse."

Evelyn swore quietly under her breath, then thanked the woman. They got back into the jeep to drive to the French section of the city.

"What is it?" David asked.

"Let's just hope I'm wrong," Evelyn replied.

They pulled up to a series of crumbling red-brick houses. Evelyn got out of the car and walked down the block to stand in front of one that had been burned to the ground.

"Before we were sent into Berlin, Nick and I were given a list of safe houses in different parts of the city. They were only to be used as a last resort—their addresses never written down, their locations never discussed."

"What happened?"

"Rumor was the SS learned about them in late 1942."

"Right around the time Hannah and Sophie went into hiding," David said.

"Not sure if one of our people turned or if the information was tortured out of them. Five of the houses burned to the ground. Their owners were shot in the street as an example to others. Their inhabitants were sent off to the camps—Dachau, and Buchenwald."

"Then eventually Auschwitz?" David guessed.

"If they lasted that long," Evelyn said.

"There's no guarantee Hannah and Sophie were there."

"True," Evelyn admitted. "The Red Cross has lists of camp inmates and those who were murdered, but we didn't find anything about the Vogels. There's gotta be something more."

"I can get the original records from Dachau and Buchenwald, as well as the others in the western part of the country," David said. "The allies liberated those. There were more camps than I can name throughout Poland and the other eastern countries, including Majdanek and Auschwitz. I don't think the Soviets are going to just let you come over and peruse the documents."

"What if I ask really nicely?"

"You're going to get me into trouble, aren't you?"

Evelyn just smiled.

# Chapter 19

Nick was returning from a client interview when he saw Helen pacing on the sidewalk outside his office. Her heels made a sharp staccato across six squares of concrete. Though she was as well-dressed as ever, people gave her a wide berth, not wanting to catch her obvious ire.

"This is becoming a habit," Nick said.

"Where the hell have you been?" Helen snapped. "That asshole kidnapped Julia. I want her found. I want him dead."

"Come inside," Nick said, leading her upstairs to his office.

Helen entered and began pacing the floor.

"Tell me what happened," Nick began.

"Gallo took her. I know he did."

"Helen—"

"Don't 'Helen' me. Go find her."

Nick grabbed her, gently turning her to face him.

"I will, but before I can do that, I need to know exactly what happened. The sooner you tell me, the sooner I can get started."

For a moment, it looked as though his words had not

sunk in. She twisted her shoulders as if to shake him off, then she took a deep breath and let Nick steer her toward a couch. He grabbed a glass, poured an inch of Scotch, and handed it to her.

"Start from the beginning," Nick said after she belted down her drink. "What is Julia's full name?"

"Martinez. Julia Martinez. She's my bartender," Helen began. "The best I've ever seen. Doesn't let anyone get away with shit, but they all love her for it. I think a lot of times men come in just to chat. She's a great listener and even when it's busy, they feel like they've got her full attention."

"Not an easy skill."

"One that can't be taught," Helen agreed. "I know it sounds like I'm upset that she'll miss her shifts, but it's not that. I care about the people who work for me."

"I know you do," Nick said.

"They're like family," Helen continued. "I don't really have anyone else. Which feels so goddamned pathetic to admit. But it's true. It's my job to take care of them and I'm failing."

Helen stood up to pace again, and this time, Nick let her.

"How do you know she's missing?" Nick asked.

"She didn't make it home last night. Her family called the cops."

"You have contacts in the department?" Nick asked.

"Some of them are clients," Helen explained. "They're not going to take this seriously because they know where she works."

"Normally, she'd get home around what? One or two in the morning?" Nick asked.

"About then," Helen said.

Nick checked the time. It was almost noon.

"So, she's only been missing about ten hours."

"Don't you start," Helen began, her hackles rising.

"I'm trying to get an accurate timeline. I have to ask these questions. Even if they seem stupid or obvious. Is it possible she went to stay with a friend or had a long night with a client?"

"Julia doesn't have clients. When she first came to me, I gave her the option to earn some extra money, but it was a nonstarter. She comes from a strict Catholic household and made it clear she intends to stay a virgin until she's married."

"And she's comfortable working at your club?"

"She's pragmatic," Helen said. "She has a strong faith, very specific morals, but keeps them to herself. I asked her about it once and she replied with scripture."

" 'Judge not lest ye be judged'?" Nick guessed. " 'Let those without sin cast the first stone'?"

"Something like that. She never tries to save anyone or convert them, just serves drinks with a smile. Everyone likes her. It's impossible not to."

"I'm guessing she makes decent tips."

"And then some," Helen replied.

"Any chance it could be a mugging? Someone who knew she'd have a lot of cash on her?"

"No. Gregory makes weekly deposits into people's accounts if they choose. Most do. It's safer than leaving at night with their earnings. Plus, many of the women are glad to have an account their families don't know about. Gives them independence and makes it so they don't have to explain the unexpected money."

"You really do have it all figured out," Nick said, impressed. "Does Julia have a boyfriend?"

"What does that matter? It had to be Gallo," Helen said. "First, he starts by beating girls up. Now this . . . ?"

"It's a big escalation," Nick said.

"He's probably pissed you went around his back to Norman Roth."

"If he's smart, he'll be afraid of Norman Roth," Nick replied.

"Has Gallo ever impressed you with his intellectual capabilities?"

"I'll find him. If he has Julia, I'll get her back."

"I want you to kill him. This has to stop."

"That's not what I do," Nick said.

"You've done it before."

"In war."

"And before."

"That was a long time ago," Nick said quietly.

He was thirteen when a drunk man cornered him in a dark alley wanting more than his pocket money. Terrified and pinned to the ground, Nick grasped frantically for anything to protect himself. His fingers found a broken bottle and he slashed it upward. The jagged glass sliced through the man's carotid artery. Death was quick and messy. Not knowing what to do, Nick showed up on Helen's doorstep, covered in blood and shaking from shock. She got him cleaned up, gave him his first glass of gin, and put him to bed. Even more than when his parents abandoned him, Nick realized this was the end of his childhood. Years later, when he signed up for the army, he felt confident he could do what was necessary. Yet every time someone died by his hand, no matter how deserving, even if it was to protect his team, it still tore away a piece of his soul.

"I'll find Julia and make sure the person who took her sees justice," Nick said. "If you're looking for revenge, I suggest you go elsewhere."

Helen thought for a moment, looking like she wanted to argue. Finally, she nodded.

"Just get her home safely," she said quietly.

Nick wanted to promise that he would, but they had both seen too much of life to believe in false hope.

# Chapter 20

Nick walked up to a small house just south of San Vicente. The front porch was dotted with red and white geraniums and a birdhouse hung from the awnings. The exterior was freshly painted a cheerful yellow, with white shutters. Gauzy curtains fluttered in the breeze and Nick could swear he smelled bread baking. This was not what he expected when he set out to find Gallo at home. Nick rang the doorbell and a young woman in her early twenties answered. The first thing Nick noticed about her was her warm, friendly smile. The second was that she was at least seven months pregnant.

"Sorry to bother you," Nick said, turning to go. "I think I'm in the wrong place."

"Who are you looking for?" she asked. "Maybe I can help."

"Man named Gallo."

"Oh, no, you have the right house. Do come in, Mr. . . . ?"

"Gallagher," Nick said as he stepped over the threshold.

The inside of the house matched the domesticity of the outside. The striped wallpaper in the living room echoed the damask stripes on the pristine couch. Pastel pillows rested on every soft surface and the coffee table was polished within an inch of its life.

"I'm Mary Gallo. Can I get you some coffee, Mr. Gallagher?"

"No, thank you," he said.

Nick had come over, ready to put the fear of God into Gallo to find Julia, but now he was uncertain how to behave.

"I just made it," Mary offered. She looked at him with hopeful eagerness, desperate to be a good host.

"How can I turn that down?" Nick replied.

"Won't be a minute. Please, make yourself comfortable," she said, gesturing to the living room. As she disappeared toward the kitchen, she called upstairs, "Joey, you have company."

"Who is it?" Gallo's voice called from upstairs.

"Mr. Gallagher."

Joey Gallo thundered down the stairs, shaving cream still flecked across his ear, a small pistol in his hand.

"You!" he hissed as he glanced at the kitchen door. "How dare you come to my house and threaten my—"

"You're one to talk about threats," Nick said, quietly matching his tone. "Where is Julia Martinez?"

The kitchen door opened and Mary came out holding a cup of coffee on a saucer. Gallo tucked the gun into his pocket before she could see it.

"I'm so sorry!" she exclaimed. "I forgot to ask how you take it."

"Black is wonderful," Nick said. "Thank you."

"Honey," Gallo said, moving to Mary's side. "What have I told you about inviting people into the house?"

"I know, but it just seems so rude to keep them out on the front step."

"How many times I gotta say it? No one comes into the house unless I let them in."

"But . . ."

"Don't fucking argue with me!"

Tears hovered at the bottom of her eyes and she sniffled.

"I'm sorry, Joey."

Gallo's expression softened.

"No, I'm sorry. I shouldn'ta yelled," he said. "It's just that I need to keep us safe. There are some not great people out there. We gotta be careful."

"But why? I don't understand," Mary pleaded.

"You don't need to understand," Gallo replied. "All you need to know is that it's my job to protect you and the baby. No one comes through that door unless I say it's okay. Even if you've met them before. Even if they've been here before."

"You worry too much, Joey."

"I worry just enough," he said.

"Well, what's done is done. Can I get you any refreshments?" Mary asked Nick. "We have some coffee cake, or it's almost time for lunch."

Nick glanced to Gallo, who glared at him.

"That's not necessary," Gallo said. "Mr. Gallagher isn't staying."

"Coffee cake sounds lovely," Nick said, needling Gallo.

A few minutes later found the three of them sitting around a polished dining room table, each with a slice of cinnamon coffee cake in front of them. Mary looked at Nick expectantly as he took a bite.

"Just delicious," Nick said. "Homemade?"

"Fresh this morning," she said brightly.

"You are a lucky, lucky man," Nick said to Gallo. "I wasn't aware you were married."

"What you don't know could fill an ocean," snapped Gallo.

"Joey is my brother-in-law. He's staying with me until . . ." She broke off with a ragged sigh, gently rubbing her belly.

"We'll get Bobby out of that hellhole," Gallo promised, taking Mary's hand.

"My husband's in prison," Mary explained to Nick. "But he didn't do what they said. He wouldn't. You don't know him. He's a good man."

"Why don't you go upstairs and get some rest?" Gallo said. "Mr. Gallagher and I have some things to discuss."

Mary looked between the two men, then nodded, realizing it was not a suggestion.

"It was lovely to meet you, Mr. Gallagher."

"You, too, Mrs. Gallo."

Mary headed upstairs, and it was only after they heard the bedroom door shut that Nick and Gallo turned to each other.

"The hell are you doing at my house?" Gallo demanded, reaching for his gun.

"You don't need that," Nick said. "I'm not here to hurt you. At least not yet. Tell me where I can find Julia Martinez."

"I have no idea who the fuck that is."

"The bartender at Helen Brecker's club."

Gallo looked genuinely confused.

"Come on. You beat up two girls already. You really expect me to believe you haven't escalated to kidnapping?"

"You, I'm happy to screw over, but I'm not about to cross Cohen. I might not have much book learning, but I do know enough to save my own skin," Gallo insisted.

"So, it's a coincidence that immediately after you beat up two women another goes missing?"

"Don't care what you call it, it wasn't me."

Nick studied him for a long minute.

"I took a shot. Didn't work out," Gallo explained, shaking his head. "My own fault, really. Only needed one photo to get the guy. But no, I had to get greedy."

"How do you mean?" Nick asked. "What guy?"

"Don't matter. I'll find another way," Gallo said. "There's a baby on the way who needs me. Sure, it's all fun and games when I'm out with the boys, but my old man was never around. Just me and my brother. Not gonna let this kid grow up that way. Certainly not because I was dumb enough to get on Cohen's radar. I'm keeping my head down and doing what I'm told."

To his surprise, Nick believed him.

"Please thank Mrs. Gallo for the coffee and cake. It really was delicious," Nick said as he stood to go. Gallo escorted him to the door. As Nick stepped out onto the front porch, he heard the dead bolt lock behind him.

# Chapter 21

"Absolutely not," General Gibson raged.

"I told you. It's always better to ask forgiveness than permission," Evelyn said to David.

"We had to return the jeep to HQ," David replied.

"You could be court-martialed!" Gibson shouted.

"That, too," David agreed.

For someone with the potential to lose his military career, David looked particularly sanguine. Perhaps Evelyn and Nick had influenced him a bit too much.

"The Russian sector is off-limits. Especially now. All it takes is one misstep to set off the next world war," Gibson threatened.

"That's a little dramatic," Evelyn said.

"It's the truth. This whole place is a powder keg."

"I'm very good with explosives," Evelyn replied.

"This is not the time to get cute," Gibson said.

"Nor is it the time for you to start being someone else," Evelyn retorted. "You trusted us throughout the war to get stuff done our own way. This is no different."

"Of course it is," Gibson said. "Back then, we were already at war. What? It was going to get worse?"

"You're not responsible for an American socialite look-ing for cheap thrills. That's how every newspaper in the world will report it if I get caught."

"You're not a rich socialite. You're the president of one of the largest companies in the world," Gibson snapped.

"Please, almost no one thinks I'm capable of doing the job."

"Then they clearly don't know you."

"Was that . . . a compliment?" Evelyn gasped, pretend-ing to swoon.

General Gibson just grunted.

"I can do this," Evelyn said softly. "You know I can."

General Gibson studied her for a long moment, before grumbling, "If you die, I'll kill you."

Evelyn and David borrowed a car from one of the clerks at the embassy. It was an old VW Type 3 from the 1930s. Considering the state of the roads, Evelyn wondered if it would actually get them to the Russian sector. They stopped at a secondhand store to change out of anything that looked remotely American. All the clothes Evelyn brought with her were too new. Few people in Berlin had the lux-ury of the latest styles—especially where they were going. Evelyn chose a green dress with a square neckline and a straight skirt that was frayed around the edges. David changed out of his uniform into worn gray slacks, brown boots, and a dark blue shirt. Together, they looked like a young couple out on a date.

"So, what's it like to be in the middle of all the in-trigue?" Evelyn asked as they drove across the city.

"Don't know," David said. "After the OSS was dis-banded, I followed General Gibson, which meant signing up for the regular army. It's not quite as much fun."

"I'm surprised you didn't join the CIA."

"Please. It's so new, they can't even figure out their acronyms. It's nothing but a bunch of preppy Ivy League assholes pretending to be secret agents."

"Aren't you a preppy Ivy League asshole?" Evelyn teased.

"Yes," David said. "But at least I have some clue what I'm doing. I don't know if they'll hold it together long enough to figure it out."

"You could teach them."

"I don't want that to be my life," David admitted. "It was a great adventure during the war. The work is still important, but I don't have to be the one doing it. I wasn't joking when I said I want what you and Nick have. A family and a career that will let me be home for dinner every night."

"We still don't have the last one," Evelyn commented.

"But you have each other," David insisted. "When you first meet Nick, you think he's going to be one thing. This tough guy who's learned not to care. Then I got to know him and saw you two together—all that love and your partnership. After everything, you found each other again. It's *beshert.*"

Evelyn frowned at the unfamiliar word.

"Yiddish for 'meant to be,'" David explained. "You're both incredibly capable people who are fine on your own. Together, however, you're more than that. You make each other better."

"It's not always easy," Evelyn confessed. "But I suppose nothing worth having is."

"I doubt I'll find who I'm looking for in Berlin," David said. "Especially since it's important to me to marry someone Jewish. My contract is up right around the time Gibson's planning on retiring. Seems a good time to go."

"Don't think you could work for anyone else?" Evelyn asked.

"You and Nick ruined me for the regular army." David laughed.

He parked the car a few blocks away from the bar. Evelyn got out first and was halfway up the street before David followed her. It was best not to be seen together. Should anyone recognize David as an American army captain, it did not bode well for the life expectancy of their contact.

Like any good former OSS officer, Gibson still kept a large ring of informants. They knew the habits of every higher-level Russian officer, especially those in the MGB, the Soviet secret police. That is how Evelyn and David knew to look for Alexei Antonov in a bar where he could take off his uniform and blend into the crowd. A man of average height and weight, with dark hair and brown eyes, he had a face that rarely imprinted on a person's memory. It was amazing what he overheard when people forgot his existence, which was how he justified his nightly excursions. Mostly, though, he sought an escape from his compatriots. He never bought into any organization, even his own, which often put him at odds with his superiors.

Alexei was seated on the far side of the bar with his back to the wall, where no one could sneak up behind him. Old training, Evelyn supposed as she walked toward him. They had worked together several times during the war. It was a productive relationship but rarely an easy one. Their countries were too different. The place was crowded with people talking loudly over the raucous music. Unobtrusively, David sat down and ordered a beer. Evelyn reached Alexei and kissed him on both cheeks.

" 'Of all the gin joints in all the world . . .' "

"Still got a love for American movies," she said with a smile.

"Ingrid Bergman. Humphrey Bogart. How can you go wrong?"

Alexei caught the eye of the bartender. A moment later, a bottle of vodka and two glasses appeared. Alexei picked them up and led Evelyn to a table hidden in the back corner. They sat down and he poured the drinks. Evelyn noticed David pick up his beer and move so he could watch them from the corner of his eye.

"Heard you were in town," Alexei said.

"I couldn't come all this way without stopping to say hello."

"It's good to see you, Evie. I appreciate you not flaunting your American soldier."

"Is he that obvious?" Evelyn asked. "David will be so disappointed."

"Only to me. I've kept track of young Captain Bernstein. US Army, formerly of the OSS. I know he was on your team, though I never did have the pleasure of a formal introduction."

"Would you like one?"

"Oh God, no," Alexei said with a laugh. "I've never been a fan of the cold and I don't think exile in Siberia would suit me."

"I've missed you," Evelyn said, raising her glass to his.

They toasted, and downed the vodka in a single swallow. Alexei poured two more.

"So, you're officially a part of the big, fancy capitalist system," Alexei said.

"I'm surprised your spies didn't tell you that during the war."

"You never shared your last name. Who expects to find an American socialite in a tank trench in the middle of the Belgian countryside?"

"Ah, but weren't you glad I was there?" Evelyn asked with a smile.

Alexei tapped his chest where three bullets had almost killed him.

"At the time I thought you were an idiot," he confessed. "Why the hell would you risk your life pulling a total stranger to safety? Then, why would you stay to patch him up when the SS was looking for us both?"

"You'd have done the same for me," Evelyn said lightly.

"No, I wouldn't have," Alexei replied.

There was truth in his statement, but Evelyn chose to ignore it.

"Perhaps I was saving my own skin by not letting them interrogate you," she said.

"It's hard to question a dead man."

"You could have survived. At least for a little while."

"For all I knew, you were a French farm girl having a very bad day," Alexei insisted.

"Maybe I just felt sorry for you."

"Then you're definitely a fool."

"There's that Russian sentimentality I've read so much about," Evelyn joked. "I'm feeling the love."

"I love my grandmother and my dog," Alexei replied. "Though occasionally I feel a slight fondness for you."

"I knew it! You adore me!" Evelyn exclaimed. A small smile turned up the corner of Alexei's mouth. Evelyn took it as a good sign, switching over to the purpose of her visit. "So help me out. What can you tell me about Berlin?"

"It's a lovely city," Alexei began. "Thought to be established sometime in the eleventh century. It became the home of the royal palace in the thirteenth century, before being destroyed during the Thirty Years' War. Later, Frederick the Great—"

"All right, all right," Evelyn said, holding up her hand. "I should've been more specific. What can you tell me about Berlin right now? Why the blockade?"

"That's above my pay grade."

"Best guess?"

"Soviets don't relish the idea of an American outpost in the heart of their territory."

"And you? What are your thoughts on the situation?"

"There are some things America does better than Mother Russia," Alexei said, holding up a package of Lucky Strikes. "It's nice being able to get them on the black market. The movies aren't terrible. They make it seem like it's always summer. That's certainly not true of Moscow."

"Come visit me in California. It's sunny and seventy-two almost every day."

"Are you trying to recruit me?" Alexei asked. "Is that an official offer?"

"It's an offer from one friend to another. Politics isn't always kind to men like you."

Loyalty purges in the Communist system were not uncommon and it was easy to end up on the wrong side.

"My home is my home, even when it's no longer home," he said quietly. "Now tell me why you're really here?"

"Needed a vacation," Evelyn said. "This seemed relaxing."

"The airlift?" he asked.

"It's a terribly useful cover, but no. Not entirely," Evelyn said. "During the war Nick and I rescued a scientist, but his wife and daughter didn't make it out. I'm trying to discover what happened to them. Everyone believed they were gone, but the scientist recently received a postcard from Berlin."

"What is his name?"

"Kurt Vogel."

Alexei's eyes shifted slightly. It was a momentary tell. He sat back in his chair and refilled their glasses.

"Alexei?" she asked.

"There are some things you should not concern yourself with."

"Why not?"

There was a long pause. Alexei tossed back his drink and poured himself another.

"I've always liked you, as much as one spy can like another."

"What do you know, Alexei?"

"Only that in California right now, it's sunny and seventy-two."

"Will you help me?" Evelyn asked.

"I am helping you," he said. "Don't pursue this."

"Too late."

Alexei thought for a long moment, then held his glass up to Evelyn.

"To old friends," he said as he threw back his shot. "I'll find out what I can."

# Chapter 22

The next morning, Nick drove through Boyle Heights, past the Brooklyn movie theater, and turned onto a shady street. He pulled up in front of a pale blue two-story house with a wrought-iron fence. There was a child's bike parked neatly on the front porch beside a red wagon. For a place that obviously had children, it was eerily quiet. Nick let himself in through the gate and rang the doorbell. After a moment, a teenage girl looked out. She was the spitting image of Julia. Nick introduced himself and explained that he was a private investigator searching for her older sister.

"Please wait here," she said.

After a minute, a man in his midfifties appeared. Nick recognized the calluses on his hands. He was solid in the way of a person who performed manual labor. Standing in an untucked white T-shirt, there was a surgical scar down the center of his chest.

"What do you want?" he asked, his voice rough.

Nick began to explain, but the man cut him off.

"Private investigators are expensive. Who hired you?"

"The woman who runs the—"

"Coffee shop near the university?" the girl asked quickly, her eyes pleading with Nick. "She's always been fond of Julia."

"Exactly," Nick said.

"This isn't her business. Yours either. I can take care of my own."

He started to close the door, but the teenage girl stopped him. They had a quick conversation in Spanish. Nick only understood every fourth word, but the essence was her trying to convince her father to change his mind. What harm could come from Nick looking into Julia's disappearance? At least let her mother have some hope. Finally, the man relented.

"I'm Diego Martinez," he said, ushering Nick inside. "This is my daughter Camila."

A boy and a girl who looked to be eight and ten played quietly in the living room. Camila shooed them upstairs. They glanced sideways at Nick before following her orders. Then Camila disappeared into the kitchen. Diego and Nick stood awkwardly for a moment.

"We should wait for my wife," Diego said.

Nick nodded and looked around the room. On one wall was a wooden cross between two pictures of young servicemen. Beneath their photos were folded American flags. Diego followed Nick's eyes.

"Did you serve?"

"Yes, sir," Nick said. "Mostly in northern France."

"My sons were in Italy," Diego said in a voice that worked hard to remain steady. "At least they were together."

"I'm so sorry," Nick said.

Diego nodded, but didn't reply. The door to the kitchen opened and Camila came in with her mother, who was red-eyed from crying. She sat down beside Diego and introduced herself as Elizabeth.

"I can't lose another child," she said, glancing at the pictures of her sons. "And I don't trust that officer they sent over."

"From the LAPD?" Nick asked.

"Yes. Camila, find his information," Diego ordered.

She went to a table in the hall, returning with a card.

"Brian Caruso?" Nick asked as he wrote down the name in his notebook.

"Useless man," Diego growled angrily. "Refused to start looking for Julia. Said she was an adult."

"He asked all kinds of insulting questions. Like did we get along? Did she feel trapped at home? Was there any reason for her to leave?" Elizabeth said. "Implied that I drove her away because we were too strict. What does he know about us?"

"Julia's a good girl," Diego added. "She takes care of her younger siblings, helps around the house . . ."

"We all do our best to contribute," Camila said.

"I do fine," Diego snapped.

"Of course, Papa. I just meant that you and Mama raised us right. We learned to be responsible."

Diego softened slightly.

"The only thing that cop wanted to know was if Julia had a boyfriend," Elizabeth said. "Just kept coming back to it, over and over again."

"I'm afraid I have to ask some of the same questions," Nick said. "These questions are not a reflection on her or you. They're just the standard things I need to ask when someone goes missing. I'm trying to see if there's anything, no matter how small or insignificant it may seem, that might give me a place to start looking for her."

"She didn't run away," Elizabeth said.

"I believe you," Nick replied. "I think someone took her and I'm trying to find out who. Can you tell me about her daily routine?"

"She was always a late sleeper," Elizabeth began. "I still have to rouse her in the morning. She eats breakfast with us and helps with the dishes. Then she goes to her job with Mark Morales."

"The car dealer?" Nick asked. They nodded.

Camila sang the jingle that haunted the airwaves of every local radio station:

> *"Zeus and Hera needed a ride.*
> *Had to be big and plush inside.*
> *There was just one that they adored.*
> *And they got it at Olympic Ford."*

"What does Julia do for Mr. Morales?" Nick asked.

"She's his secretary," Elizabeth said. "It's a wonderful job with a wonderful man. When Diego had heart issues, he sent flowers and checked on us all the time."

"Our families come from the same town in Oaxaca. His just got here a generation earlier," Diego explained.

"What time did Julia finish work?" Nick asked.

"Around five, then she went to school," Elizabeth said with obvious pride. "She's getting her bachelor's degree from UCLA. She got a scholarship and takes night classes. Set to graduate in the spring. First person in our family."

"I don't know what she'll do with an economics degree," Diego grumbled. "But she's worked damned hard to get it. Stays late at the library almost every night. At first, we worried about her, but her friend Rosa often dropped her off at home."

"Rosa?" Nick asked.

"Hernandez," Elizabeth clarified. "They met at church, then realized they were in the same school. Sometimes she comes to Sunday dinner. Nice girl. I like knowing Julia has someone looking out for her."

"Do you have Rosa's number or any way to get a hold of her?" Nick asked.

"She's gone home to Texas," Camila said.

"What? She can't have. She's not done with school," Elizabeth insisted.

"I think her mother got sick," Camila lied smoothly. Nick caught her eye and Camila looked slightly chagrinned.

"Is Julia dating anyone?" Nick asked and realized immediately it was a mistake. Both Diego and Elizabeth glared at him. "Statistically speaking, if a woman disappears, her boyfriend or husband is responsible."

"When Julia is ready to marry, then she will be allowed to date, with a chaperone," Elizabeth explained. "She wishes to finish her degree first and we respect that."

"We'll find her a nice man from the community," Diego said. "Our daughters will not end up pregnant out of wedlock. We are a God-fearing family and we did not come to this country for her to shame herself. She knows what's expected."

"Do you know of anyone threatening her?" Nick asked. "Did she have any unexpected bruises? Or seem like she was hiding something?"

Elizabeth quickly crossed herself.

"No," Camila answered. "We didn't have secrets between us."

"Did you see anything unusual the night she went missing?" Nick asked.

Diego and Elizabeth shook their heads no, but Camila hesitated.

"Anything, no matter how small, can help," Nick said.

"Julia and I share a room. I'm a pretty light sleeper and I usually wake up when she comes home. Last night, I heard her voice outside, like she was talking to someone. I thought it was Rosa, then I heard a man's voice. I looked out the window, but there was no one on the street."

"There was a man?" Diego asked. "Why didn't you tell us sooner?"

"You should have told that police officer," Elizabeth insisted.

"He'll just say I'm crazy."

"What time was this?" Nick asked.

"Around one in the morning."

"Did the man sound like anyone you knew?"

"No," Camila said. "But a few weeks ago. Rosa had just dropped off Julia. She was walking toward the front door when she yelled in surprise. I think it was the same man."

"There was a man here in the middle of the night?" Diego snapped.

"She didn't invite him," Camila insisted. "She asked him what he was doing and how did he know where she lived? Her voice was strange, like when Papa was in the hospital. Afraid, but trying not to show it."

"Was it someone from the neighborhood?" Elizabeth asked.

"I don't know," Camila said. "Julia just looked really uncomfortable. He was standing between her and our house, blocking the way. She had her arms crossed and he kept touching her on the shoulder. Finally, she got around him and came inside."

"Can you tell me anything else about him?" Nick asked. "Maybe what he looked like? Tall, short?"

"He was taller than Julia, but he had his back to me."

"Hair color?" Nick suggested.

"He was wearing a hat," Camila replied apologetically. "I know that's not helpful."

"Was there anything else to their conversation?"

"I asked Julia about it when she came in that night, and she told me to forget I saw anything. It wasn't her brushing me off or trying to keep a secret, it seemed like she was trying to protect me," Camila explained. "My sister is tough as nails. If someone scared her, there was a really good reason."

Nick pulled out his card and handed it to Diego.

"I don't know Detective Caruso," Nick said. "I'll meet with him in case he has any insight about Julia's disappearance. See if I can't get him to take this seriously. The LAPD has a lot more resources, but I have the time to give this case my full attention. In the meantime, if you think of anything that might be helpful, please let me know. Even if it seems small or unimportant. If you get a ransom note or hear from the kidnapper, tell me as soon as possible. I'll reach out when I know more, but don't hesitate to call . . . even if it's just to check on my progress. You have my word I'll do everything in my power to find Julia and bring her home safely."

Diego looked at the card, then nodded. "At least you listened to us," he said.

Nick was at his car when Camila came running after him.

"Here," she said, handing him a recent picture of Julia. "So you don't forget there's a real person with a family who loves her."

"I won't. I promise."

Camila bit her lip, nervously.

"Mr. Gallagher," she began, "can I trust you?"

"Of course," Nick said. "I'm guessing there are some things you didn't want to say in front of your parents. Whatever it is, I'll keep your confidence."

"Julia doesn't work for Mr. Morales, at least not anymore. I think she works as . . . well, I don't know for sure. But Rosa is a . . . The other night she was . . ."

"I know," Nick said. "Rosa and Julia's boss was the one who hired me. Julia tends bar. That's it."

Camila looked relieved.

"Do you think she ran away?" Camila asked in a small voice.

"No," Nick said. "Do you?"

Camila shook her head. "Do you think she's alive?"

"I sure as hell hope so."

# Chapter 23

Olympic Ford stood out from its neighbors by virtue of a full-size car rotating slowly on the roof. Nick spared a thought for the poor worker whose job it was to climb up there and keep it polished, then he headed into the showroom. There were several different cars on display. A young man in a black suit with a crisp white shirt approached the moment Nick was through the door.

"Hello, sir! Which car can I get you to drive home today?" the young man asked.

"That was a fine opening line," Nick replied. "But unfortunately, I'm not car shopping."

"Just because you're not shopping doesn't mean you won't find something that catches your eye. Surely you'd like to take a spin in this beautiful little coupe. It has a three-speed manual gearbox and a rear-wheel drive, with a top speed of seventy-nine miles per hour."

"I'm looking for Mark Morales," Nick said.

"Or perhaps you're a family man and would prefer a Super Deluxe," the young man insisted, jealously guarding his commission. "Ask me anything and I'll have an answer for you."

"Can you tell me details about a missing college girl?" Nick asked.

The young man shut his mouth with an audible snap and blinked a few times before pointing towards the rear of the showroom.

"Mr. Morales's office is back through there."

Nick nodded his thanks and wound his way through the showroom until he stood in front of a secretary's desk. The woman behind it was young and pretty. She wore a red dress that cinched at the waist and her dark hair was meticulously curled. Nick approached and introduced himself.

"I'm sorry, sir, but Mr. Morales is very busy today," the secretary said brightly. "Would you like to make an appointment?"

"Please tell him this is regarding Julia Martinez."

The secretary lifted the receiver and relayed Nick's message.

"You may go in, sir."

Mark Morales stood as Nick entered his office. He was a handsome man in his early fifties. Wearing a three-piece suit with gold cuff links, he projected the air of success. His warm smile was meant to put people at ease.

"Come in, come in," Morales said, ushering Nick to a chair, before sitting down behind his desk. "How can I help you?"

"Julia Martinez is missing."

Morales's eyes widened.

"My God!" he said. "What happened?"

"I'm trying to find out," Nick said. "Where were you last night?"

"You can't think I'd have anything to do with—" Morales exclaimed before noticing Nick's impassive expression. "Sorry, of course you have to ask. My daughter and I grabbed a quick dinner at Ernie's, then went to see *The Luck of the Irish* at the Brooklyn Theater."

"After that?"

"We went home. I did some work and went to bed," Morales said.

Nick nodded and wrote it down. Even though the information was not particularly helpful, Nick found that putting a person's words to paper often made them uncomfortable. It was useful to have them slightly off-balance.

"The Martinezes don't deserve this," Morales said, shaking his head.

"No one does."

"I didn't mean—" he broke off again. "They're good people, kind, hardworking. We attend church together. It's a small community and we look out for one another."

"Like you did giving Julia the job at your dealership."

"Exactly," Morales replied.

"As your secretary."

"Yes . . ."

"Were you concerned when Julia didn't show up this morning?"

"Well, of course, but I, uh . . ."

"Cut the bullshit," Nick said. "I saw you at Helen Brecker's club a few nights ago. I'm guessing you got Julia her job there."

Morales leaned back with a sigh.

"What was it?" Nick asked. "You wanted to sleep with her and thought that would be a good way to do it?"

"Don't be disgusting. She's young enough to be my daughter."

"That doesn't stop a lot of men. In fact, it seems to be an added bonus."

"Not for me. Even though my daughter is in college, she's still my little girl. I can't imagine . . ." Morales shuddered with distaste. "I suggested Julia for the bartending job because I thought it would be a good place for her. You know Helen?"

"I do."

"Can you imagine someone who takes better care of her employees?"

Nick had to admit Morales had a point.

"Besides, it's not just a brothel, it's a gentleman's club where I entertain business associates. You have no idea how hard I worked to become one of the largest car dealerships in Los Angeles. Why should someone buy from me when they can go across town to a white guy? It's about relationships. I take a specific type of client there, say, for instance, the man who makes purchasing decisions for the city. Helen's has the kind of atmosphere he might appreciate. Private, upscale, with good drinks and attractive women. At the end of the night, I go home to my family. If the client decides to take advantage of the other opportunities the club provides, it's not my concern. I don't ask questions and he refers his friends."

"You still haven't told me why you sent Julia there," Nick said. "Was she a bad secretary?"

"She was the best. A year ago, Diego began having chest pains and needed heart surgery. I try to pay my employees a fair wage, but Julia needed a lot of money, fast. We could have taken up a collection at church, but Diego is a proud man. It would have humiliated him. Instead, I introduced Julia to Helen. She makes more in tips from a single night than I could pay her in a week."

"Didn't her parents ask about the extra cash?"

"She went behind her father's back to the president of the hospital, who's also one of Helen's clients. She convinced him to tell Diego there'd been a mistake when calculating the cost. Julia paid the bulk of the bills directly, without her parents ever knowing."

"Impressive," Nick said.

"You have to admire someone who will not only take on that responsibility but also protect her father's pride," Morales said.

"Did you notice anything at the club that Helen might have missed?" Nick asked.

"Not a chance. That woman has eyes like a hawk," Morales replied. "And if she didn't see it, Gregory did."

"What about something that might have seemed innocuous? Someone flirting a bit more than they should. You knew Julia pretty well. Was there anyone she seemed uncomfortable around?"

"No. She was impressive and intimidating. I'm pretty sure all of my salesmen had a crush on her."

"Anything more than a crush?"

"A few got up the nerve to ask her out. She told them that church was an important part of her life. If they liked, they could show up on Sunday. The hopefuls arrived, only to meet Diego. She never had to say no and everyone's ego stayed intact."

"Did you ever notice any tension with the other women who worked at Helen's?"

"From what I can see, the girls do their best to look out for one another. Julia told me there's a kitchen in the back where they take their breaks. If you ignored what people were wearing, it was almost like the local soda shop."

Nick laughed at the image, but it was easy to picture in his mind. Growing up, he'd spent a lot of time with Helen and her friends.

"You know how she got home most nights?" Nick asked.

"If I was there, I'd give her a ride. Otherwise, it was usually Rosa or one of the other girls."

"She didn't have her own car?" Nick asked.

"No," Morales said. "Diego has the family's only car and he takes it to work every morning."

"She ever ride the streetcar?"

"To the club. By the time she had finished work, they'd stopped running. Even in the best of situations, she had three transfers to get home. Young woman alone at night . . . ? It's not ideal."

"Anything else? Do you know if she had a boyfriend or anyone else in her life I should know about?"

"Julia never said anything about dating, but then again, she wouldn't. Her parents are very strict. There was something about her, though. In the past few months, she's seemed happier. If I didn't know better, I'd say she looked like a woman in love. She also started wearing a silver locket. Never at home or in church, where there would be questions, but at work. She'd touch it, almost like a talisman. My guess is someone special gave it to her."

Nick thanked Morales and left his card.

"Will you keep me informed?" Morales asked. "I genuinely thought sending Julia to Helen's club would be a good fit. If it turns out something happened because of her work there, I'll never forgive myself."

# Chapter 24

Evelyn stopped over for six hours in Washington, DC, on her return from Berlin. Using all her powers of persuasion, she convinced General Clay she could get him the airplane replacement parts faster than her competitors. It was not quite the five million dollars in new orders she wanted, but it was still significant.

She arrived home feeling grimy and exhausted. Setting her bag on the stairs, she kicked off her shoes and headed into the kitchen. The food on the flight was less than culinary excellence. She could not complain, though. After Berlin, she was grateful to be anywhere without ration cards. Evelyn opened the refrigerator to find Nick's leftover gnocchi. Technically, she knew enough about a kitchen to reheat it, but she couldn't be bothered. Instead, she grabbed a fork and ate it cold over the sink. Still good. On the counter were daily reports from the factory Ruth had dropped off for her review. She flipped through several pages before deciding she was too tired to concentrate.

Evelyn was washing her dishes when Taffy swept into the kitchen in a cocktail dress.

"You're back! Wonderful," she said, giving Evelyn a quick kiss on the cheek. "If you run upstairs and change, you can still accompany me to the fundraiser for the Philharmonic."

"I'm exhausted," Evelyn replied. "It's taking everything I have to stay vertical."

"Then get some rest," Taffy said. "We have a big day tomorrow."

"We do?"

"Yes. I told you about it. I even cleared it with Ruth."

"Taffy," Evelyn started, "I love you dearly, but right now I'm seeing two of you. Please, please, please, help me out here."

"Dress shopping," Taffy said.

"I have dresses," Evelyn said, rubbing the heels of her hands into her tired eyes.

"Wedding dresses," Taffy amended.

Evelyn lifted one hand and stared at Taffy from underneath.

"You're kidding, right? Tell me you're joking."

"These things take months to make and we're nearing the deadline for anything halfway decent."

The French doors leading to the pool house opened and Nick entered. Evelyn offered him a wan smile, then turned back to Taffy.

"Can we put it off? I just got back and I'm—"

"Insanely busy," Nick finished. "What needs to be done?"

"She needs to find a wedding dress."

Nick studied Evelyn for a minute. Then looked down at himself. Then looked to her again.

"I don't think I have the figure to pull off a cinched waist. Don't get me wrong, I look amazing in white organza, but this is something you really need to take care of yourself."

"You cleared it with Ruth?" Evelyn asked Taffy.

"Twice."

"Fine," Evelyn said, throwing up her hands.

"You know," Taffy said, "this is something most brides look forward to."

"It's also something most brides get to do with their mothers," Evelyn snapped, then realized what she had said. Even Nick saw the hurt on Taffy's face.

"Yeah, well, I wanted a daughter of my own. I guess we're the best each other has," Taffy replied icily, then stalked out of the room.

"Shit," Evelyn swore under her breath. She was about to chase after Taffy when they heard the front door slam.

"You should go easier on her, Ev. She knows she's not your mother," Nick said. "But she's doing everything she can to fill that void."

"I know," Evelyn said. "I'm just so tired. And overwhelmed. And . . . and I miss her. I miss my mother every day. Dad, too. I always thought he'd be the one to walk me down the aisle."

Nick opened his arms and Evelyn stepped into them, resting her head on his shoulder. Then, Nick took a few sniffs.

"I'm thrilled to see you. Don't get me wrong. But you really stink."

"Twenty-eight hours on a plane."

"Come on," Nick said. "I'll draw you a bath."

Fifteen minutes later, Evelyn was immersed in hot water. On a low table next to her was a glass of Scotch. Nick sat on a footstool beside the tub, his back against the wall. Evelyn got him caught up on everything that happened in Germany.

"I thought about staying a few more days," Evelyn said, "but I couldn't see it doing any good. General Gibson promised to locate the team they sent for Kurt's wife. He's going to check the records and find out exactly when the safe house was discovered by the SS. It's possible Hannah and Sophie were still there. Alexei is looking through the records on his side and David promised to check out the displaced persons camps."

"How is David?" Nick asked.

"All grown up," Evelyn said. "He's not a kid anymore."

"He never was. He's only three years younger than you."

"I know, but coming onto the team when he did, after Theo died . . . ? I felt ancient and he just seemed so . . . innocent."

"How do you think I felt when you stepped into my office that first time?"

"I think part of you knew that I was the person you'd spent your life waiting for."

"Well," Nick admitted, "that's true."

Evelyn reached out her soapy hand and Nick took it in his.

"Tell me about your week," Evelyn said.

Nick started with Julia's disappearance.

"Am I crazy for believing Gallo when he says he didn't do it?" Nick asked.

"Norman Roth is formidable. Not someone I'd want to cross," Evelyn replied. "Gallo's family situation seems like good motivation to toe the line."

"Helen thinks I'm a fool."

"You are," Evelyn teased. "But only about certain things. You can read people better than anyone I've ever met."

"Can't read Helen, though. I've never been able to."

"How long have you known her?" Evelyn asked.

"Since I was twelve."

Evelyn sat up in her bath, sloshing water onto the floor.

"Is she the one who . . . ?"

"Kept me alive. Kinda raised me. Took my virginity?"

Evelyn nodded.

"Yes. Although I think she saw the last one as nothing more than a life lesson."

"And you?" Evelyn asked.

"I was fifteen. I pretty much wanted to sleep with everyone when I was fifteen," Nick said. "Besides, she left shortly after."

"Did you think it was because of your skills?" Evelyn asked with a wry smile.

"Oh, I had no skills back then," Nick admitted. "No illusions of greatness. But it had nothing to do with me. She got a chance to escape. She had to take it."

"Did you wonder where she went?" Evelyn asked.

"Sure, but it was easier not to know. I liked imagining some Prince Charming came and swept her off her feet. Or maybe she got a scholarship to some fancy university. Or maybe . . . I don't know. I just knew that if she stayed, she probably wouldn't have survived."

"You did."

"I wouldn't call it surviving. I had a steady paycheck. Roof over my head," Nick replied. "These aren't things to be taken for granted, but I felt purposeless. I was so angry all the time. I hated the world and I hated myself. It was slowly killing me from the inside out."

Evelyn reached out and traced his face gently.

"So, you went into the army. I don't know what I would've done if I hadn't found you."

"You'd have managed," he said with a smile.

"Honestly, I don't think so," she replied. "In the war, we worked so well together because we trusted each other. I know you better than anyone else in the world. And you know me. Without that partnership, I don't think we would have made it out alive."

"You had Carl."

"And I love him to pieces, but he wasn't in command. You were."

"Wait, wait, wait," Nick said, faking astonishment. "You acknowledge that I was in charge."

"Was," Evelyn stressed. "Was."

"Where was this admission back in London and France?"

"Couldn't let you get a swollen head. Would have wrecked you."

"And now?" Nick asked.

Evelyn motioned him closer. Then closer still. She reached up as if to examine his head more closely.

"Hmmm. Still a risk," she said with a laugh. Then, with a tug, she pulled him into the bath, clothes and all. For a moment, Nick sat there, absolutely soaked to the skin.

"You've made a mess."

Evelyn shrugged then kissed him.

"It'll be worth it."

Later, when they were both dry and lying in bed, Evelyn looked over at Nick.

"Can I meet Helen?"

Nick nodded. "I'm not hiding her. We've both been so busy."

"I wish we had more time together," Evelyn said. "My father wasn't always at work."

"We'll figure it out," Nick replied. "We have the rest of our lives."

Evelyn kissed him, then snuggled down into bed. Nick knew she was exhausted and about to close her eyes. It wasn't the best time to bring it up, but he couldn't help himself.

"Evie?"

"Hmm?"

"Why didn't you ask me about the prenuptial agreement yourself?"

Evelyn frowned. "What?"

"I'm happy to sign it," Nick said. "It's not that. I just wish it was something we discussed, rather than Taffy springing it on me."

Evelyn looked at him. "What are you talking about?"

"The prenuptial agreement."

"You said that already."

"You really don't know?"

"Love," Evelyn began. "I've barely slept in the past week. I'm jet-lagged and so tired the whole room is fuzzy. When I tell you I don't know about any agreement, please believe me. . . . Or at least argue with me about it in the morning."

"So, Taffy did that all by herself . . . ? Wow," Nick said.

He looked back to Evelyn to see how she responded to Taffy going behind her back, but she was already asleep.

# Chapter 25

Sitting in her office at Bishop Aeronautics, Evelyn filled Ruth in on the new orders. Then Ruth updated Evelyn on everything that happened since she left. Logan had hired incredibly competent people and, as a result, when problems arose, nine times out of ten, they solved them without her input. It also helped that Ruth was a more than capable second-in-command. She had been there so long, she knew almost every answer and very little flustered her.

"Are you certain you have to retire?" Evelyn asked for the hundredth time.

"I'm setting up more interviews for next week," Ruth replied.

The phone on Evelyn's desk rang and Ruth reached over to answer it. She listened for a moment, then turned to Evelyn.

"There's a Kurt Vogel at the front gate."

Evelyn nodded, and Ruth told the security guard to send him through. Ten minutes later, Kurt was ushered into the office. Ruth left to give them privacy and quietly shut the door behind her.

"Did you find them?" he asked without preamble.

"No," Evelyn said. "I can't tell you where the postcard came from or whether it was sent by your wife. One way or another, though, I'm going to find out what happened to Hannah and Sophie. You have my word."

Kurt laughed humorlessly. "I've heard that before."

"Not from me. Tell me what I don't know," Evelyn said. There was something more than grief to Kurt's anger.

"What you don't know could fill an ocean."

"That's certainly true," she replied. "But let's focus on you and your family."

"Did you ever wonder what happened after you dropped me off in London?" Kurt asked.

"No," Evelyn said.

"Didn't expect you to be so honest."

"After we got you to 70 Grosvenor, I went home, took a shower, then slept for twenty-eight hours. Three days later, I was heading to France on another mission."

"You just assumed there was a happy ending."

"I needed to believe that risking my life meant something," Evelyn replied. "I didn't know your real name. I didn't know why you were important to America. I was told to get you, so I did."

"I spent ten days in London recovering from our trip," Kurt began. "They gave me food, medical care, but absolutely no answers when I asked about Sophie and Hannah. Finally, a general came in to see me. He said that he knew where my family was, but extracting them would take a little bit longer. In the meantime, I had to keep up my end of the bargain. They were sending me to the States to help build rockets.

"Late one night, they woke me up and rustled me onto an airplane. I fought it, but . . ." He trailed off with a shrug. "We landed at an army base in the desert. I was taken to a laboratory where I worked every day, developing more efficient fuel. At night, I wrote letters and tried to reach someone with answers. Finally, after a year, I gave up. I refused to go to the lab. I refused to do anything until I got word of my family. Do you know what they did?"

Evelyn shook her head no.

"They threw me in prison. It was a military work camp, where we literally broke rocks as punishment. It was like I'd never left Nazi Germany."

"How long were you there?" Evelyn asked.

"Five weeks before I finally relented. In there, I had no power. No paper or pen to reach out. No access to a telephone. At least at the lab, I had status. I could keep looking for them."

"No one told you anything more about your family?" Evelyn asked.

"I'm sure, like you, they got busy with other things," Kurt replied bitterly. "This postcard was the first I'd heard from my wife in six years. Leaving her and Sophie in Berlin was the biggest mistake of my life. I'd give anything to go back and insist they come with us. Hell, I'd even go back and work for the Nazis if I thought it would have kept them safe."

"If you feel that way, why are you still at JPL?" Evelyn asked.

"It's the only leverage I have. Would you be looking into my case if General Gibson had not asked?"

"No," Evelyn admitted.

"Would you even care?" Kurt snapped.

Evelyn was exhausted and frustrated. It felt as though her trip to Berlin had been a waste of time and there was already so much on her plate. If she had slept more than twenty hours in the past week, she might have been kinder.

"I understand what it's like to lose someone you love," Evelyn said. "That ache never fully goes away. Sometimes, I think it will consume me. But your loss is not unique, nor is your anger. I know because I feel it, too. Every. Single.

Day. You're a brilliant man with opportunities others would kill for. You escaped Nazi Germany. You have a home that is more than crumbling ruins. You have enough food to eat and you have a job that gives you so many privileges. More than all that? You still have hope. So, choose. You can stop feeling sorry for yourself and help me find your family, or you can wallow in your anger and hate. I don't care, but make your decision and get out of my office. I have things to do."

Kurt stared at Evelyn, shocked by her words.

"You're a real bitch."

"Yep," Evelyn replied, turning to the paperwork in front of her. She looked through reports from her absence and made notes for other projects. The silence went on so long that Evelyn almost forgot Kurt was there.

"You said there was a safe house in Berlin," he said finally.

Evelyn looked up.

"I doubt Hannah would have stayed more than a few days," Kurt said. "Especially if her guides did not return. It was hard enough for her and Sophie inside our apartment. A strange place without the comforts of home would have been impossible. Hannah's a fighter. She wouldn't have waited for the worst to show up on her doorstep. She would've gone on the run."

Evelyn slid a pad of paper and a pen across the desk.

"Give me a list of the people she trusted."

Kurt picked up the pen and began to write.

# Chapter 26

Detective Brian Caruso looked like he should be on a recruitment poster for the LAPD. In his early thirties, he was unusually handsome in an all-American way. Tall and fit, with deep blue eyes, his blond hair parted neatly to the side. He had a polished smile with just enough warmth to seem friendly and noncommittal. His suit was expensive dark gray merino wool with a crisp white shirt underneath. Gold cuff links peaked out from under his sleeves and a gold pin secured his burgundy silk tie. Even Nick, who rarely gave a thought to the trappings of wealth, could see Caruso came from money.

"I appreciate you coming to see me," Caruso said, leading Nick through the bullpen toward his desk. "I didn't realize the Martinezes had the resources for a private detective."

"They don't," Nick replied.

"Then who hired you? If you don't mind me asking."

"I do."

"Do what?"

"Mind."

Caruso's smile faltered slightly. He was not used to getting so little response to all his charm.

"They told me about you," Caruso said. "Washed out of the LAPD in less than a year."

"Yup."

"What was it? Girls? Booze? Something else?"

"Take your pick," Nick said with a shrug. It was no longer a sore subject.

"You're wasting your time," Caruso said. "There's not much of a case here."

"How do you figure?" Nick asked.

"Julia's a young woman in her twenties. Probably met a guy and shacked up with him."

"From what her family says, that's unlikely. They're very worried."

"They're immigrants."

"And . . . ?"

"Come on. Those people don't get how America works."

"How does America work?" Nick asked, his voice low and tense.

"Don't get your hackles up," Caruso said. "I admire how hard those people worked to get here. It's just that Mexicans are strict Catholics. When their girls finally cut loose, they go wild. She'll limp home eventually."

"Or maybe she was kidnapped in front of her house."

"What?" Caruso asked, suddenly alert.

"I have a witness who says Julia was on her front walk when she was stopped by a man who forced her into a car."

It wasn't exactly what Camila told Nick, but if it lit a fire under Caruso's ass, he was willing to stretch the truth.

"What did they see? Did they get a look at the person? Maybe a license plate?"

"No," Nick said. "But I don't think Julia's going to 'just turn up.' "

"Why didn't anyone tell me that?" Caruso asked, pulling a notebook from his coat pocket.

"How many people did you talk to?" Nick asked.

Caruso had the decency to look ashamed.

"Right, so maybe you should start treating this like a real case, rather than just some brown girl gone missing."

"I resent that," Caruso said.

"Feel free," Nick replied.

"Okay, okay. What do you know? Does she have a boyfriend?" Caruso asked. Nick didn't reply. Seeing his intransigence, Caruso threw up his hands. "It isn't an unreasonable place to start."

"Are you going to look for her?" Nick asked.

"Fine. You're right. I should've taken this more seriously," Caruso said. Then, musing to himself, "Think about what happened with Elizabeth Short."

"The Black Dahlia?" Nick asked.

"The person who solves that murder is going to be famous. This one might be the same. I know she's Mexican, but she's still pretty. The papers might pick it up."

Nick didn't bother to hide his disgust.

"Whereas I'm hoping to find her alive," he said, setting down his card on Caruso's desk.

Nick walked out of the bullpen and straight into the captain's office. Wharton was a graying man in his early fifties with a gruff, unsmiling face. Nick reported to him during his brief tenure as a cop and he generally considered Wharton a good man. Sure, he had thrown Nick out on his ass, but in retrospect, he deserved it.

"Please tell me you haven't come to beg for your job back," Wharton said.

"Yeah, because I'm a masochist," Nick replied.

"I've known that for a while, but I don't think you're a complete idiot."

"Thanks?"

"So why are you darkening my doorstep?"

"Julia Martinez."

"Ah, yes. Detective Caruso's case," Wharton said wryly.

"Not a fan?" Nick guessed.

"I'd never say anything bad about my officers," Wharton replied.

"You've said plenty of shit about me."

"I said plenty of shit *to you*. It's not gossip if you say it to someone's face. Then, it's helpful criticism."

"Yeah," Nick replied. "Felt helpful."

"Was I wrong?" Wharton asked. "About any of it?"

Nick thought for a moment, wanting to disagree, but he couldn't.

"No," Nick admitted. "So, what can you tell me about Caruso that you'd say to his face?"

"He graduated Stanford with honors."

"Comes from money?" Nick asked.

"Oh yes. The shoes give it away."

"I noticed the cuff links."

"Those, too," Wharton replied. "He's had a meteoric rise through the LAPD, starting in vice and now in robbery-homicide. He doesn't brag about it, but he's gotta be well-connected at the mayor's office, or even higher. Everyone knows he's the golden boy."

"You must be in hell."

A rare smile cracked Wharton's face, but he didn't answer.

"He gunning for your job?" Nick asked.

"Hell no. He's gonna be a senator one day."

"Lucky us," Nick said. "He doesn't seem that interested in Julia's case."

"He wasn't supposed to get it," Wharton said. "Another detective asked to trade shifts. Caruso can be a team player. Knows how to make friends."

"He any good?"

"When he wants to be. Closes cases."

"Legally?" Nick asked.

"Doesn't have any complaints from internal affairs."

"Not the same thing."

"No," Wharton admitted. "It's not. There are rumors, but no one's said anything to me. I think most of the guys really look up to him."

"Enough to protect him?"

Wharton shrugged. "He helps the new guys get their feet underneath them, kisses the veterans' asses, and the DAs love him."

"But you don't?"

"What we do saves lives and gets justice for victims," Wharton said. "No one should treat this job as a way station to somewhere better. I don't give a shit who gets credit, so long as girls like Julia Martinez come home."

"I knew it," Nick said. "You're a teddy bear underneath it all."

"Get the fuck out of my office," Wharton replied.

With a smile, Nick did.

# Chapter 27

Evelyn stood on a low pedestal in front of a three-way mirror. Instead of her usual sleek business suit, she was wearing a cupcake. Not an actual cupcake, just an incredibly puffy dress made of white silk with several crinoline petticoats. Taffy circled her with an appraising eye. Nearby, Lily and Colette sat on a gold brocade couch sipping champagne. Evelyn called them that morning for moral support. She hated shopping on a good day. This was her definition of hell.

"It's marvelous," Barbara the saleswoman cooed. "You look like a dream."

Evelyn was tempted to retort that it felt more like a nightmare, but she caught Taffy's stern gaze in the mirror.

"I just . . ." Evelyn began, trying to politely frame her hatred for this dress. "I don't think it's quite me. Maybe something with less volume . . ."

Barbara nodded sagely. "A really beautiful gown came in yesterday."

A few minutes later, Evelyn was standing in a dress that weighed at least twenty pounds. It was covered in beading and looked more like armor than fashion.

"Work of art," Evelyn said. "But heavy."

Barbara nodded again. "Don't worry. We'll keep going till we find the perfect one!"

Barbara pulled a dress made from a satin so shiny it could serve as the mirror to a lighthouse. Evelyn's eyes widened in horror.

"*Mon dieu,*" Colette gasped with barely suppressed laughter.

"Evelyn's style is more like Schiaparelli or Balmain," Lily explained.

Barbara gave her a blank stare.

"Smooth, clean lines, beautifully tailored, with a surprising element to make it stand out."

"Show me everything." Taffy sighed.

Barbara looked horrified.

"We don't do that. This is a boutique experience."

Taffy looked at the tag on Evelyn's dress.

"When we're paying this much, it's whatever experience we want," Taffy replied.

Evelyn glanced at the number and her eyes widened.

"That's what it costs? For a dress?"

"Don't forget the tailoring," Lily said. "It almost doubles the price."

"Insanity," Evelyn insisted.

"You can afford it," Colette teased.

"It's not about the money. It's the principle of the thing. Nick's tux will cost a fraction of this and he'll wear it for the next twenty years. This'll be worn once, then shoved in a closet."

"Ignore her," Taffy said.

Barbara sighed and opened the door to the storeroom, where there were rows upon rows of fluffy white gowns. As she and Taffy disappeared inside, Colette helped Evelyn out of the dress. Evelyn sighed, rolling her shoulders back to loosen them up. Lily handed her a silk robe and a glass of champagne.

"Did you have this many problems finding a dress?" Evelyn asked.

"I fled France with nothing more than the clothes on my back," Colette said. "By the time George and I reached New York, I wanted to start our lives together as soon as possible. We checked into our hotel, went to Bergdorf Goodman, where I bought the first thing I saw, then we headed to city hall. My wedding wasn't anything like I imagined, but I got to marry George, which made it perfect."

Colette dabbed her eyes, thinking of her late husband. Even months after his death, she still wore black as a sign of her mourning. Evelyn reached out for Colette's hand.

"You're lucky." Lily sighed. She was also a widow, but unlike Colette, the day she found out her husband was killed in the war was one of the happiest of her life. He was an abusive man who terrorized her every day. She knew he would never grant her a divorce, so his death felt like freedom.

"Did you at least get a good dress?" Colette asked.

"I was ready to make it myself. Knew exactly what I wanted, but my mother-in-law insisted that I wear light blue because it was practical and I could wear it again . . . which I never did. I absolutely loathe that color now. In retrospect, I should have run for the hills, but I was seventeen. I thought I was in love. I thought I needed to be settled. I thought it was what everyone did."

"I want to go back and give your teenage self a hug," Evelyn said.

"I want to go back and tell her she's an idiot," Colette replied.

"She could have used both." Lily laughed. "It all worked out, though. I love my work. I love my friends. I love my life. How can I regret the things that brought me here?"

"Would you ever get married again?" Evelyn asked.

"Never," Lily replied definitively.

"Maybe," Colette said. "I can't imagine loving anyone as much as I loved George. Once you have that, it's impossible to settle for anything less."

"Is that how you feel about Nick?" Lily asked.

Evelyn smiled. It was the kind of smile that started deep down in her stomach and worked its way up to her face, where it glowed.

"Yes," she said.

"Then pick something to wear," Taffy said, catching the tail end of their conversation.

Barbara, looking significantly less perky, trailed behind, rolling a rack of seven dresses. Taffy had found ones that were simple and elegant.

Evelyn chose a white silk crepe dress. It was cut on the bias, with long sleeves, a sweetheart neckline, and a short train. Simple and stunning. Lily helped her into it and Evelyn turned to look in the mirror. It was gorgeous. If someone had asked Evelyn what she wanted, she would have described this dress. And yet, it still wasn't right. She did not know how to put it into words. Lily, Colette, and Taffy all nodded encouragingly. Barbara, the saleswoman, looked something akin to desperate.

"It's really beautiful . . ." Evelyn began.

"Oh, for God's sake," Taffy said, throwing up her hands in the air.

Barbara glanced between them, slowly realizing her commission was going up in smoke.

*    *    *

Outside the bridal shop, Evelyn turned to Lily, Colette, and Taffy.

"I'm so sorry for wasting your time. Lily, maybe you could find something for me?"

"After witnessing that disaster? No, thank you," Lily shuddered. "Besides, this is the best bridal salon in the city. If you didn't find it here, I don't know what to tell you."

"Well, I always enjoy a glass of bubbly," Colette said. She gave Evelyn a hug goodbye. "Let me know the next time you need me to watch you reject everything in a store. It's strangely fun, though I do believe poor Barbara is probably crying in the stockroom."

"She's definitely drinking the rest of that champagne all by herself," Evelyn replied.

"Look through some magazines." Lily sighed. "If you find something you like, perhaps I can make it for you. But once it's done, you can't reject it. Do not make me ban you from my store."

"Where would I get all my clothes?" Evelyn asked in horror.

"Exactly," Lily replied.

They all said goodbye, then Colette and Lily headed in one direction while Taffy and Evelyn walked in the other.

"Your mother never got to go dress shopping," Taffy said. "When she and your father eloped, there wasn't much time to make preparations. She just picked her favorite dress and wore it to the ceremony. She was beautiful. It had nothing to do with what she was wearing; she was just so happy. All I want is for you to be that happy. Are you?"

"Yes," Evelyn replied.

"Really? Planning this wedding seems like a chore. If you can't get excited about this, how are you going to get excited about your marriage?"

"They're two very different things," Evelyn said. "I think the better question is why are you working so hard to plan this wedding if you don't think my marriage will last?"

"What do you mean?" Taffy asked.

"Nick said you asked him to sign a prenuptial agreement."

"Of course I did."

"How dare you go behind my back like that?"

"Because I knew you wouldn't do it."

"I'm not going into my marriage with an eye toward the exit," Evelyn insisted.

"Even with the best intentions, people change. Lives go in different directions. Sometimes there are events you can't even imagine that will pull you apart through no fault of your own. We can't predict the future. Once you're married, everything you own is his according to the law. The prenuptial agreement isn't just protecting you, it's protecting Bishop Aeronautics . . . and everyone who works for you."

Evelyn stopped in surprise. She had never thought about it that way.

"Even so," she said after a moment. "You don't belong in the middle of my relationship. How did you think he would react?"

"If he tore it up and stormed away, then he's not half the man I believe him to be. Nor would he be half the man that you deserve."

"So, it was a test?"

"That wasn't its original purpose, but yes, I suppose. Every day people tell us who they are; we just have to pay attention to see it."

"I know who Nick is."

"Sometimes it's good to have a second opinion," Taffy replied.

"I'm not asking for your blessing and I don't need your approval," Evelyn said before stalking away. She needed time and space away from her aunt.

# Chapter 28

The campus of UCLA always felt a bit surreal to Nick. It was beautiful, with wide green lawns and neoclassical buildings. The students wandered with ease, sometimes lying on the grass with a book in hand, sometimes sitting on benches, deep in conversation. It was hard to imagine a world where people had no responsibilities beyond their coursework. Sometimes, Nick wondered what it would be like to go to college. It was an experience so far out of reach when he was a child that he never allowed himself to long for it. Now, he just felt too old.

Having asked Camila for Julia's schedule, Nick was waiting outside her Advanced Economic Theory class. At exactly 11:05 a.m., a flood of students came out of the building. Nick had Julia's picture ready and began asking everyone if they knew her. A few people stopped.

"She wasn't in class today," a young man offered.

"Yeah, James, that's why he's looking for her," another replied dismissively.

"What's she done?" a third man asked.

"She's missing," Nick replied.

"Wait, what?" asked one woman, clearly distressed.

Two others stopped beside her. "What do you mean, missing?"

Twenty minutes later, Nick and the three women were sitting at a table in the cafeteria. They introduced themselves as Elena, Denise, and Sara. There weren't many women who majored in economics, so they stuck together. They all knew that Julia was a bartender, but they did not know where.

"She said it was a private club in Brentwood," Elena said.

"I got the feeling she made good money, too," Sara added.

"Why do you think that?" Nick asked.

"Tuition ain't cheap," Sara replied. "I know she's on a scholarship, but it doesn't cover everything."

"And she's not from a wealthy family," Denise added.

The other women glared at her.

"What?" Denise asked. "I'm not supposed to notice her clothes are a few seasons out of date? It's not a criticism. I admire her for figuring this out."

According to them, Julia was always busy, running from one thing to the next. Sometimes it was work. Sometimes family. Sometimes it was just trying to keep up with her studies. Unlike the others, Julia did not have a dorm room, so she usually secluded herself in the library. At the end of most days, she took a bus to her job.

"Do you know if she's dating anyone?" Nick asked.

The women looked between themselves and nodded.

"Well, she did spend a lot of time with one guy," Sara said. "He volunteers over at the community health clinic."

"Got a name?" Nick asked.

"Gabe something," Elena guessed. "She never actually said that they were together, but she's always leaving our

Thursday study sessions early to meet up with him when he gets off his shift."

"He's in the med school," Denise said.

"She seemed really happy," Sara added. "Like when she said his name, her whole face lit up. We'd ask her about him, but she never said anything besides the fact that he was kind and treated her well."

"I guess her parents didn't let her date," Denise said. "I have no idea what that's about. He's going to be a doctor. My folks would kill for a doctor as a son-in-law."

"Anyone else?" Nick asked.

Again, the girls looked between themselves, as if silently asking permission to confide in Nick. Finally, Elena said, "There was another guy who came around sometimes."

"Tall, maybe former army," Sara guessed.

"Everyone's former army," Denise said.

"Hair color?" Nick asked. "Eye color?"

"He always wore a hat and stayed pretty far away," Sara said. "Julia seemed really uncomfortable around him. The first time she saw him, she wondered what he was doing here."

"I think her exact words were, 'How did he find me?'" Denise said.

"When was this?" Nick asked.

"Some time last semester. Maybe six months ago?" Denise said, looking to the other women for confirmation. They nodded in agreement.

"She was always annoyed when he showed up. But she always went to talk to him," Elena said. "Almost like she had to."

"She smiled, but not a real smile," Sara said. "The kind you give someone when they offer to buy you a drink you don't want."

"The please-don't-get-mad smile," Denise said.

"That's a thing?" Nick asked.

"Of course it is," Elena replied. "Guys can be . . ."

"Scary," Sara said bluntly.

"Am I scary?" Nick asked. "Do I make you uncomfortable?"

The women, again, looked at each other, then shook their heads no.

"You seem like you're not interested in us," Denise said.

"Or you are," Sara added. "But you're interested in what we have to say. You're not thinking about . . . you know."

"I do," Nick said. "What was it about this guy that made Julia so uncomfortable?"

"He didn't take a hint," Sara said. "She tried to keep her distance. If he stepped closer, she'd take a step backward. One time, she almost fell into the street."

"She was afraid of him," Denise said. "There was no rhyme or reason to when he came. Sometimes it was after this class or another one of our classes. Sometimes he was just waiting on the steps of the library."

"It wasn't every day," Sara added. "Maybe a few times a month?"

"We didn't always see him," Elena said, "But you could tell when he'd been here. She was rattled. Those were the days she'd head to work early. I guess they had a kitchen in the back where she could study until her shift started."

"And a security guard who kept them safe."

"Can you tell me anything else about this guy?" Nick said.

"He seemed too old to be in college," Sara said.

"Looked like a businessman," Denise said. "Banker? Lawyer? The kind of man who doesn't get his hands dirty."

Nick nodded and wrote it all down in his notebook. Then he passed out his business card.

"If you think of anything else or you see that guy hanging around, let me know."

The women nodded.

"Please find her," Denise said. "I know bad things happen to women all the time. I just never thought it would be one of us."

# Chapter 29

Following the women's directions, Nick headed over to the community health center. It was a low brick building with a line out the door and a harried nurse at the front desk, triaging people as they arrived. Nick asked about a volunteer named Gabe and the nurse pointed to a slender man in his midtwenties with dark, curly hair. He wore glasses that were slightly too big and made his eyes seem beady in comparison. Though he had clearly shaved that morning, his face embodied the term five-o'clock shadow. He wore neat clothes that were worn and appeared to be handed down from an older relative. Nick watched Gabe for a moment, seeing his warm expression and the gentle way he spoke with people. Fairly tall, Gabe always knelt down to meet his patients on their level. Nick studied him for a minute more, then went outside to wait.

An hour later, when he finished his shift, Gabe walked out of the clinic. He blinked against the bright sunlight, then frowned as he checked his watch.

"Waiting for Julia?" Nick asked.

Gabe was suddenly alert. "Who are you?"

Nick introduced himself.

"A private detective?" Gabe said warily. "You have any identification?"

Obligingly, Nick pulled out his wallet and showed Gabe his detective license. He studied it, then examined Nick.

"What do you want with Julia?"

"Do you know Helen Brecker?" Nick asked.

"Her boss?"

"Do you know what she does for work?"

"Why are you asking these questions? What's going on?" Gabe demanded.

"Julia's missing. She's been gone two days."

"I don't understand. She always meets me after my shift. Should be here any minute."

He glanced down the street hopefully, then back at Nick. He checked his watch and looked in the distance again. This time, however, he seemed more concerned.

"Shall we start over from the beginning?" Nick asked.

Gabe nodded.

Nick took Gabe to a nearby coffee shop. Across the table, Gabe's brow furrowed with worry. He had kind eyes that projected a sensitive soul. Statistically, the majority of crimes against women were committed by a boyfriend or husband, but Nick could not wrap his head around the idea of Gabe as threatening.

"I'm sorry for being strange back there," Gabe began. "It's just that some guy's been bothering Julia. She won't tell me anything about him, but . . ."

"Better safe than sorry," Nick finished for him. "I gotta ask, just to cover my bases. Where were you two nights ago?"

Gabe thought for a moment, then shrugged helplessly.

"I had dinner at home alone, studied until midnight, then went to bed. Not a great alibi, is it?"

"Most honest ones aren't," Nick replied. "How often do we go out of our way to make sure people see us in the middle of the night?"

Gabe nodded gratefully.

"How can I help?" he asked. "Should I go look for her? I can talk to people. I can . . . I can do whatever you need."

"What I need is information," Nick replied.

"Anything."

"How come you didn't know Julia is missing? You say that you two are close, but . . ."

"We don't get to see each other that much. She joins me after my clinic twice a week. We have an early dinner before she goes to work."

"How did you meet?"

"It was about eight months ago. I prefer the back section of the library, where it's usually empty. One day, I found Julia sitting in my favorite carrel. It was annoying. I like things the way I like them, and I kept glaring at her. She finally looked up with this incredible smile and asked if I wanted to switch. I felt weird about saying yes, but she got up and moved over. Somehow, she understood and didn't judge me. Do you know how rare that is? We both went back to work, but I couldn't get anything done. I kept thinking about her smile. It was like sunshine. When she left, I didn't say anything. I didn't know how. She had probably walked out of my life forever. Yet the next day she was back, sitting two seats away from my usual carrel. At the end of the week, I asked her to dinner.

"You know that moment, when you look across the table from someone and realize your life would be complete if you could spend the rest of it with them?"

"I do," Nick said.

"It was like that," Gabe said. "I knew within the first five minutes."

"You want to marry her?"

Gabe reached into his bag and pulled out his wallet. He withdrew a recent picture of Julia smiling and pointed to her silver necklace.

"I gave that to her on our six-month anniversary. It's not a ring, but it is a promise. I want to wait until I've finished medical school and she wants to wait until she's done with college. It's only until June."

"Your families must be thrilled."

Gabe's expression wavered.

"My parents really like Julia, but they struggle with her not being Jewish. To be honest, I do, too. My family fled to the United States in 1918, after my uncle was killed during the Lwów pogrom. Who'd have guessed we were the lucky ones? I was six years old, and my family started over with almost nothing. It was a struggle to learn the language, find a place to live, get work. There were so many kind people who helped us, and my parents are very grateful for our community."

"It's something you and Julia have in common. Immigrant families."

"We talked about that on our first date," Gabe replied. "Our backgrounds couldn't be more different. I'm a Polish Jew. She's a Mexican Catholic. I asked her straightaway if she was okay with that difference. Religion is important to me and to her. I didn't want to start something that would only break my heart."

"What did she say?"

"She said that our faith brought both of us comfort and a sense of belonging. If we could each find that, wouldn't it be beautiful to share it with our children? Besides, as she pointed out, my sabbath is Saturday, hers is Sunday. There's no overlap. We can make it to synagogue and church."

"What about her family?" Nick asked, testing Gabe's honesty.

"She hasn't told them about me yet. I think they're hoping to find a nice young man from their neighborhood and have her future wrapped up in a tidy bow."

"You sure that's not what she wants, too?"

"Julia's not a neat and tidy person. It's part of what I love about her. She likes exploring the world and finds beauty in everything. If there's an adventure to be had, she's first in line. She loves her family and feels a great deal of responsibility toward them, but she doesn't want to live up to their expectations at the risk of losing herself. It's a hard struggle."

"What about her work?" Nick asked.

"What about it?"

"You're okay with it?"

"Why wouldn't I be?"

"It's at a gentleman's club. You're not worried she's doing more than just pouring drinks?"

"No," Gabe said with the unshakable faith of a man in love.

"Do you know anyone who would want to hurt Julia?"

"No," he said again. "She's the kindest person I've ever met."

Then, unexpectedly, Gabe started to cry. Dropping his head in his hands, his shoulders shook as small puddles formed on the table. Nick sat awkwardly, not knowing how to help. After a few minutes, Gabe pulled a few paper napkins from the dispenser, wiped his eyes, and blew his nose.

"Sorry, all of this is just so . . . I love Julia and I'll do anything for her. The thought of her . . ." Gabe broke off, as if it was too painful to consider her being mistreated. "I just feel so powerless. How can I help?"

"Sit tight and let the cops and me do our jobs," Nick said, then handed Gabe his business card. "If you think of anything. If anyone contacts you. If you see her mystery man, please let me know."

Gabe took a notebook and pen out of his backpack. He wrote down four carefully labeled phone numbers on the paper, then tore it out from the spiral binding.

"The first one is my apartment. The second is my parents' house. The next is the med school and the last is the clinic. Other than the library, they're the only places I go. Please tell me as soon as you know anything."

Nick nodded. Gabe looked at him expectantly.

"Isn't this where you promise you're going to find her?" Gabe asked.

"I don't make promises I can't keep."

# Chapter 30

After dress shopping, Evelyn decided to finish her day working from home. She sat behind her father's large mahogany desk in the library. The room had dark green wallpaper, and the late afternoon sun made her feel a bit like she was hiding away in a forest glen.

Earlier in the day, she had called Berlin and given David the list of names Kurt provided. David promised to track them down to see if there were any further leads. He had gone through the records of the concentration camps in the areas the Allies had liberated without discovering anything about Hannah or Sophie Vogel. Nor was there anyone by those names in the displaced persons camps. It was almost as if they had vanished completely. Then General Gibson took the phone and told Evelyn he had tracked down the name of the surviving team member who was supposed to get Hannah and Sophie out of Berlin: Tom Rivers.

"That sounds familiar," Evelyn said.

"It should." Gibson laughed. "He tried to get you thrown out of the OSS after you gave him a black eye."

"Oh," Evelyn remembered. "That guy was a real asshole."

Evelyn first encountered Tom Rivers in a bar in London in late 1943. He was drunk and hitting on a woman. She kept trying to escape, but he wasn't taking no for an answer. Evelyn stepped in, and the rest was written up in an incident report that earned her a formal reprimand.

Rivers' last known address was his hometown in Iowa, but David reached out to some of his contacts. They told him that after the war, Tom disappeared for a while, before winding up in Encinitas. Evelyn thanked David for the information, then called Ruth to cancel the assistant interviews for the next day. Ruth's exasperation was audible and she threatened to quit at the end of the week if Evelyn did not meet with more people.

"Friday," Evelyn promised before hanging up. She saw Nick in the doorway and gave him a broad smile.

"Ruth's not happy with me," Evelyn said, turning her face up for a kiss. He obliged, then took a seat in front of the desk.

"How did dress shopping go?" Nick asked.

"It's a work in progress," Evelyn said. "I've discovered what I don't like, which is a step in the right direction."

"How's Taffy holding up?"

"Oh, you know, fine. Just fine. Totally fine."

"I'll bet that's exactly how she would describe it," Nick teased. "She's on her third gin and tonic."

"I asked about the prenuptial agreement," Evelyn said.

"Wasn't sure if you were awake for that part of the night."

"It was the last thing I heard before I drifted off. You know I don't care about any of that. We've been through so much already. I trust you."

"It just surprised me," Nick replied. "I thought you asked Taffy to bring it up and I hated the idea of someone between us. If there's stuff we can't talk about, that's a bigger issue than who gets what. I'll never leave you, and if you left me, my world would fall apart. No amount of money would hold it together, so what does it matter?"

"We'll tear it up."

"Keep it," Nick insisted. "It'll give you peace of mind when it comes to Bishop Aeronautics and make the chain of command clear."

"You know, that was Taffy's whole argument, too."

"She's a smart woman."

"You like her, don't you?" Evelyn asked, faintly surprised.

"How can I not like a woman who has your best interests at heart? Besides, under all those fancy clothes and expensive jewelry, that woman's tough as nails. I admire that."

"She's . . . opinionated," Evelyn admitted. Then, seeing Nick's smile, "Fine. She's exactly like the rest of the Bishops."

"Taffy's trying really hard," Nick offered. "She's done a lot of the planning that neither of us have time or interest in. We should be more grateful."

Evelyn grudgingly nodded, then asked, "Is there anyone from your family you want to invite to the wedding?"

"No."

"Do you even know where they are? I can help you find them."

"I said no."

"Nick—" Evelyn began.

"If I wanted to see them, I would have done it already."

Whenever Nick thought about his parents, it felt like there was sand under his skin. Nick had never told anyone about the long nights he spent hoping they would come back for him. Terrified and shivering, he felt worthless because the two people who were supposed to love him more than anyone in the world didn't love him enough to stay. He tried to forget crying himself to sleep at night, huddled in the doorway of a building. At times, he was too hungry to feel scared. Others, he was too scared to feel hungry. Yet the pain, exhaustion, and cold never left him.

Later, he would read books with happy endings where an orphan ended up in a wealthy man's house. The experience of poverty turned him into a grateful child with wonderful manners. Nick knew the truth. The struggle made a person relentless. There was little room for compassion when survival was the only goal. Nick did not fool himself into believing Helen helped him simply from the goodness of her heart. She did it partially because he could serve as a distraction while she picked pockets and partially because she was lonely. The only thing worse than being homeless was being homeless without anyone to trust.

Nick did not know how to explain his youth to Evelyn, nor did he want to. Despite her best intentions, she could never fully understand, and even if she did, he hated the knowledge of that trauma living in her mind as part of him. He needed her to be separate from his past.

Nick stood, walked to Evelyn and gently put his hands on her shoulders.

"As far as I'm concerned, you're my only family. Please don't ask again."

# Chapter 31

Encinitas was a small beach town just north of San Diego. The drive down was beautiful, with much of it running alongside the ocean. Evelyn tied a scarf over her hair and put the top down on her car. The sun reflected off the waves and the fresh air felt like renewal. There was something relaxing about the open road. By the time Evelyn arrived, she almost felt like a new person. She checked her map, then drove to an address on Third Street. The building was a plain wood structure with a sliding door, opening the workshop to the street. A sign near the top of the building read **Rivers Surf Shop**. There was a sawhorse in front, with a few boards in various stages of completion. A man with a caramel tan was stripped to the waist, plaining a long board that was rounded at each end. He was very fit, with hair bleached a light brown by the sun and the salt. He looked up quizzically when Evelyn stepped out of her car. It was clear Tom Rivers did not remember her. To be fair, she would not have recognized him either had he not been the purpose of her trip.

"Help you?" Tom asked.

"Are those surfboards?"

He nodded. Each board was handmade, with ingrained designs made of different types of wood. Then the whole thing was covered in a thick resin that made it shine.

"They're beautiful," Evelyn said. "Did you make these yourself?"

Tom nodded again as Evelyn ran her hand along one.

"Not from around here?" he asked.

"Los Angeles."

"They got some waves up around there."

"I'm sure they do, but I never quite found the time."

"You gotta make the time," Tom insisted.

"That's true of most things," Evelyn replied.

"I'd be happy to take you out," he offered. "Nothing like it. Most peaceful place in the world. It's real good for getting your mind right."

"I could use a little bit of that," Evelyn admitted.

"Probably everyone could." He laughed. "So, if you're not looking for a surfboard, what are you looking for?"

"The man I once knew. I don't see him anywhere in you."

"Have we met?" Tom asked. "You seem like someone I'd remember."

"I'm worth remembering."

"So, help a fellow out."

"London, 1943," Evelyn said. "I gave you a pretty good shiner."

Tom's smile disappeared. "How did you find me?"

"I have friends."

"Whatever it is, I don't want any part of it. I'm not that guy anymore."

"None of us are," Evelyn said.

"Don't tell me that. You have no idea what it was like."

"I know you thought I was a secretary giving you a hard time, but did you ever stop to wonder where a secretary got such a good right hook?"

Tom stared at her.

"Hand to hand combat. Part of the OSS training. I was in the field, just like you," Evelyn said. "I went behind enemy lines, just like you. In fact, we worked on a mission together, without ever meeting each other. It was 1942, there was a scientist who needed to escape Berlin. My team took him. You and your partner were responsible for his wife and child."

"I don't know what you're talking about," Tom snapped.

He began to pack up his tools, carrying them into the shack.

"You went to a grand apartment building in the Dahlem district. Up to the fifth floor. There you found beautiful mosaics on the wall that had been painted to make a five-year-old girl forget the ugliness outside her door. Maybe you stopped to admire them. Maybe you just grabbed the woman and her daughter and fled down the back stairs."

Tom moved the surfboards inside.

"The Gestapo was already on the doorstep and you were running for your lives," Evelyn continued. "That was the last anyone heard of Kurt Vogel's family."

Tom stacked the two sawhorses in his workshop, then slid the large door closed and secured it with a padlock.

"Vogel got a postcard from his wife two weeks ago."

"What?" For the first time since she'd started speaking, Tom stopped and looked at Evelyn.

"I'm just trying to find out what happened to them," she said.

"I can't help you," he replied.

"You can. And I'm going to keep coming back here every day until you do. It looks like you've built yourself a good life here. I don't want to ruin that."

"Then leave me the hell alone," Tom snapped. Evelyn saw a flash of the man with whom she had fought all those years ago. There was a raw, uncontrolled anger in his eyes. He stormed down the street. Evelyn hurried after him.

"What if it was your wife or child? It's been six years and Vogel can't even mourn them properly. That sliver of hope is killing him."

"Goddamnit!" Tom roared as he turned back toward Evelyn.

For a moment, she thought he was going to hit her, but then he sat down on the bumper of a car and dropped his head into his hands. His breath was ragged, his eyes wide and his pupils dilated. Evelyn knelt beside him. She didn't want to touch him and break what fragile control he possessed. Instead, she just waited, her gaze level with his. He slid off the bumper until he was sitting on the sidewalk beside her. It was another few minutes before he managed to catch his breath.

"Do you know how long it's taken me to simply exist? Not find happiness or even peace. Just exist?" Tom asked. "I went home after the war, and people were so happy to see me. They tried to wrap me in a flag and tell me I was a hero. Everyone wanted to hear the stories of daring exploits, but no one wanted to know the truth. What we did was hard and terrifying, and sometimes inhumane. I killed people and I let others be killed. My whole team died in an ambush and I survived. Why me? Why the hell was it me? Everyone back in Iowa wanted me to be the man I was before I left. I couldn't do it.

"I'd wake up in the morning and think, 'Today is the day I'm going to kill myself.' It was the only thing that'd get me out of bed. It was the peace that came from feeling like I didn't have to keep going. At the end of the day, I'd promise I could let go tomorrow. One day, I was with my niece, and she asked me what the ocean was like. I told her it went on forever. You could start swimming and never reach the end. I liked the idea of that and it became my new mission. I'd come to California and swim until I couldn't anymore.

"I packed a few things onto an old motorcycle I bought off my best friend's parents. They didn't need it anymore. His body was left in an unmarked grave in France. At first, getting here was my only mission, but then I started to wonder why I was in such a hurry. I'd put off killing myself for a few months already, what was a couple more weeks? I took some detours, headed up to San Francisco, then drove down the coast. You ever done that?"

"No," Evelyn said.

"It's beautiful. There are places where you're flying along, above the clouds. I stopped at the beach in Los Angeles, thinking I'd do it there, but it didn't feel right. So I kept going, until I ended up here. I was ready. I parked my bike by the shore. Took off my jacket and boots and started toward the water. The sand was so white, it felt pure and clean. When I got to the water, it was warmer than I expected. I felt something deep inside me, the sun on my face, the wind in my hair. It was almost like happiness. Of course, that couldn't be right. I didn't deserve happiness. I took another step into the water and saw an older man gliding across the waves. He rode his board all the way up to the shore. I wondered for a minute if he was a mirage. Instead, he asked if I wanted to give it a go. He taught me to surf and, eventually, the water was what got me out of bed in the morning."

"After V-E Day, I didn't come home for a year," Evelyn said. "I didn't know how to reconcile the two parts of my life. How could the woman I'd become slip back into the life of the girl I'd left behind?"

"And now?"

"People see what they want to see." Evelyn shrugged. "But I know the truth. The pain, the fear, the heartache—

It never goes away. Not really. Even on my best day, it's still part of me."

Tom nodded and thought for a minute. Finally, he stood up and offered Evelyn a hand.

"Come on."

Tom led Evelyn down to the water. They sat watching the waves in silence for about twenty minutes before he began to speak.

"We parachuted into Denmark just outside Kolding. Our contact met us with a car and identification papers. We drove down through Hamburg and then onto Berlin. It was an easy drive, but of course . . ."

"Nothing is easy," Evelyn said.

"Every time we went behind enemy lines, I was terrified. The smallest thing could trip you up, from the way you pronounced a city name to the way you tied your tie. We were exhausted, all the time. It's easy to make mistakes when you're that tired. The month before, my commander was killed. He was searched and they found a candy wrapper. That's all it took for him to end up with a bullet in his brain."

Evelyn waited, knowing all stories had their own rhythm. Tom stared out at the waves crashing against the sand.

"We got to Berlin the day before we were supposed to make contact and checked into our hotel. It was my first time in the city, and it's hard to describe the way it made my skin crawl. Everything about the place felt evil. I was constantly looking over my shoulder, wondering if that old man reading a newspaper at the coffee shop or the pretty girl selling flowers would turn me in for thinking or even breathing wrong.

"I don't know whether the Nazis followed us or if one of the neighbors tipped off the Gestapo when they saw the scientist leave. We must have arrived shortly after you left because the two of them—mother and daughter—were sitting next to their suitcases, anxiously waiting. The little girl was silent and still. It was unnerving to see a child whose eyes have seen the worst in people. We heard the cars pull up outside. The screech of brakes and the shouting voices. The sound still echoes in my nightmares. Next came boots marching up the stairs. Leaving everything behind, we fled down the back staircase. A cleaning woman looked out to make sure the alley was clear.

"Once we were free of the building, we walked to the side street and away from the Gestapo. I didn't trust returning to the hotel. They recorded our identification papers when we checked in and we couldn't know if they were compromised. We took the woman and the girl around the city, hopping different trams to make sure we weren't followed. By that point, my partner Andrew and I felt more like a liability. At least that's what I told myself. Their papers were clean, but if they were with us and ours had been reported, we'd endanger them. So, we gave them their documents and took them to the safe house."

"Do you remember the names on their passports?" Evelyn asked.

"Lina and Emma Muller," Tom answered. "They're seared into my brain."

"Where did you go after the safe house?" Evelyn asked.

"Andrew and I went to look for a forger who'd done work for the OSS before, but he was gone. We didn't know what to do. You have to understand how scared I was the whole time we were in Germany. I couldn't think straight. Finally, we decided to just get out of there. We got in the car and started driving, praying our exit visas would get us over the border."

"What about Hannah and Sophie? If the forger was gone, there's a good chance the safe house was also compromised. You went back for them, right?"

Tom didn't meet her eye.

"Right?"

"What if we had led the Gestapo right to them?" Tom asked. "Or what if the Gestapo was already there waiting for us? We would have been killed, too. Later, I heard the safe house was burned to the ground."

"That and four others," Evelyn confirmed. "Do you know if they got out?"

"No. With those new IDs, they could have started over," Tom said. "Or tried to escape on their own. We did the best we could. And when we got home to London . . ."

"What?" Evelyn asked.

"I wanted to go back, I swear," Tom said. "But we weren't allowed. Once the scientist was in the States, his family was no longer a priority. They sent us on other missions and I tried to forget about it."

"And you never wondered . . . ?"

"I wondered every goddamned day," Tom snapped. "Eventually, they just became one more thing I couldn't change."

Evelyn looked out at the ocean, then picked up a handful of sand and let it slip through her fingers.

"I never asked, either," Evelyn said quietly. "I never followed up on any of my missions. I just . . . I needed to believe in the happy ending."

# Chapter 32

Nick sat at his desk with several index cards scattered in front of him. On each, he had written the names of everyone he spoke to, along with the information they provided. He arranged and rearranged the cards, hoping different configurations would show him a pattern or something he had missed. There were footsteps on the stairs, and Nick quickly gathered the cards, shuffled them into a neat pile, and set them face down. Brian Caruso entered Nick's office without knocking. Dapper as ever, his suit was neatly pressed. The collar of his light blue shirt was starched and straightened with tabs that highlighted the perfect Windsor knot in his silk tie.

"Detective," Nick said. "To what do I owe the pleasure?"

"I feel like we got off on the wrong foot," Caruso began. "You were right. I wasn't taking Julia's case seriously enough. It's just sometimes young women fall in love and run off—the excitement of being young and getting carried away. Most of them return home, maybe a little worse for wear, but it's not a police matter."

Nick did not agree or disagree. He simply watched Caruso long enough to make him uncomfortable.

"Well," Caruso continued. "Thought I might come by and we could share information. Two heads are better than one and all that."

"Sounds great," Nick replied. "You start."

Caruso blinked. It was obvious this was not how he hoped the meeting would go, but he pulled out his notebook.

"I talked to a man named Mark Morales. Julia was his secretary," Caruso said. "Until she wasn't. He got her the job at a gentleman's club. Apparently, there were money problems at home. Says she was just a bartender, but come on. A pretty girl like that?"

Nick did not answer. Caruso cleared his throat, uncomfortable.

"Met some of the people around the neighborhood. Said Julia's father was very strict. His daughters were kept like nuns in a convent. And, uh . . . everyone said she was very nice," Caruso finished.

"Thanks for sharing," Nick said. Caruso waited until it was clear Nick was not about to return the favor and share what he had learned.

"Come on, man," Caruso snapped. "I get it. You don't like me, but it's not about us. It's about the girl. At the end of the day, no matter what happened, someone's going to prison and I'm gonna be the guy arresting him. You help me out, I won't forget it."

"Is this about finding Julia?" Nick asked. "Or your case closure rate?"

Caruso's face flushed.

"Is your attitude about Julia or your dislike of me?" Caruso countered. When Nick didn't respond, Caruso continued. "I guess I'll have to dig deeper into the work angle. Maybe visit her family again and tell them she fucked men for money. See if that gets me any further."

"You're a real asshole," Nick said.

Caruso shrugged. Nick debated what he could say without having Caruso stomp all over it. He was the type of cop who would bully witnesses into silence and ruin any potential lead.

"Apparently, there was a man hanging around Julia's school who kept bothering her," Nick said.

"Boyfriend?" Caruso asked.

"No, some random guy. Her friends say he's a creep."

Caruso looked up sharply. "You got a name?"

"Julia didn't tell them."

"What about where she knows him from?" Caruso asked.

"No, but her friends think she's scared of him."

"This guy a student? Or maybe a professor?"

"Too old to be a student. He was well dressed. They thought maybe a banker or a lawyer."

"Probably someone from the club."

"Maybe, but Helen doesn't remember anyone singling Julia out," Nick said.

"Well, she's just an old whore. What does she know about men?"

"A lot more than you or me," Nick said wryly. He wondered if Caruso ever stopped to think before he spoke.

"But does she have a boyfriend?" Caruso asked.

"You seem awfully fixated on that question," Nick said. He felt it was unfair to set Caruso on Gabe. Nick had a suspicion the young medical student would end up in prison as a sacrifice to Caruso's case closure rate.

"It's just statistics," Caruso countered.

Before Nick could respond, the phone on his desk rang. He answered it to hear Helen's voice.

"Speak of the devil," Nick said.

"I got the ransom note!" she declared.

Her voice was loud and carried through the wire. Nick glanced over his shoulder at Caruso, who moved closer.

"He wants all the photos and the negatives," Helen said. "It has to be Gallo."

"The gangster?" Caruso asked.

Nick waved him away.

"He seemed terrified of Mickey Cohen when I spoke to him," Nick replied.

"Who else could it be?" Helen asked. "This is exactly what he was after."

"It's certainly worth another chat," Nick said. "Let me make a couple of calls."

"You have to find her," Helen insisted. "I keep thinking about what might be happening to her. Where she's kept. If she's eating or sleeping. What if she's hurt? What if—"

"We're doing everything we can," Nick assured her. "Letting your mind go down that dark path won't do you or her any good."

"It's just . . . No one protected us," Helen said. "I thought I could do better for them."

"I know."

Nick hung up and turned to see Caruso pretending to browse Nick's bookshelves.

"So, you're going to get Gallo?" Caruso asked.

"Yes."

"Mind if I come along?"

"I do, actually. He's more likely to talk to me than the police."

Caruso started to protest, but Nick held up his hand.

"If Julia turns up in his basement, I promise you can arrest him."

Caruso sighed, then fished his card out of his pocket. "You hear anything, call me. We're a team. Right?"

"Right," Nick said, taking the card.

The moment Caruso's footsteps were no longer audible, Nick picked up the phone and called the Brown Derby. The bartender who answered was more than happy to inform Nick that Gallo was sitting at his usual table.

Twenty minutes later, Nick entered the restaurant and was greeted by a dazzling smile from the hostess. She clearly remembered him from the other night and gestured toward Gallo's table in the back. Gallo's eyes narrowed when he saw Nick and he stepped out of his booth to intercept him.

"The fuck you doing here?" Gallo asked.

"Good to see you, too," Nick replied. "Helen Brecker just got a ransom note for Julia Martinez."

"And?" Gallo asked.

"They're not asking for money. They want Helen's photographs and negatives."

Gallo's eyes widened as he realized what this meant.

"It wasn't me," he insisted.

"I trusted you last time you said that. Now I feel like a proper idiot."

"You gotta believe me," Gallo said, fear creeping into his voice. "Roth told me to stay away, so I stayed away."

"It's a nice cover. You put on a good show of following orders, but you already got the girl. Can't let her go because she's seen your face and knows who you are. You figure, what the hell, might as well get something out of this?"

"Please," Gallo said, almost begging. "I'm gonna be an uncle any day. I swear on that baby's life I didn't have nothing to do with this. I made my brother a promise and I'm not going to let him down."

"I'll give you a one-time offer. You take me to Julia, we set her free. She might run to the cops, but she might not. Either way, you'll still be there for the kid. It just might be from behind bars. Isn't that still a better option than whatever Cohen has in store?"

"If I could, I'd give her up so fast, it'd make your head

spin. I get it, I took it too far when I beat up those girls, but I was desperate. I needed leverage."

"For what?" Nick asked.

Gallo sighed and glanced over his shoulder to check no one was listening to their conversation. "A bunch of guys hit up a gambling joint protected by the LAPD. My brother was nowhere near the place, but he'd been picked up a few months ago and the cop didn't like his attitude. They say my brother drove the getaway car, but you know how many black Chevys there are in the city? Magically, they pull him over, nowhere near the crime scene, and find a gun in his glove compartment.

"You gotta understand. My brother and I got into the rackets when we were kids. Ma did her best, but it was hard keeping a roof over our heads. When Bobby found out Mary was pregnant? That was it. He was done with this life. Found a job working as an electrician's apprentice. His kid was going to have a better life than either of us. But it's all right, I'm gonna get Bobby out of prison. I learned something about—" Gallo broke off, seeing the commotion behind Nick.

A dozen cops flooded into the Brown Derby. They crowded around Nick and Gallo, who both put up their hands, not wanting to provoke anyone into doing anything stupid. Gallo looked to Nick.

"Arrest him," came a voice from behind the group.

"Which one?" one of the cops asked.

Caruso pushed through, a satisfied smile on his face.

"I'd love to say both, but I guess I owe Gallagher for leading me straight here."

"I was handling it," Nick said with clenched teeth.

"You motherfucker," Gallo roared. "I'll kill you. I'll fucking kill you."

He lunged, but three policemen grabbed him, while a fourth slapped on handcuffs.

"Take him outside," Caruso said. Gallo struggled mightily against the officers. Finally, one of them pulled the blackjack off his hip and cracked it across Gallo's head. He slumped forward, and the cops dragged him out to the street.

"You used me," Nick said.

"I'll do whatever needs to be done to keep the streets safe," Caruso said pompously.

"I'm not a reporter, so stop giving me that Captain America shit. I was questioning him. He was going to tell me everything, then you come in like a bull in a china shop. Now what?"

"Now I find out where the girl is," Caruso said. "One way or the other. Although, knowing a man like Gallo, she's probably buried in the desert somewhere."

"That's not his MO," Nick replied.

"You don't know shit about these types of guys. If you're lucky, maybe I'll tell you the date of his trial."

# Chapter 33

Evelyn looked at the résumé, then back to the young man sitting in front of her.

"So, you graduated Harvard a year ago?" Evelyn asked.

"Yes, ma'am!"

Evelyn clocked the crimson and black tie knotted neatly at his throat. The collar on his shirt was pressed and his jacket freshly brushed. He wore his hair slicked back, with a razor-edge part on the side. The cuffs peeking out from his sleeves were monogrammed with his initials.

"Tell me about your last job."

He looked slightly startled, then pasted the ingratiating smile on his face once again.

"After college, I went to Europe for the year."

"To help rebuild?" Evelyn asked.

"Well, no. I think a grand tour is an essential part of any classical education. I saw the Elgin Marbles in London, then the Parthenon in Greece. Van Gogh in Amsterdam and wandered through the Louvre. That's in Paris."

"I'm aware."

"Let me tell you this," he said. "I'm eager to learn. I think this position can offer me a great chance to see how a large organization like this is run from the ground up. The experience I gain here would be invaluable."

"And what do you bring to the table?" Evelyn asked.

For a moment, the young man looked confused.

"Why should I hire you?" Evelyn said bluntly.

"I went to Harvard," he explained, as if she had somehow missed this essential fact.

Evelyn stood up to signal the meeting was over. He jumped to his feet as well.

"What time do you want me here on Monday?"

"I don't," Evelyn replied as she escorted him out of her office. "I'm afraid it's not going to work out."

The young man stared at Evelyn blankly. She wondered if he had ever heard the word "no" before. Ruth ushered him toward the stairs.

"There you go. Best of luck," Ruth called to his back as the phone rang. Evelyn picked it up.

"Evelyn Bishop."

"Evie?" David asked.

"You're burning the midnight oil," Evelyn replied, checking her watch.

"I have news," David said, his voice barely containing his excitement. "I found Hannah and Sophie."

For a long minute, Evelyn sat silent, stunned.

"Are you still there?" David asked.

"Yes, I . . . I never really believed it was possible," Evelyn said. "This is incredible. How did you do it?"

"Luck, hard work, and annoying all the right people," David said. "Just like you taught me. They were in the camps. When the Russians finally marched through, Hannah was at death's door. The Red Cross took Sophie and put her into school at a displaced persons camp. It took Hannah over a year to recover; then she set about searching for her daughter. Everything was more complicated because Sophie learned to go by the fake name on her documents. During the war, Hannah was terrified of them being discovered, so she drilled it into her."

"Which is why they didn't show up in any of the records for the concentration camps."

"Exactly. Once you gave me the information from their identity papers, I reached out to all the aid societies for Lina and Emma Muller, looked into our records, and eventually got a note to Alexei."

"He must have been thrilled to hear from you," Evelyn deadpanned.

"He appreciated the four cartons of Lucky Strikes. Came through, in the end. Don't know how he did it, but he got me an address in the French sector."

"That's fantastic!" Evelyn said. "One thing I don't understand. It's been three years. Why didn't Hannah try to get in contact with Kurt sooner?"

"They were in the Russian occupied zone and Hannah was not about to leave without her daughter. When they were finally reunited, they made their way to Berlin, hoping to find some pieces of their old life. Their former apartment was occupied, but Hannah eventually found a professor from her university who took them in. That's when Hannah sent the postcard."

"But why not give an address? Why make us hunt for her?" Evelyn asked.

"When I spoke with her yesterday, it seemed like she's still afraid of someone or something. Wouldn't tell me what," David said. "You should ask her when you get here. You are coming, right?"

"As soon as you can get me a flight."

"Booked you on a transport tomorrow morning."

"You're incredible," Evelyn said. "I don't know how you did it."

"Aw, shucks," David joked, but she heard the pride in his voice.

* * *

An hour later, Evelyn pulled up outside Kurt's building at JPL and ran up the stairs to his office. She knocked on the closed door. There was no answer. She knocked again.

"I'm busy!" Kurt's voice shouted through the door.

"You'll want to hear this," Evelyn called back.

There was a very long pause before Kurt finally opened the door.

"I told you. I'm not to be disturb . . ." he trailed off as his eyes adjusted and he recognized Evelyn. "Come in."

Kurt took off his glasses and polished the lenses.

"You either have very good news or very bad," Kurt said.

"We found Hannah and Sophie," Evelyn said with a broad smile.

Every muscle in Kurt's body froze. The air in the room was saturated, like the sky just before the first crack of lightning. Very slowly, he put his glasses back on and turned to Evelyn.

"You found them?" he asked.

"It wasn't just me," Evelyn said. "We had a whole team. Nothing's guaranteed, of course, but so far, the story tracks."

"You found my wife and daughter?" Kurt asked again, still in shock. "How?"

Evelyn told him the full story. When she finished, he did not say a word. Evelyn had expected disbelief or joy, but his prolonged silence unnerved her.

"When can I see them?" he asked eventually.

"You're going to give me two dozen questions, something that only Hannah would know. We'll use these to make sure it's really her. Then, we get her and Sophie's paperwork sorted out and bring them back to the States."

"I'm coming with you."

"Berlin isn't safe," Evelyn insisted.

"You went."

"The US Army cares a lot less about me than they do about you," Evelyn said.

"I highly doubt that," Kurt replied. "After all, you're Bishop Aeronautics."

"I have special training, contacts in the army, and have worked in dangerous situations."

"And this is my family," Kurt said. "You promised me once that you'd bring them home from Berlin. Forgive me if I don't trust you a second time."

Evelyn wanted to argue it was the US government who betrayed him. Not her, personally. However, she was beginning to realize that to Kurt, there was no difference. She leaned over and picked up the phone.

"May I?"

Kurt nodded. Evelyn dialed the number and waited what felt like an eternity as the call was routed from one branch to another. Finally, she heard the staticky beep of the German telephone system. After several double beeps, a sleepy voice finally answered.

"Lieutenant Wallace," the voice said by way of greeting.

"This is Evelyn Bishop. Please tell Captain David Bernstein we're going to need another seat on tomorrow's flight."

Lieutenant Wallace made a grunting sound of assent, then Evelyn hung up.

"Eleven a.m. Fort MacArthur."

# Chapter 34

"I'm here! I'm here!" Evelyn called as she rushed into her house.

Seeing the cars in the driveway reminded her that she was late for the meeting with the florist. At least she had not missed it entirely. Hurrying into the dining room, she found Nick, Taffy, and Carl sitting with a fussy woman in her early fifties. Dressed in a cinched-waist, polyester satin dress, she wore heels and had her hair twisted up intricately at the nape of her neck. With a perfect bright red manicure, there was no indication she had ever sunk her hands into the soil.

"This is Evelyn, our perpetually late bride," Taffy said. "Evelyn, this is Mrs. Farnsworth, the florist."

"Sorry for keeping you waiting," Evelyn said.

"Mrs. Farnsworth was about to tell us her ideas for the centerpieces," Taffy said, gesturing to a chair between her and Nick. Evelyn took it, gave Nick a quick kiss, and waved at Carl, who smiled back.

"Can't wait," Evelyn said.

Mrs. Farnsworth laid out several photographs of floral arrangements. There were white roses in a tiny bowl. A larger bouquet, made of roses, lilies, and other white flow-

ers, in the center of the table. The final picture reminded
Evelyn of the hanging gardens of Babylon.

"How are our guests going to see one another?" Evelyn
asked.

"Surely they're not about to shout across the table like
savages," Mrs. Farnsworth said. "It's proper etiquette to
speak to the person directly to one side or the other."

"Of course. Silly me," Evelyn replied. Beside her, Nick
let out a small cough of laughter.

Mrs. Farnsworth picked up the picture of the small bowl
of roses, barely touching the edges, as if it were distasteful.

"I only brought this for comparison. Considering the
stature of the wedding, I think it would be completely
overwhelmed by the place settings. This middle option is
really the smallest we can go."

Evelyn wanted to insist on the smallest option just to be
ornery, but Taffy jumped in.

"It certainly is an elegant display, don't you think,
Evelyn?"

"It's still awfully tall."

"Perhaps you could do something wider but still low,"
Carl offered. "My cousin had beautiful arrangements that
looked like overgrown flower boxes."

"I don't think—" Mrs. Farnsworth began.

"That's a great idea," Evelyn said. "Small enough to see
over, large enough not to get lost. Carl's always the best at
finding a middle ground."

"I worry it will look messy," Mrs. Farnsworth said.
"Though, if we uniformly go with white . . ."

"Oh, no," Evelyn said. "That's not going to work."

"It's traditional," Mrs. Farnsworth exclaimed.

"It's for funerals. This is a happy event. Let's have something bright to reflect that. Red and pink. Orange and yellow. Maybe peonies or marigolds. Gardenias . . . ? I don't
really know the different types of flowers."

"It's a difficult season for such things," Mrs. Farnsworth said.

"It's spring," Nick replied dryly. "Isn't that traditionally when flowers bloom?"

"I'll see what I can manage," Mrs. Farnsworth huffed. "Next up is your bouquet. Red roses are most appropriate, though calla lilies are an elegant option."

"I'm going with roses."

Both Nick and Taffy looked at her in surprise. Mrs. Farnsworth sighed in relief.

"I've actually given a lot of thought to my bouquet," Evelyn said. "I want to carry the flowers from our front gardens. The ones my mother planted. I think it's a nice way of having her with me."

"That's a wonderful idea," Taffy said.

"Absolutely not," Mrs. Farnsworth replied. "They are not bred properly and they have no uniformity. I'd hate for someone to think me capable of such sloppy work."

"There's a simple solution," Nick said as he stood up. "We'll go with someone else."

"Surely you must understand . . ."

"What I understand," Nick said, "is that my fiancée has expressed an opinion on something regarding this wedding . . . for the first time, I might add. We are going to do what she wants."

Mrs. Farnsworth looked at Taffy.

"You've just been fired, dear," Taffy said primly.

It took Mrs. Farnsworth a moment to realize there was no recourse. Then, with an indignant huff, she gathered her things and Nick escorted her out.

"I'm sorry," Evelyn apologized. "The one meeting I attend I manage to ruin."

"Nonsense," Taffy replied. "It's your wedding; you should have it as you imagine."

"Thank you," Evelyn said.

"I have a dinner I must get ready for," Taffy said, standing as Nick reentered the room. "However, this does bring up the question of who will be walking you down the aisle?"

"A year ago, I would have said my father." Evelyn sighed.

"Do give it some thought," Taffy instructed, then headed upstairs to change.

"So, what has the great chef prepared for us?" Carl asked, turning to Nick.

"Unfortunately, the great chef must dine elsewhere. With all the developments in Julia's case, I promised I'd swing by Helen's club."

"Guess I'm cooking," Evelyn said. Then, clocking the horrified look on Carl's and Nick's faces, she started laughing. "Kidding, kidding."

Thirty minutes later found Evelyn sitting across from Carl at Cole's downtown. Sitting in a booth towards the back, they were both sipping a Manhattan while waiting for their French dip sandwiches. Carl had a craving and Evelyn was more than happy to oblige. The restaurant, located a few steps below street level, had a bright and friendly atmosphere with leather seats and well-varnished wood tables. It was more of a place to stop after work rather than haute cuisine. It fit them perfectly. Plus, the drinks were second to none.

Evelyn was telling Carl all about her case with Kurt.

"His reaction was just so strange," she said.

"Perhaps it hurts too much to hope," Carl said. "The reunion, even in the best of circumstances, is going to be incredibly difficult. He's established a life in Pasadena that's going to be thrown into turmoil. No matter how happy he'll be to see them, his wife is a different person; his daughter is a stranger. Give him space."

"You are a very wise man," Evelyn said.

"I know," Carl replied with a smile.

"How is work?" Evelyn asked.

"Work is . . . work," Carl said unenthusiastically.

"Wow. Don't bowl me over with the wonders of the FBI," Evelyn teased.

"No one's supposed to know, but there are rumors Russia has a nuclear bomb," Carl said. "Could be testing it any day."

Evelyn sat back in her seat, stunned. "I didn't think . . ."

"None of us did," Carl said. "They're at least four years ahead of schedule."

"That changes the whole ball game," Evelyn said.

"We have reason to believe someone in the Manhattan Project leaked more than a few secrets."

"Are you heading to New Mexico?"

"Nope," Carl said. "Not to Los Alamos or Oak Ridge, Tennessee, or even the University of Chicago. I spent ten hours today in a small room listening to tapped telephone calls of various movie stars gossiping about one another. I swear, my brain is turning to mush."

"I don't understand," Evelyn said.

"Neither do I. Say, for instance, Fred Astaire was secretly a communist. Or Humphrey Bogart. Sure, people look up to them, but I don't think they're secretly slipping Russians information about the type of camera used to shoot *Casablanca* or *Ziegfeld Follies*."

"So, you're not a true believer?" Evelyn asked.

"We both know that Communism is horrible—the lack of food, the back-breaking work, the political purges, and the anti-intellectualism. A repressive society is the last thing we want here, yet if we keep going down this road, we're going to turn into the thing we hate. Thoughts cannot and should not be regulated. Only actions."

"Wait, wait, wait. You want spies to actually spy before they're thrown in prison?"

"Crazy, right?"

"I think you're out of step with the times, my friend," Evelyn said.

"I want to wake up in the morning and feel like I have purpose to my days. I want my work to mean something."

"You want to save the world."

"It sounds ridiculous when you say it like that, but yes. At least a little part of it."

Evelyn took Carl's hand. Nothing she could say would make it better, but she wanted him to feel less alone. He gave her a smile that did not quite reach his eyes.

"You could always go into business with Nick," Evelyn finally suggested.

"I haven't gotten that desperate." He laughed.

# Chapter 35

Helen's club was busy, with full poker tables and women dashing back and forth to refill drinks. There was laughter as couples made their way upstairs, and a few people danced to the latest music on the radio. The mood in most of the house was that of celebration. Inside Helen's private office, it was much different.

"You got a ransom note, which is good," Nick began. "We'll ask for proof of life. It's standard in all kidnapping cases and might help us figure out where to go next."

"How?"

"Almost all communication is good communication. Each time we talk to the guy, we learn a little bit more. It's another chance for him to screw up."

"I'd rather burn all the photographs and negatives than give them to Gallo," Helen raged.

"I don't blame you," Nick said. "But I'm still not convinced he took Julia. He seemed sincere in his desire to get his brother out of prison."

"So he's looking for something on the LAPD."

"Or the DA's office or judges or local politicians. Could be any number of people. I got the sense he has something else up his sleeve."

"Well, if it's not him, then who?"

"I don't know. You said it yourself—those photos could be extremely damaging to a lot of people. I'm willing to bet there are more than a few people who would love that kind of power. Can you give me a list of everyone who knew about them? And who they might have talked to? Maybe they're not going after them for blackmail; they could be trying to take away any leverage you or others might have over them."

Helen sat down behind her desk, pulled out a sheet of paper, and began to write. Nick recognized most of the names from the business and society pages. Before Helen finished, there was a commotion out front.

From the other room, Gregory yelled, "You can't come in here!"

A voice answered, "We got a warrant."

Nick turned back to Helen. In an ashtray, he saw the flaming remains of the list. She swept past him into the main room, where twenty police officers stood in the foyer. The dealers at the poker tables stopped in midshuffle. Helen marched up to the officer.

"I'd like to see that warrant," she said.

"I don't gotta show you shit," he barked.

"According to the fourth amendment, you do, Officer Wells," Gregory said, noting the man's name tag.

The cop whipped out his nightstick and smashed it across Gregory's face with a slur that could have come out of a Confederate general's mouth. Helen rushed to kneel at Gregory's side.

"Get back up, boy, I dare you," Wells snarled.

There was a deep gash across Gregory's cheek and it looked like his eye socket might be broken. Helen turned toward the nearest woman.

"Alice, please get us some ice and clean towels," she

instructed. Then she stood up to face Wells. "Do you have a search warrant or an arrest warrant?"

"I got a fuck-you warrant," he said, pushing past her as the cops spread out through the room.

"Man's got a way with words," Nick said sarcastically.

Some of Helen's clients and employees fled toward the back exit, only to be confronted with more cops blocking the way. Helen watched helplessly as the police toppled the poker tables, shattered liquor bottles, and raced upstairs to roust people out of bed. They came down in various states of undress, with one woman wrapped in only a sheet. Officer Wells and a few others pushed through to Helen's office. Helen followed them, poorly contained rage in her eyes. The police pulled books off the shelves and packed away her papers in boxes. Leaving the emptied drawers strewn across the floor, they "accidentally" stepped through the bottom. Nick put his arm around Helen, partially as comfort and partially to hold her back from doing something stupid.

The cops finally located the safe behind a bookshelf.

"Give me the combination," Wells said to Helen.

"No," Helen replied.

"Gimme the combination or I pull the whole fucking thing outta the wall."

Helen shrugged. Officer Wells nodded to two other policemen. "Get the axes."

"Come on," Nick said, leading Helen out to the main room. "You don't want to see this."

"I know exactly how much money is in there," Helen yelled. "I expect every penny returned."

Nick directed Helen towards a space on the floor beside Gregory. Gently, she pulled away the ice he was holding up to his face and examined his eye. It was already swollen so badly he couldn't see through it. Helen looked to one of the younger cops.

"This man needs a hospital," Helen demanded.

The young cop glanced around nervously. An officer went through, checking IDs. A few of the more powerful men he waved away. They grabbed their coats and hurried out the front door.

"I . . . I'm sorry, ma'am. I can't allow that," the young cop replied. "I'm just doing what I'm told."

"What's the point of paying off the cops if this is what I get?" Helen hissed to Nick.

He didn't have an answer.

It was another half hour before the safe, held aloft by four cops, was finally paraded through the main room.

"You didn't have the photos in there?" Nick asked.

"Don't be an idiot. Of course not," Helen said. "They're somewhere secure."

"Load them up," Officer Wells said to the remaining cops, as he nodded towards the motley group remaining.

"You have to take Gregory to a hospital," Helen insisted again.

Wells smiled maliciously. "I'd be happy to separate him out."

"No," Gregory insisted quickly. "I'm fine."

Nick stepped up beside Gregory as the men and women were divided into paddy wagons.

"Look after Gregory," Helen whispered.

Nick nodded, helping Gregory into a seat beside a well-dressed man. The man looked over at Gregory, then back down at his shackled hands.

# Chapter 36

The persistent ring of the telephone woke Evelyn. It was still night and Nick was not beside her. She answered warily. Calls this late rarely offered good news.

"Hello?"

"Hey, Evie," Nick said.

"What's wrong?" she asked, instantly alert, her mind fearing the worst.

"I seem to have gotten myself arrested. Bail me out and I'll buy you breakfast."

Evelyn quickly dressed in a sweater and chinos. Shoving her feet into driving loafers, she pulled her hair into a low ponytail. Not bothering with makeup, she went downstairs to the library. Next to the desk was a hidden floor safe where she kept a couple of thousand dollars for emergencies. She grabbed the cash, tossed it in her bag, and was out the door within ten minutes of hanging up the phone. The streets were largely empty as she drove. Sunrise peaked over the mountains to the east. It would be beautiful flying weather.

The lobby of the police station held several chairs and benches pushed up against the wall. A few people slept with their heads pillowed on their arms. Paper coffee cups and discarded newspapers littered the room. Evelyn supposed this was the calm after an evening's chaos. She walked to the front desk where a bleary-eyed clerk greeted her without enthusiasm.

"Whaddya want?"

"I'm here to bail out Nick Gallagher," Evelyn replied.

The clerk grabbed a clipboard. He ran his eyes down it until he found Nick's name, then sniggered slightly.

"Lemme get his paperwork."

The clerk disappeared for a moment, and when he returned, he had a few documents. Evelyn read them quickly. The bail agreement held her responsible for ensuring Nick made his court appearance. She signed it and handed over the cash.

"Wait here," the clerk said as he picked up the telephone and called the holding cells in the back of the building.

Evelyn was restless, pacing back and forth across the lobby. Sleep was for the weak, she reminded herself sardonically. There was a lot to do before she left for Berlin and she still had a few instructions to give Ruth.

"Evelyn Bishop!" a loud voice called.

Evelyn looked up to see Captain Wharton enter the room and she smiled broadly, giving him a kiss on the cheek.

"It's good to see you," she said.

"And you. Come back to my office while you wait."

When they got there, she took a seat and he offered her coffee.

"Yes, please. I didn't have time before I left the house."

Wharton got drinks for both of them, then sat down behind his desk.

"Why are you here so early?" Evelyn asked. "I thought captains got to make their own hours."

"They call me when a cop or former cop gets arrested,"

Wharton replied. "Gallagher always did know how to get himself in trouble."

"Everyone's gotta have a talent," Evelyn said.

"Do you know what he was brought in for?" Wharton asked gingerly.

"No. He didn't say."

Wharton sat back in his chair, tenting his fingers as he considered how to break the news.

"Nick was found in a brothel that was raided by the vice squad," Wharton said eventually.

"Huh. That's not something you want to write home about."

"Are you okay?" Wharton asked.

"He's a private investigator," Evelyn replied. "I know the life as well as anyone. It can take you some strange places."

"Even so. You're awfully calm. Most people, finding out their fiancé was caught with whores . . ."

"Was he in bed with them?"

"Well, no."

"Nick and I have been to literal hell and back. You trust someone or you don't," Evelyn insisted. "And if you don't, then why are you with them?"

Wharton shook his head at her seeming naïveté.

"Was Helen Brecker arrested, too?" Evelyn asked.

"Along with quite a few of her employees."

"I'd like to pay their bail."

"Why?"

"I know how important Helen is to Nick. Setting her free will be the first thing he does once he's out. Let's just save time."

Wharton sighed but picked up the phone and called down to the front desk to get everything in order.

"I know we haven't known each other that long,"

Wharton began. "I'll never understand what you see in Gallagher. But I like you. I don't want you to get hurt."

"I appreciate that," Evelyn replied. "And it's absolutely fine if you want to remind Nick that he's a lucky son of a bitch."

Wharton laughed.

"One other thing . . . seeing our engagement was front-page news, I'm guessing this might be, too. Any chance you can keep Nick's name out of it?"

"And by extension yours?"

"I believe in Nick, but I also know how it looks. People will say if I can't keep my personal life sorted, how the hell will I keep the company on track? There are already a lot of people who doubt my competence. I don't want to give them any more ammunition."

Wharton nodded. "I'll do what I can."

Evelyn filled out the paperwork and paid the rest of the bail. By the time Nick came around the corner, the world was already bright with the morning sunshine. She went to him and he enveloped her in a huge hug.

"Thanks for coming," he said, then kissed her. He looked at her like she was fresh and new, the best thing in the world, miraculously walking into his life again each morning.

"Next time, I'm bringing a toothbrush."

Nick laughed as Helen and her employees entered the lobby. Most of the women left immediately, but Gregory stood uncertainly, his face and clothes coated in dried blood and his eye swollen shut. Helen went to him, however he pulled back when she tried to touch his face.

"It looks even worse than last night," Helen said.

"Feels worse, too," Gregory replied.

"That fucking bastard. I'll have him written up and—"

"They'll say I fell on my way to the paddy wagon," Gregory said. "It's not worth it."

"But there are eyewitnesses!" Helen insisted. "This is how they get away with it!"

"I know, but right now . . . I'm just so tired."

The exhaustion was more than simply a night in prison. It was soul deep. The weight of trying to convince people to see beyond his skin color was a burden no one should have to carry. Helen bit her tongue and nodded. Then she looked to Nick.

"Thanks for getting us out."

"Wish I could take credit, but it was Evelyn," he replied.

"Well, thank you, Miss Bishop," Helen said.

"Oh, wow. So formal." Evelyn laughed. "Please, call me Evelyn."

"Why don't we celebrate our freedom by grabbing some breakfast?" Nick said. Then, glancing at Gregory, "Perhaps in a hospital cafeteria?"

"I still haven't packed for Berlin and my flight's in a few hours," Evelyn said as she led them outside. "I'm going to have to take a rain check. Can we give you a ride, though?"

"No, thanks. We'll get a taxi," Helen replied as she raised her hand to hail one.

"It's really no problem," Evelyn insisted.

Helen shook her head.

"No. Thank you, though."

A taxi pulled up and Helen helped Gregory into the back seat, before getting in herself and slamming the door. They took off down the street. Nick slipped his arm around Evelyn's waist and they walked towards the car.

"Thank God you got arrested last night instead of tomorrow," Evelyn teased. "What would you do without me?"

"That is something I never want to find out," Nick said as he leaned down and kissed her.

# Chapter 37

Evelyn and Kurt sat across the aisle from each other on the army transport plane. He was rigid in his seat, working out calculations in a small black notebook. After their first layover, Evelyn suggested he try to get some rest. He merely grunted. Knowing the plane would be cold, she had brought a thick cashmere shawl and used it as a blanket as she curled up in her seat and fell asleep, rocked by the steady hum of the engines. Several hours later, their arrival in Newfoundland jolted her awake. She looked over to see Kurt still in the same place, his small writing filling page after page.

"Do you want to talk about it?" Evelyn asked when their next flight reached altitude.

"About what?"

"Any of it. This is your first trip back to Berlin, right?"

He nodded.

"A lot's changed. I'm sure seeing your family again will be hard."

"I'm fine," he said curtly, then turned back to his work, clearly wanting to be left alone.

Evelyn nodded and picked up the novel she had brought. An hour later, she glanced over to see Kurt slumped down, his head resting on his chest as he snored quietly. His notebook had fallen off his lap, onto the floor. Evelyn reached across the aisle and picked it up. There were equations and notations written in his native German. Evelyn flipped through the pages, looking at a variety of chemical equations that went into the creation of rocket fuel. Then she set it on the seat next to her and continued her reading. Eventually, the plane hit turbulence and Kurt woke abruptly. He looked around his seat, standing up and checking his pockets.

"Where's my notebook?" he asked sharply.

Evelyn handed it over.

"It was on the floor. Must have slipped off your lap when you fell asleep."

Kurt glared for a moment, eyeing Evelyn uncertainly. He flipped through the pages to see nothing amiss, then tucked the book into his jacket. Folding his arms across his chest, he stared straight ahead for the remainder of the trip. At Rhein-Main Air Base, they checked in at the command center. The captain in charge looked down at the schedule.

"We've got flights every three minutes. You let me know when you're ready."

"Let's get on with it," Kurt said.

"Perhaps the lady might like to freshen up?" the captain asked.

Kurt glowered and Evelyn suppressed a smile. She would love to see his face if she asked for time to redo her hair and apply makeup.

"The people we're meeting have seen me look much worse than this," she said.

The captain summoned a corporal who led them down to the airfield. The soldier was young and Evelyn wondered if he had seen any fighting during the war.

"Don't really get many civilians down here," he said, trying to make conversation.

"I've heard Berlin is lovely this time of year," Evelyn joked. "Perfect for a vacation."

"Oh, no," the corporal said earnestly. "It's a real mess. Prepare yourselves."

Evelyn sighed. It always hurt her heart a little when people did not appreciate her humor.

They drove out to a waiting Skymaster, where they took seats behind the pilot and copilot. For the first thirty minutes, the pilots and Evelyn chatted about the planes. She asked what they liked, and what they would do differently, if it was theirs to design. Most pilots had strong opinions about what they flew, and Evelyn promised to pass their notes along to the design team.

When the plane reached the Soviet sector, the beeping fell silent and the pilots tensed in their seats. It was another forty minutes before they reached the outskirts of Berlin. Kurt looked out the window, with an expression of stunned disbelief as he saw the ruins of his former hometown. He did not notice the tears streaming from his eyes.

"I didn't know what to expect," he said quietly. "Hannah and I used to have picnics in Treptower Park. Or go ice skating in Tiergarten. There's nothing left. All our memories . . . Our whole life was here."

Evelyn reached over and took his hand. He grasped it tightly for the rest of the journey. The plane landed at Tempelhof and David was there to meet them as they disembarked. Evelyn gave him a hug and introduced Kurt.

"How was your flight?" David asked.

"Long," Kurt said.

"The last leg was a bit rough," Evelyn replied.

David nodded in understanding.

"It's always a shock to view the city from above," he

said. "At least on the ground, you can see how some things have returned to normal."

"You're making good progress," Evelyn offered.

"Or we were before the blockade. It'll be interesting to see what effect the presidential election will have here. Truman's all in, but Dewey . . . ?"

"He's leading in the polls," Evelyn said.

"Do you think there's anything worth saving here?" Kurt asked.

"Yes," David answered without hesitation. "The people. The culture. The possibility of a democracy in this part of the world."

"The Russians have you surrounded," Kurt noted.

"True," David agreed. "If the people didn't want us here, I'd say we should pack it up and go home. But they do, and we've made a commitment."

"America always honors its commitments," Kurt replied, bitterness creeping into his voice.

"It didn't for you," David admitted. "But it's an ideal we try to embody."

"You're young, are you not?" Kurt commented, studying David intently. "When did you join up?"

"I did my training at the end of 1943 and shipped out in 1944."

"So, you were not there when I was extracted," Kurt said.

"No, but I've worked very hard to find your wife. I know how important it is to General Gibson to make this right."

"Speaking of," Kurt began. "I'd like to see him, if I may."

David hesitated for just a minute before he said, "Sure, we can swing by HQ."

\* \* \*

Kurt was silent as they drove through the streets. Evelyn glanced over at him and wondered if the detour to see General Gibson was a delay tactic. The longed-for meeting with his family carried its own perils, and the threat of disappointed expectations. He wore a stoic expression that offered no insight. When they arrived at American headquarters, David led them to the back offices. General Gibson looked up in surprise, then quickly stood and came around his desk. He held out his hand to Kurt.

"Herr Vogel, welcome back to Berlin. I'm—"

"General Henry Gibson," Kurt said. "I remember you from when I was extracted in 1942. I asked you about my wife and daughter. You had no answers."

"That side of the mission was run by a colleague. I'm eternally sorry I didn't follow up more closely on their well-being. We failed you."

"Thank you," Kurt replied softly. "I appreciate your words. As well as your actions to locate my family now. After all this time, I'm hoping you'll join us for this reunion—the culmination of my extraction."

General Gibson glanced at the pile of work on his desk. Evelyn could tell he wanted to refuse, but he believed in taking personal responsibility, even if the mistake was above his pay grade.

"Let me get my coat."

Evelyn, Kurt, David, and General Gibson pulled up in front of a small townhouse in the French sector next to the Russian border. Everything felt a bit too quiet. The tension of potential enemies existing in close quarters.

"Ever feel like you're being watched?" Gibson asked.

Evelyn glanced around, then pointed to three buildings on the Russian side.

"If it was me, I'd set up there."

Gibson put his arm around Evelyn.

"It's good to have you here, kid. Almost like old times."

"Almost," Evelyn replied. "But I expect real coffee tomorrow morning to help with the jetlag."

"You're in luck. It's still considered an essential good."

Kurt got out of the jeep and propped his foot on the edge to tie his shoes. Evelyn noticed his shaking hands as he struggled with the laces. He took something out of his pocket, then wiped his forehead with a handkerchief. His nerves were getting the better of him.

"It's this way," David said gently.

David led them across the street and up the front stoop. He knocked on the front door. After a minute, it opened.

"Yes?" asked a woman in her late thirties. She was thin to the point of fragility and wore a knee-length dress patched in so many places it was difficult to tell the original pattern. For a moment, she surveyed the strangers in front of her, then her eyes landed on Kurt and her whole face lit up.

"Kurt!" she exclaimed.

She pushed past David and wrapped Kurt in a huge hug. For a moment, he stood uncertainly.

"Hannah?" he asked.

She nodded, and he pulled her close, burying his face in her hair. Then he began to sob. They were great, bellowing cries that shook his whole body. Kurt's eyes were closed, as if reality was too much. Evelyn, David, and Gibson stepped aside to give them space. Gibson smiled awkwardly at Evelyn.

"You old softy," she whispered.

Gibson shrugged. "My secret's out."

"Mama?" a small voice asked.

Hannah broke off the embrace and turned to a girl standing in the doorway. Evelyn knew she must have been eleven, but she looked barely eight. Her brown hair was plaited neatly into two braids, tied with string. Her wrists jutted out awkwardly from the sleeves of her threadbare dress. Like her mother, she was too thin. Kurt looked down at the girl, then sunk to his knees so he could be at her level.

"Sophie!"

He opened up his arms, but she held back, frightened. She looked to her mother, and Hannah pushed her into Kurt's arms.

"Don't be shy. Give your papa a hug."

Sophie let herself be held by Kurt. While tears streamed down his cheeks, she stood stiffly, her face devoid of emotion.

"Tell your father how much we've missed him," Hannah prompted.

"We missed you, Papa," Sophie repeated. "I'm so glad you're back."

Gibson looked around and saw a few Russian soldiers patrolling the border.

"Why don't we head inside?" he said.

"Of course, of course," Hannah said, opening the door wider and ushering them into the apartment.

There was a small living room, wallpapered in a bright design with flower trellises. It was possible to see where bookshelves once stood. Evelyn guessed they had been fed to the fire in a desperate attempt to survive the past winter. Two low couches sat across from each other, with a reading chair in the corner by the window.

"My old professor was kind enough to take us in," Hannah explained. "I looked him up and he invited me to stay with him and his wife. I don't know what we would have done otherwise."

Hannah motioned to the couches. Evelyn and David sat on one, while Hannah and Kurt took the other. General Gibson, restless, hovered near the door. Kurt took Hannah's hand in his, staring at it as if it were precious and ephemeral.

"How did you survive?" he asked.

"We were supposed to leave an hour after you," Hannah began. "Someone must have tipped off the Gestapo. They arrived only moments after the American agents. We fled to a safe house. They gave us fake identification papers, then told us they were going to get new ones for themselves. They promised to return, but . . ."

Hannah sighed, gathering herself.

"We stayed there two nights, waiting for them. Then we heard trucks pull up outside. It was like fleeing from our apartment all over again—rats chased from one hole to another. We escaped out the back window and I realized we were on our own."

"Where did you go?" Kurt asked.

"Do you remember my friend Ilsa?"

"From university?" Kurt asked.

Hannah nodded. "It was a gamble, but we took a bus to her home in Schleswig-Holstein. There were so many people fleeing the bombing in the big cities that we blended in with them. When our papers were checked, I held my breath, but the soldiers just nodded and handed them back. It felt like freedom. Even though the Americans never returned, I thought we could ride out the war as a widow and her daughter.

"Ilsa was surprised to see us, but with her husband away at the front, she was grateful for the help on the farm. We worked all day, and at night we talked and laughed like family. She had a daughter not much younger than Sophie and they became like sisters. For a moment, it was almost possible to forget the danger."

"But you ended up in the camps . . . ?" Kurt prompted.

"Ilsa's husband was injured at the front and sent home to recover. Better that he should have died," she said bitterly. "It didn't take long for him to realize who I was. He turned us into the Gestapo for a few extra ration cards."

"Then what happened? How did you survive?" Kurt asked.

"Forgive me. I can't. I just can't talk about it. Not yet." Hannah gathered her daughter close, drawing strength from the little girl. Then Hannah reached out to Kurt.

"I missed you so much. In my head, I composed all these letters to you but never put anything down on paper for fear of someone finding them. Instead, I inscribed the words on my heart, so I could say them when I saw you again. We're together now, my darling. That's all that matters. Take us home and we can finally be a family again."

Kurt reached for Hannah's hand. Then he turned it over and brushed his fingers along the inside of her arm.

"Do you remember the night you made your mother's brisket?"

"When you proposed?" Hannah said.

"Before then. It was in our early days. We were going to visit your family in Hamburg for Passover and I was so nervous. I wanted to make a good impression."

Hannah smiled, covering Kurt's hand with hers.

"You planned a whole seder so I'd know what to expect," Kurt continued. "No one had ever put in that much effort so I would feel like I belonged. It was the night I fell in love with you. I knew then that I wanted us to spend the rest of our lives together. Do you remember what you said when you pulled the brisket out of the oven?"

"I told you I loved you," Hannah said.

Kurt pulled his hand out of Hannah's, then laughed to himself, a bittersweet smile on his lips.

"It's not supposed to be quite so fuzzy."

Hannah frowned, confused.

"That's what Hannah, my Hannah said. She lost her grip on the pan. The brisket slid sideways and ended up on the floor," Kurt said with a laugh. "Trying to catch it, she burned herself badly, right across the inside of her arm. The scar barely faded with the years."

The woman looked down at her arms, free of blemishes. "How did you know?" she asked softly.

"Hannah never called me darling. She knew I hated it because that's how my mother referred to me when she had been drinking. No, Hannah said *neshama*. It means soul in Hebrew, because that's what we were. Each other's souls. I didn't let myself hope she was still alive, because if she were, I'd be able to feel her. When I saw you, I wanted it to be true. I wanted so badly for it to be true," Kurt said. "Who are you?"

"Ilsa," the woman answered. "Hannah came to me when she fled Berlin. We had several good months, the four of us on the farm. Her and Sophie, me and Johanna."

The girl looked up at her mother, hearing her name.

"My husband didn't just turn in Hannah and Sophie. He handed me over to the Gestapo, too. We were taken to the local police station. I was put in one room, they were taken to another. From there, I was sent to Ravensbrück, but Hannah and Sophie were not with me. I don't know what happened to them, but I survived, barely. When the war was over, I went looking for my daughter. She was still living with her father. I took her from school and we fled to Berlin. I didn't know what to do, but my old professor took pity on us and invited us to live with him. One day, he came home and said people were looking for Hannah. I figured this was my chance for us to leave and start over again in America. Hannah was my best friend and we told each other everything. I could have been here for you. I could have been close enough."

Ilsa reached out and grabbed Kurt's hand.

"Please," she begged. "Please, let me try."

Kurt pulled his hand free in disgust, then stalked out of

the apartment. Ilsa turned toward David and General Gibson, pleading.

"I know it was wrong, but I'm desperate. If my husband finds us, he'll kill me. Can you help?"

David and General Gibson looked at each other, then Gibson gave a small nod.

"You sheltered Hannah Vogel and her daughter when we failed them," David said. "You paid a terrible price for your courage. I'll see what I can do."

"Thank you," Ilsa cried. "Thank you."

"Don't contact Kurt Vogel again," Evelyn said. "It was cruel to get his hopes up."

"I'm sorry. I truly am," Ilsa said. "I wish Hannah survived. I spent the war hoping, but the first thing she would have done is look for Kurt. She would have written him every day, reached out to the Americans, the British, the Russians and searched every list imaginable until she found him. They loved each other like nothing I've seen before or since. If she was alive, he'd have found her by now."

Walking to the jeep, the silence between Evelyn, David, and General Gibson was heavy. Kurt was already sitting behind the driver's seat, his arms crossed, seething.

"This was my fault. I'm so sorry," David began. "She was convincing and looked so much like the picture I had—"

"Let's just go," Kurt snapped.

David nodded and got behind the wheel. General Gibson took shotgun while Evelyn climbed in the back. David turned the key and the engine coughed, almost unwilling to start. He waited a moment, then turned the key again.

The jeep exploded.

# Chapter 38

Nick sat behind his desk, reading over the lists of names Helen gave him. One contained those who knew about the photos. The other was people who had the power to have her club raided. The first was about a dozen names, but the second had at least thirty of the city's top judges, cops, prosecutors, and politicians.

"All of these men are clients?"

Helen nodded.

"Anyone not on the list who could have ordered it?"

"Sure," Helen replied, "hundreds of people. These are just the ones I know personally."

"A few of Mickey Cohen's people are on here," Nick said.

"Err on the side of caution. Some of Cohen's lieutenants have enough pull in the LAPD to make it happen. One of the other club owners in the city ran afoul of Mickey and he was hit over and over until he went bankrupt. He's now serving time in Lancaster."

"You forgot Gallo's name," Nick said.

"Gallo couldn't get the department to forgive a parking ticket," Helen said.

"Wasn't your tune the other day."

"I always knew he was a low-level enforcer, I just thought he saw an opportunity and took it. Now, I'm not so sure. This bust had to come from someone with influence. It would be an awful coincidence if the person who sent us the ransom note and the person who ordered the raid had no connection. Cops seemed like they were specifically looking for the safe."

"Do you think there's any other reason vice might've raided the club?" Nick asked.

"Sometimes a new guy comes in and decides to crack down. Usually, they just smash a couple of liquor bottles and help themselves to the ready cash. A week later, everything's back to normal and a third of the guys who knocked up the place are at the poker tables. They've never taken the safe before."

"Gregory and I were tossed into a cell," Nick said. "There were no questions. You?"

"No, but then again, I've never been sprung so quickly. Thank Evelyn for me."

"I will," Nick replied.

"She wasn't mad, was she?" Helen asked, genuinely curious.

"No, why?"

Helen gave him a look and Nick laughed.

"A house full of beautiful women is not something Evelyn finds threatening," Nick said. "She's never been competitive like that. Her theory is that being a woman is hard enough. Why cut yourself off from the only people who understand what you're going through?"

"Easier to say when you're rich and beautiful."

"Most things are," Nick conceded. "How do your clients find partners for the evening?"

"With the regulars, my employees have a list of men

they're willing to entertain and a list of men they don't care for. If a client asks for someone and he's on her yes list, off they go."

"And if he asks, but is on her second list?"

"If he's on someone else's yes list, I'll try to direct him toward her, saying the first woman is already engaged for the evening. If he's on everyone's no list, there's probably a reason. I'll tell him everyone is booked. After a few evenings, they usually take the hint."

"Do they ever get upset? Feel rejected?"

"I try to frame it as a scheduling issue, but sure, sometimes they've had too much to drink or are just arrogant enough to show their true selves."

"Then Gregory throws them out?"

"Often, it's not necessary. As I've said, I work hard to make mine an upscale establishment, where people can conduct business. If someone causes trouble, the regulars will shame them into leaving quietly."

"What if someone's new or a guest of a member is interested in company for the evening?"

"All requests are handled discreetly. The men write me a note. The woman then says yes or no. If it seems like two people are connecting, I might ask her preemptively. At the end of the night, every employee who had a rendezvous puts a short note into a book regarding that particular man. For example, it might read, 'Same as always.' However, if he requested something different, couldn't perform, or was especially bad or good, that is mentioned as well."

"Do you know of any disgruntled employees?"

"A couple are afraid after Ilene and Rosa were attacked. Especially with Julia still missing. Beyond that, we handle complaints as they arise. There have never been any serious issues. This job isn't for everyone. When it's not a good fit, we recognize it quickly and part on good terms."

"Do the women know about the cameras?"

Helen hesitated, guilt crossing her face.

"No," she said finally. "Keep in mind, these are students, starlets, and mothers. They want their pictures out in the world even less than my clients."

Nick glanced over the names again, then stopped.

"Brian Caruso?" he asked. "I got the impression he'd never heard of your club before this whole thing started."

"You don't expect him to jump up and announce that he visited a brothel, do you?"

"No," Nick said. "I suppose not. How was he?"

"Fine. Behaved like a gentleman."

"Did he have any favorite?" Nick asked.

"Not really. He was only in a few times."

"How recently?"

"I'd have to look at my records, but it's been six? Eight months?"

"Can I see the book the girls use to keep records? I'd like to know more about each of these men. Specifically, who might be strong enough to force a girl into his car and who might—"

Nick stopped, hearing the sound of a man's footsteps taking the stairs two at a time. He stood and reached for his gun, not certain who was coming through that door. Motioning Helen behind him, he squared his stance, ready for a fight. Then, Carl burst through the door. Nick blinked a few times, surprised by his urgency.

"A jeep exploded in Berlin. Evelyn was inside," Carl declared.

For a moment, Nick's world stopped spinning. It was as if he heard the words from a far-distant place. His body felt numb.

"I . . . I don't understand," he said, willing his mind to catch up. "What happened?"

"I'm not sure. I just heard about it at the bureau."

"Where's Evie?"

"They were all taken to a hospital outside Frankfurt."

"Is she hurt?"

Carl paused. It was an agonizing moment. "There's a report of one dead. Two critically injured."

"*Who?*" Nick demanded.

"I don't know."

"What do you mean you don't know? What happened to Evelyn?"

"I don't know," Carl repeated gently. "I came here as soon as I heard the news. Everything is still up in the air. They're still trying to figure out exactly what happened."

"Is she—"

Unable to complete the thought, Nick stumbled to a couch and dropped his head in his hands. Carl sat beside him, not willing to offer false hope. To the side, Helen watched uncertainly. She opened her mouth a few times, but could not find the words. Finally, Nick looked up.

"I have to get to Germany."

# Chapter 39

Evelyn woke in a strange bed to hear shouting. It was a voice she would recognize anywhere, despite the fact that she rarely heard it at this register.

"I am her goddamned fiancé!"

Someone else replied too low for Evelyn to decipher.

"Take your regulations and shove them up your—"

"Enough!" David's voice broke in. "Nick, let me remind you that we are in a hospital. You need to stay calm or they will escort you out of here and you will have flown thousands of miles for nothing. Corporal, you either let this man in to see Evelyn Bishop right now or I'll bust you back to private before you finish your shift."

There was more grumbling, then Nick pushed open the curtain around Evelyn's bed. For a moment, he just stared, relief filling his eyes. Then he took in her elevated leg, the bandages around her ribs, the shrapnel wounds across her face, and the white gauze hiding the burns on her arms. His breath was shaky. She understood what was going through his mind because she had been at his hospital bedside less than a year ago.

"Making friends?" she asked.

"Always," he said, pulling up a chair.

"What was all the commotion about?"

"Nothing."

"I'm pretty sure they heard that nothing in Munich."

"Idiot told me I wasn't family because we're not married."

"Well, that's ridiculous," Evelyn replied.

"I may have used slightly stronger words than that," Nick admitted.

Evelyn reached out her hand and Nick took it, bringing her palm to his lips.

"How are you feeling?" he asked.

"They're keeping me on a pretty generous morphine drip."

"As well they should. A concussion, broken ribs, second-degree burns, a torn ligament in your knee? You scared the hell out of me, Evie."

"It was never my intention," she said.

"When Carl found me, they didn't have all the details. I flew halfway around the world not knowing if you were . . ." He broke off, emotional. "It was the longest trip of my life."

Evelyn brushed away his tears.

"What do you remember?" Nick asked.

"Not much. Just . . ."

"Just what?"

"Pain," Evelyn admitted. "I was lying on the ground and there was too much silence. It was probably the ringing in my ears. Blood was everywhere, and I didn't understand why no one was helping us. I tried to move, but I couldn't. I didn't know if I ever would again. It's horrible to feel so vulnerable."

Careful not to jostle her injuries, Nick slid into bed beside her and took her in his arms.

"I'm here now," he said.

She wanted to cry but felt too empty and tired. They lay together silently—her unable to stop thinking about the explosion, him trying to quiet his mind after a day and a half of the worst fear he had ever known. Only holding her could calm the storm inside him. Finally, Evelyn mumbled into Nick's chest. He pulled away and looked at her.

"General Gibson is gone," she repeated.

"I know," Nick said quietly.

Nick got the full story from David. When the jeep exploded, David was thrown free, landing hard and dislocating his shoulder. Besides some cuts and bruises, he was otherwise unharmed. Kurt caught some shrapnel and had to have his spleen removed. There was internal bleeding, but the surgeons expected him to make a full recovery. The lower half of Evelyn would have been crushed had she been sitting further to the left. As it was, only time would tell whether the ligaments in her knee would heal or whether she would walk with a limp. General Gibson, however, caught the full blast. There was nothing anyone could have done to save him.

Nick waited until Evelyn fell back asleep, then left the room. David was curled up across a few chairs. Nick did not have the heart to wake him, so he walked down the hall, too restless to sit still. Near the end, he found an open door. Inside the private room Kurt was propped up in bed, staring into space. Nick knocked and Kurt was startled out of his reverie. It took his eyes a moment to focus, but when he did, surprise filled his face.

"Herr Schmidt," Kurt said, calling Nick by his code name from the war.

"Actually, Nick Gallagher," he replied, then motioned to a chair by the bed. "May I?"

"Yes, of course."

Nick entered and sat down.

"How are you feeling?"

Kurt shrugged.

"David told me what happened with the woman claiming to be your wife. I can't imagine how difficult that must have been."

"It would have been better if the bomb took me, too," Kurt replied. He looked defiant, as if daring Nick to argue. Nick did not. He understood the sentiment all too well.

"What are you doing here?" Kurt asked, gesturing at Nick's travel-worn clothes. "You don't look like a man who still serves."

"Oh, no. The army and I parted ways immediately after the war. I'm here for Evelyn. When I heard she was injured . . ."

"You're not just colleagues, then?"

"No. Not for a long while."

"I always thought there was something between you two," Kurt said. "Maybe not at the beginning of our journey together, but certainly by the end. You reminded me of the early days with my wife. That feeling of discovery, when everything is new and exciting. Where it seems like real life will never intrude."

"Real life was all around us. It was war."

"No, that's simply hell," Kurt admonished. "Real life is arguing over who has to do the laundry, scrub the bathroom, or cook dinner at the end of a long day."

"That last one's always an easy decision in our house, but I see your point."

"It must be nice to come out of the war with so much intact."

"I didn't," Nick said. "Evelyn and I . . . we lost each other for a while. I came home without much reason to live. My circumstances were no worse than when I left, but by then, I knew what I was missing."

"My wife and daughter are gone," Kurt said quietly. "I think I knew it before, but I allowed myself a sliver of hope. What a fool I am."

"There's nothing foolish about hope," Nick said.

"I just wish . . ." Kurt trailed off.

"What?" Nick asked.

"I wish they didn't suffer."

Nick did not know how to respond. The silence that filled the space between them was heavy with sorrow.

"Do you know of anyone who might want to hurt you?" Nick asked eventually.

Kurt looked up in surprise.

"The possibility of finding your wife and daughter is a strong incentive to lure you back to Berlin."

"You think I was the target?"

"No, but we have to consider all possibilities."

"Some of my old colleagues might not have approved of my fleeing the country, but I can't imagine any of them still caring enough to go through the bother of setting a bomb. As far as I knew, Hannah and I had no personal enemies. Our biggest conflict was with our downstairs neighbor when her dog's barking woke Sophie. Certainly not something to hold a grudge over. Especially with everything that's happened since then."

"I'm just wondering who sent you the postcard," Nick said.

"It wasn't that woman? Ilsa?"

"She's been thoroughly questioned. According to David, she took advantage of the fact that people were looking for Hannah. She didn't create the situation."

"Then, no," Kurt said with a frown. "I have no idea who sent it. Who would be so cruel?"

"I'll look into it and see if I can get any answers. Maybe in the process, we'll discover exactly what happened to your family."

"Does it matter now?" Kurt asked.

"The truth always matters," Nick replied. He stood up to leave and was at the door when Kurt called out.

"You and Evelyn were close to General Gibson, weren't you?"

"He was like family."

"It's horrible to lose those we love and have to keep going," Kurt said. There was something in his tone that made Nick turn back. Kurt held his eye with an expression Nick couldn't define. They stared at each other for a long moment and Nick had a strange feeling it was almost a challenge. Then Kurt broke off and turned to stare out the window.

Nick walked out of the room. He checked on Evelyn, who was still asleep. He went back into the hallway and sat down beside David, who opened his eyes, groggy and tired.

"You should get some rest," Nick said. "In a real bed."

"Probably," David replied. "But it can wait. We're going to Berlin, aren't we?"

Nick nodded.

# Chapter 40

A casual observer would not know a jeep had exploded on this street. The remains of the vehicle were taken to a large warehouse where army investigators would go over every inch of it, looking for clues. The shattered glass and other debris were swept to the side and the scorch marks on nearby walls were indistinguishable from the previous damage of war. In the hours immediately after the explosion, the MPs spoke to everyone in the neighborhood. It was the middle of the day and the few people who were home either saw nothing or were not interested in helping the Americans. Nick looked over to the Russian sector and noted the same three buildings Evelyn had pointed out to Gibson.

"I'll bet you anything the Russians were watching the border," Nick said. "Someone saw something."

"Unfortunately, we can't exactly march over to high command and ask them," David said.

"You'd think they would come forward with information, just to prove it wasn't them. Something like this, so close to their sector? It's bound to ratchet up tensions."

"Right now, the story is that it was a bad alternator. If the press gets wind that a US Army general was killed in an intentional bombing, they'll lose their minds and our options for how to respond become limited."

Nick walked the streets, looking for anything the MPs might have missed.

"Kurt couldn't think of anyone who might want to lure him here," Nick said. "I tend to agree. He's been out of the city for six years. Any of the SS or Gestapo who once hunted him are now either in prison or in hiding. There's no more Fatherland to serve, so why bother?"

"What about Evelyn?" David asked. "You two had a few missions here."

"It's possible. One time in 1943, everything went south. We killed two SS soldiers to escape. They might have families, but if Evie was the target, why not go after her when she was last here?"

"General Gibson makes the most sense," David said. "Someone was either targeting him and followed us there. Or it wasn't about General Gibson specifically. They just saw an opportunity to destroy a fragile peace. It would be easy to cross over from the Russian sector and plant the bomb."

Nick stopped walking and bent down to look more closely at a sewer grate.

"Help me lift this," he said to David.

They struggled with the heavy iron and finally pushed it aside. Nick kicked away the broken glass, then wrapped his hand in his handkerchief. Getting onto his stomach, he reached into the storm drain and pulled up a small, singed metal cylinder with wires extending from the top. It was the detonator marked with Cyrillic writing.

"Doesn't mean it was the Russians," David said. "Someone could have planted this."

"Perhaps," Nick agreed.

"But you doubt it?" David asked.

"I don't know," Nick said as he slid it into his pocket.

"I need to change, and we could both use some sleep and food before tonight," David said.

"Tonight?" Nick asked.

"I'm sure as hell not letting you go to the Soviet sector on your own and Alexei Antonov doesn't start drinking until seven p.m."

Nick was snoring on a camp bed when David shook him awake. The first thing he did was call the hospital to check on Evelyn. The nurse told him she was drugged into a dreamless sleep. He envied her refuge. For a short while, she could forget the pain of losing General Gibson. Nick knew his solace lay in figuring out what had happened. Wordlessly, he took the clothes David offered and changed into them.

As David drove to East Berlin, Nick looked over and saw his eyes ringed with exhaustion. Though he covered it well, he still moved gingerly, protecting his injured shoulder.

"Did you get any sleep?" Nick asked.

"There were about a hundred messages waiting for me when I got back to the barracks. I took a shower and went to the office. There's just so much to do without—"

"You want to talk about it?" Nick offered.

"Not yet," David said. "I can't afford to fall apart right now."

"Just make sure you don't put it off too long," Nick said. "It's one thing to break. It's another to shatter."

"Why did you leave the service?" David asked Nick.

"Never wanted to be here in the first place. I joined up because it seemed better than my life at the time. Then, war came and leaving wasn't exactly an option," Nick said. "Why did you stay?"

"Truth, justice, the American way," David said with a wry smile. "Honestly, it was General Gibson. My dad wasn't really around much. The general was . . . well, I guess I never told him what he was to me."

"That's true for a lot of us," Nick said. "So, what happens now?"

"Don't know. I'll get a new CO and . . . ?" David trailed off. "No sense in borrowing trouble. It finds us all in its own time."

They crossed into East Berlin, and David parked near the bar.

"The one with the red sign," David said.

Nick nodded but didn't move.

"What is it?" David asked.

"Just gearing myself up to face Alexei. He was a son of a bitch during the war and that's when we were on the same side."

David reached between the seats and pulled out a carton of Lucky Strikes. Nick looked at it and snorted.

"Screw him," Nick said, then got out of the car, leaving the cigarettes behind. He entered the bar and saw Alexei in his usual seat with his back against the wall.

"Why am I not surprised to see you?" Alexei asked as Nick approached.

"Probably because you've had eyes on me ever since I touched down at Tempelhof," Nick replied.

Alexei smiled humorlessly. "You Americans, so paranoid."

"Practical," Nick corrected.

"I take your presence to mean the rumors are true. You and Evelyn Bishop are to be married."

"I'd be here regardless."

"I was sad to hear you broke up at the end of the war," Alexei said. "But sadder to find you are back together. She could do better."

"That seems to be a common sentiment," Nick replied. "What do you know about the bombing?"

"Ah, yes. Tragedy. Gibson was your commanding officer, was he not?"

"Cut the shit, Alexei. I don't like you. You don't like me. The only thing we've ever had in common is Evelyn. That bomb could have killed her."

Alexei gestured to the bartender, who returned with a second glass and a bottle of vodka. He poured them shots and left the bottle. Alexei slid one to Nick.

"I did warn her that Berlin is not a safe place," Alexei said, then threw back his drink. "How is she?"

"You should go see her yourself," Nick said.

"It's not quite that easy."

"Not like looking out the window of an apartment building into the French sector?"

Alexei raised his eyebrows and nudged Nick's untouched drink toward him. Nick knocked it off the bar. It shattered on the floor and everyone turned in their direction. From the looks of the people around them, Nick knew he was outnumbered, should everything go sideways. Alexei shrugged and poured himself a refill. Nick pulled the detonator out of his pocket.

"Someone used Russian supplies, Alexei. Rather careless, don't you think?"

Alexei took it, turned it over in his hand, then gave it back to Nick.

"There were quite a few of these lying around after the war," Alexei replied. "Could have been anyone."

"Do you think your government will say the same thing when the US Army accused them of breaking the peace? We're four months into this idiotic blockade and nothing's changed. The Americans aren't leaving and the Berliners haven't begged you to take over. It's one thing to start a war intentionally, it's another to fall ass-backwards into an armed conflict."

"You always did have a way with words," Alexei noted dryly.

"Help me find out what happened," Nick said. "Do you know anyone who would want to hurt Kurt Vogel?"

"No."

"How about General Gibson?"

"More people than I can name."

"What about Evelyn? Is there anyone who would want to hurt her?"

Alexei did not answer.

"She saved your life once," Nick reminded him.

"That is her check to cash, not yours."

"Well, she's in the hospital right now, so your options are limited," Nick said.

Alexei picked up the shot in front of him and drained it slowly. He threw a few marks on the bar and stood. Nick blocked him and again, the bar fell silent.

"War is a horrible time," Alexei said eventually. "Perhaps some things are best left in the past. Evelyn should not have come back. Nor should you."

# Chapter 41

Unsurprisingly, Evelyn was a terrible patient, especially after they got home. Though she tired easily, she was restless, wanting to do more than her doctor allowed. No one would let her go to Bishop Aeronautics, afraid of her trying to walk the factory floor or climb the stairs to her office. Instead, she was lodged in the library at home, resting on a couch with a lap desk and a low table filled with work. Nick and Taffy tried to anticipate her requests because she was not above doing things herself and reinjuring her leg.

The only person remotely happy about Evelyn's incapacitation was Ruth, who took advantage of her forced idleness to bring in a string of potential new secretaries for interviews. They ranged from "not terrible" to "what were you thinking?" There were girls fresh out of school and women who had worked as executive assistants for the presidents of major corporations. Evelyn found something wrong with every single person. Some were too young, others too set in their ways. Still others Evelyn worried would want to retire soon and leave her with the same problem a few years down the line. Finally, Ruth sat down with Evelyn and handed her an envelope.

"This is my official letter of resignation. I'm giving you six weeks. At the end of it, if you haven't found a new secretary, I'm leaving. You're on your own."

"There's so much going on," Evelyn protested. "And I'm injured and—"

"If I don't do this, you will never choose someone," Ruth said. "Figure it out."

In the week since she got home, Evelyn called Kurt twice, leaving messages at his office. He did not return her calls and Evelyn could not blame him. Her last message was simply information regarding the memorial for General Gibson, which was to be held in Oxnard.

Late one night, Nick ventured into the library to find Evelyn asleep, with several reports resting on her chest, her pen uncapped, bleeding across the paper. She woke with a start, the papers cascading to the floor.

"Let me take you upstairs," Nick said.

"I have too much to do," Evelyn insisted, wincing as she levered herself into a sitting position.

"If you don't take care of yourself, you're going to be out of the office even longer."

"I know," Evelyn grumbled.

Nick glanced at the pages as he shuffled them into a pile. They were not from Bishop Aeronautics, as Nick had assumed. They were army reports about the bombing. David sent them to her, along with pictures from the site.

"I need to make sense of this," Evelyn said. "General Gibson was targeted and I want to know why."

Nick glanced down at the pages.

"Do you even have clearance for this?"

"Gibson gave me clearance when I agreed to look for Kurt's family. So far, no one's revoked it."

"Is it possible no one knows it exists?"

Evelyn shrugged. "I'm following the letter of the law."

"Have you found anything?" Nick asked.

"No." Evelyn sighed with frustration. "I've even reached out to Alexei a few times, but he doesn't have any information."

"That he's willing to share," Nick replied.

"It's strange being on opposite sides after everything that's happened."

"I don't know that we were ever on the same side. Alexei's only side is Alexei. He's always been very good at looking out for himself."

"I need to feel like I'm doing something," Evelyn said.

"Then how about helping me with Julia's case?"

"Is there anything new?"

"It took them three weeks, but they finally agreed to send over proof of life in exchange for a sample of the ransom."

Evelyn frowned. Proof of life was usually just a photograph of the captive holding a recent newspaper. It could be dropped in the mail anonymously, reducing the risk to the kidnapper. The fact that it took weeks to respond did not bode well.

"If I hadn't gotten hurt . . ." Evelyn began.

"Nonsense. This has nothing to do with you. I gave Helen Carl's number in case anything came up. There was no progress on the case while I was gone. Even if there was . . ." He trailed off, not wanting to tell her he still had nightmares about seeing her in the hospital. His greatest fear was losing her. "You come first. Always."

She pulled him close and kissed him.

"How can I help?"

"I need to alter some photographs."

"Samples for the kidnappers with faces edited out," Evelyn guessed.

Nick nodded.

"Tell Helen to bring over the negatives."

\* \* \*

An hour later, Nick answered the door to reveal Helen on the doorstep, her eyes wide.

"This place is . . ." she began. Then she saw Evelyn propped up on crutches, her leg splinted on both sides.

"It's good to see you again," Evelyn said. "Please come in."

Helen looked around, her face inscrutable.

"I didn't know real people lived like this."

"My father worked very hard," Evelyn replied. "So do I. You know, we have that in common. We're both women running businesses. From what Nick tells me, you're damned good at it."

Helen flushed with the unexpected compliment.

"I built mine from the ground up," she said. "You're just . . . lucky."

"In so many ways," Evelyn agreed, with a smile at Nick.

"Must've been nice growing up here, having everything you want," Helen said.

"You and I don't know each other very well," Evelyn replied quietly. "Let's not make assumptions. They tend to stand in the way of friendship."

"Is that what we're going to become?" Helen asked. "Friends?"

"Anything's possible. Now, let's get these photographs printed."

Moving slowly and awkwardly, Evelyn headed to the cramped darkroom and ushered them inside. Once Evelyn had everything set up, she asked Helen for the negatives.

"Number fourteen," Helen said, handing over the strip. There was a challenge in her voice as Evelyn turned on the enlarger and displayed an image of two people having sex.

"How do you want to take out their faces?" Evelyn asked. "Should I blur them or solid white circles?"

"Do white circles," Nick said. "Make it clear the kidnappers aren't getting a thing until Julia's safe."

"What if it just pisses them off?" Helen asked.

"Pissed-off people make mistakes," Nick replied. "We've been playing by their rules and they haven't even given us proof of life. The games are over."

Evelyn found two quarters, then used them to mark the spot on the enlarger. She slid a sheet of photograph paper into place and printed the image. When it was finished, the people were unrecognizable.

"He asked for five pictures," Helen said.

"Did he name specific people?" Nick asked. "Might help us figure out who he is."

"No. Just gave me a number."

Evelyn took the negative out of the enlarger and handed it back to Helen, who passed her another. The photos showed a range of different acts. As Evelyn printed the pictures, she felt Helen watching her.

"Are you waiting for me to be shocked?" Evelyn asked.

Helen started, surprised. "Well, yes."

"You seem to think that I look down on your profession. I don't. What happens between consenting adults is none of my business. Though I do think it's a scandal there aren't more ways for women to earn a good living."

Evelyn turned back to the enlarger and printed the last photograph. As Nick hung it up to dry, she turned to him and confessed, "You know how hard it is to admit you're right. . . ."

"Oh, wait for this," Nick said to Helen. "It's going to be good."

"I pushed myself. My leg is killing me."

Nick opened the door and ushered Helen out, then he swept Evelyn into his arms.

"I'm going to savor those words," he promised.

"Do you want to stay for a drink while the prints dry?" Evelyn asked Helen.

"I don't want to impose," Helen replied.

"It's not an imposition," Evelyn said. "I'm not the best hostess right now, but Nick excels at pouring Scotch."

"I can do other things, too," Nick insisted. "Vodka, gin, tequila . . . ?"

"Thank you, but no. I should get home," Helen said. "Nick, you'll do the exchange tomorrow?"

"Of course. I'll call you when it's done."

Helen walked to the door but stopped on the threshold. "I keep being in your debt," she said to Evelyn.

"Happy to help."

Helen nodded once, then left the house. Evelyn turned to Nick.

"I think she's warming up to me."

Nick laughed, then carried Evelyn upstairs.

# Chapter 42

Early the next morning, Evelyn, Nick, and Carl set off for General Gibson's funeral. The day was gray and overcast as they drove north to Oxnard.

"Did you know he was from here?" Carl asked Nick.

"Told me once that he chose all of us because he liked to be reminded of home," Nick replied.

"I never knew," Carl said. "Come to think of it, there was a lot I didn't know about him."

"That's the way he wanted it," Evelyn replied. "He was like a one-way street. We gave him all our concerns and problems and he gave us support."

"General Gibson saved our lives on more than one occasion. I don't think we would have survived the war without him," Nick remembered. "There were so many missions he refused because he knew they were suicide."

"At one point, wasn't he busted down to colonel?" Evelyn asked.

Nick nodded. "They even talked about reassigning us to someone else. I told them Gibson was our commanding officer or I wouldn't let either of you board a plane."

"They threatened to court-martial you." Evelyn laughed. "Like you would have cared."

"The team that went instead of us was slaughtered," Carl said.

"Wasn't even for something important," Nick added. "To them, we were expendable."

"Whereas Gibson always treated us like his own children," Evelyn mused.

Despite the army's rigid structure, General Gibson took them drinking and even home to dinner. Not wanting to be separated from his wife Theresa, he brought her to London and they had a flat near 70 Grosvenor Street. It was small but comfortable, with a few family photos framed on the mantel. For Evelyn and Carl, these meals were a nice reminder of home. For Nick, they were the first time he experienced anything akin to a family dinner. The time allowed them to relax and discuss their missions in a way they never would in a formal debrief. With full bellies and Theresa at the head of the table, it was easier to admit their fears. They could talk about their loneliness and longing for home. When they lost one member of their team, that apartment felt like the only place they could fall apart, knowing Gibson shared their pain.

It took almost an hour and a half to reach the church. They stepped out of the car to see dozens of people dressed in black, slowly making their way inside. Theresa, General Gibson's widow, stood in a receiving line flanked by her adult children. Nick helped Evelyn out of the car and Carl got the cane she still needed. They made their way to the receiving line, listening as others offered condolences and spoke of General Gibson's rabble rousing, sense of humor and extraordinary kindness. It was strange to hear him addressed as Henry by so many people. Despite that being his first name, in their minds, he was always known by his rank. Theresa reached out and took Carl's hand in both of hers. Then she turned to Evelyn, gently cupping her cheek and looking down at her injuries.

"How are you feeling?" she asked gently.

"Fine. I'm fine," Evelyn replied.

"Really?" Theresa said.

"No," Evelyn answered, tears prickling her eyes. "There's a hole in our hearts."

"He was the best of men," Nick offered.

"I'm glad to see you three together," Theresa said, looking at each of them in turn. "He always said you were family, and family gets us through the worst of times. He loved you, you know."

"We knew," Carl said. "And we loved him."

"As the wife of an army man, I'd made peace with the idea of losing him. After the war, though . . ." Theresa broke off, shaking her head. "I thought he was safe. It was only a year until his retirement, but I guess God had other plans."

"We'll find out who did this," Evelyn promised.

"Oh, sweetheart," Theresa said. "It doesn't matter. Not to me. Henry is gone and nothing can change that."

Beside Theresa, her daughter slipped her arm through her mother's. Evelyn, Nick, and Carl greeted her, then moved down the line into the church. By the start of the service, every pew was filled. The people giving eulogies ranged from grade-school friends to people Gibson served with in the First World War, to those who knew him from his family's farm. They all spoke of his generosity, intelligence, and good heart. There were stories of late-night poker games and early morning reveille. He went out of his way to make other people's days better and ensure they never felt alone. His was a life well-lived.

After the service, Evelyn looked down at her mascara- and tearstained handkerchief.

"I must look a mess," she said.

"Never," Nick replied.

"Let me freshen up. I'll meet you two outside."

It took Evelyn a moment to find the restroom. There, she collected herself and looked into the mirror. When she first met General Gibson, she was so young and naïve. Of course, she did not know that at the time. Like most twenty-somethings, she had all the arrogance of youth. Yet Gibson saw something in her—something more than she even suspected—and gave her a chance, changing her life forever. She wondered if he knew how grateful she was to him. She wished she had thought to tell him. Splashing water on her face, and patting it dry, Evelyn felt ready to face the world again.

Hobbling back through the church, she found Tom Rivers sitting in the last row. His eyes were bloodshot and his hands trembled.

"You came," Evelyn said, surprised. She had called him to let him know what happened but did not actually expect to see him.

"I met Gibson a couple times during the war. He was a good man," Tom replied. "I wish he'd been my CO."

Evelyn did not know how to respond. Instead, she sat down in the pew, facing him. It took Tom a few minutes to gather himself and Evelyn waited patiently. Nick looked in to check on her and she gave him a smile and a nod. Tom followed her gaze.

"Boyfriend?" Tom asked.

"Fiancé," Evelyn said.

"How do you have a relationship after everything . . . ?"

"Nick was there, beside me the whole time. I don't have to hide and I don't have to explain."

"You're lucky," Tom mused.

"I am," Evelyn agreed. "If it wasn't Nick, it probably wouldn't be anyone. Marriage feels like the ultimate leap of faith."

"I don't really have much of that left."

"You look like hell," Evelyn said, not unkindly.

"I really wanted to forget about the war. Find a way to put it all behind me. Then you showed up on my doorstep."

"I'm sorry," Evelyn replied softly. "You had found peace."

"And you showed me how fragile it actually was," Tom countered. "I hate you for that."

"I know."

For a moment, they sat in silence. Tom looked at her, as if waiting for something, but Evelyn had no words to reassure him. There was no comfort to be given.

"This was a mistake," Tom said, before standing up and fleeing the church.

With her cane, Evelyn was much slower, but she followed him out into the bright sunlight.

"Tom, wait!" she called. Her fear was that he would leave the funeral and walk into the ocean as he had promised himself two years ago. Nick went after him. Tom spun around, taking a wild swing. Nick ducked it easily and stepped out of reach, not willing to brawl at a funeral.

"Come on!" Tom shouted at Nick, his pent-up rage looking for a release. "Come at me."

He charged toward Nick, who stepped back. Carl moved toward them and Tom took a swing at him, too. Carl caught him in a bear hug, holding his arms to his sides. Tom struggled, but Carl was stronger.

"I won't let you do this," Carl said quietly. "You're not going to disrespect a good man and upset his family."

Tom struggled for a moment more before his body slumped in Carl's arms.

"Can I let you go?" Carl asked.

Tom nodded and Carl released him. Evelyn caught up to them.

"Why did you come today?"

"I don't know. I've been messed up ever since you came to find me," Tom said.

"Do you see this?" Evelyn pointed at her leg. Then at her other injuries. "And these? I could have been killed."

Tom didn't say anything.

"General Gibson died while trying to discover what happened to Kurt Vogel's family."

"It's not my fault," Tom snapped.

"I never said it was," Evelyn countered. "But you have the ability to help. Don't do it for me or Kurt or even for General Gibson. Do it for yourself. You talk about wanting to let go, but this haunts you. I know it does. You never got the chance to finish your mission. Maybe discovering what happened will finally give you a real, lasting peace."

"The last thing I need on my conscience is two more people I couldn't save," Tom retorted.

That hung between them for a long moment.

"All right," Evelyn said. "I won't contact you again."

# Chapter 43

Evelyn and Nick sat in his car, outside a small park near Los Feliz, watching a manila envelope they had set on the bench an hour earlier. It was past the drop-off time and they were both on edge. General Gibson's funeral left them emotionally wrung out. Carl offered to help Nick with the exchange of doctored photos for Julia's proof of life, but Evelyn felt fragile and wanted to stay close to him. Technically, she was in the driver's seat, but she leaned over so she could rest her head on Nick's shoulder. There was nothing he could do to make her feel better, but his presence was comfort enough.

"Thanks for coming with me," Nick said.

"I like spending time with you," Evelyn replied. "We haven't had the chance to do much of that lately. Between work, looking for Kurt's family, your case with Julia—"

"Don't forget wedding planning."

"And my being in the hospital," Evelyn added. "I miss you."

"So, a stakeout was your remedy?" Nick teased.

"Why not? It's not like we ever dated like a normal couple."

"Do you wish I had taken you out to dinner and a movie for our first date?" Nick asked.

"Did we have a first date? It sort of felt like one day we were together."

"We went drinking a lot," Nick offered.

"With Carl," Evelyn said.

"I still think taking you to a pub is considered a date."

"Only if there's food."

Nick reached into his knapsack and pulled out a small bag of almonds.

"Now it's officially a date."

"You do know how to romance a girl." Evelyn laughed.

Nick looked out the window to check on the envelope. Still nothing.

"At the end of the war, you wanted to stay in the OSS," Nick said. "Do you ever wonder what our lives would look like now?"

"The new CIA is a bunch of men who would have made me a secretary regardless of our wartime service."

"I mean, do you miss it? The spying. The adventure. The intensity of it all. Do you wish things were different?"

"No," Evelyn answered immediately. "Those years after the war were hell, but I ended up exactly where I'm meant to be. Here with you."

Nick hadn't realized how much he needed to hear her say that.

"The things that I want to be different are impossible," Evelyn continued. "I wish my father was innocent. I wish my brother was alive. I wish my mother could know the person I've become. I wish all of them could see how lucky I am to have found you."

"Is that why you've been so hesitant about planning the wedding?"

"I wouldn't say hesitant . . ." Evelyn said.

"Reluctant?" Nick asked. "Disinclined? Unenthusiastic?"

"You're a regular thesaurus."

"And you're changing the subject. I don't want to hear how busy you are. Tell me the truth."

Evelyn paused for a long minute, trying to figure out how to put her feelings into words.

"I'm not ready to be Mrs. Nicholas Gallagher."

She felt the air between them shift.

"You're not ready to marry me?" Nick asked finally, trying to keep the pain from his voice.

"I am!" Evelyn assured him. "But I'm not ready to stop being Evelyn Bishop. I know it's just a name, but it's my name. My family's name. My company's name. This is who I've been for the past twenty-eight years. It's all I know."

"So don't give it up."

"What?"

"There's no law saying you have to take my name when we get married," Nick said. "I never expected you to."

"Really?"

"I'm going to spend the rest of my life being Mr. Evelyn Bishop. I know that. I've known that since the moment I saw your life in Los Angeles. And I don't care. You are powerful and strong and incredible. You're going to re-shape the world. I don't need to be the person who does that. I need to be the person you come home to."

"You understand?" Evelyn asked hesitantly.

"Of course, I do!" Nick insisted. "I know how a lot of marriages work, but we won't become each other's property. You can't be any less of you. And I can't be any less of me. We would never survive."

Tears welled up in Evelyn's eyes and she kissed him. "I love you."

"You'd better," Nick teased. Then he glanced out the window and sat up straighter. A man in his midtwenties approached the bench. He had dark hair and a short, slight build. When he stepped under a streetlight, they saw his face.

"Do you recognize him?" Evelyn asked.

"No."

His clothes were casual and inexpensive. Khakis, a dark cotton sweater, and brown shoes. He could have been anyone from anywhere, but Nick supposed that was the point. The man picked up the envelope and dropped another one on the bench, before heading further into the park. As Evelyn turned the ignition, Nick got out and picked up the second envelope. He tucked it into his jacket and followed the young man. They walked past a baseball diamond and a small playground. The man crossed the street and hailed a taxi. Evelyn, who had driven around the outside, pulled up to the curb and Nick hopped in beside her. They tracked the man to Western Avenue, where he leaped out of the taxi and onto a streetcar headed downtown. Several stops later, the young man got off. Nick stepped out of the car and shadowed him several blocks as he walked. He knew how to lose a tail, darting down bottlenecks in dark alleys and retracing his steps. Nick was impressed. It took everything he had learned in the war to remain unobserved. The man took two more taxis, another streetcar, and walked at least a mile before he finally glanced over his shoulder and felt safe enough to go into his final destination: the police station.

# Chapter 44

Next morning, Evelyn and Nick studied the proof-of-life photo as they drank coffee at the kitchen table. Julia stood in front of a white sheet tacked to the wall, wearing a pale dress and high heels. She was holding yesterday's newspaper. Around her right ankle was a dark circle where her skin was rubbed raw.

"She's been chained up," Evelyn said.

Nick nodded. It was expected, but the sight still enraged him. Needing something to do, he stood up to pour more coffee. Taffy entered as Evelyn shuffled Julia's photo back into the manila folder.

"You two were out late last night," Taffy commented as she took a chair beside Evelyn. Nick set a fresh cup of coffee in front of her.

"Which you only know because you came home at the same time," Evelyn teased. "I swear. You've been here a few weeks and already have a better social life than I do."

"Well, that's not hard," Taffy countered. "You barely leave the house except to go to work."

"So that's what we've been doing wrong," Nick said.

"I have friends all over the world," Taffy replied. "I make

the effort to keep in touch. Wherever I go, I already have an introduction."

"When I grow up, I want to be like you," Evelyn mused.

"Don't mock me."

"I'm not. After Uncle Bill died, you picked yourself up and kept going. You've built an incredible life. I might not be interested in charity dinners and lunch at the club, but you have so many people who genuinely care about you. It's a gift."

"Well, thank you," Taffy said, slightly mollified.

Just then, the doorbell rang. Evelyn and Nick looked at each other in surprise. Unexpected visitors were strange enough, but ones who came this early were rarely a harbinger of good news. Nick reached into one of the kitchen drawers and pulled out a gun. He checked the chamber, then tucked it behind his hip before heading into the foyer. Evelyn heard the door open and Nick's surprised greeting. He returned a moment later with Norman Roth.

"I'm sorry to interrupt your breakfast, but—" Norman stopped upon seeing Taffy. Then, with a flourish, he introduced himself.

"A pleasure," Taffy replied. "Did we meet at Nick and Evelyn's engagement party? It was such a whirlwind."

"Unfortunately, I didn't have the good fortune," Norman said.

"Well, hopefully you'll make it to the wedding. If you're comfortable dropping by at this hour, you must be close," Taffy said.

Norman looked to Evelyn and Nick with a wry smile.

"I'd be delighted," Norman replied. "Thank you."

"This is how our guest list gets so large," Evelyn said to Nick.

"Gracious!" Taffy cried, glancing at the clock. "Is that the time? Forgive me for running off, but I have an appointment."

Norman gallantly kissed Taffy's hand. "Until next time."
Taffy blushed slightly, nodded, then left.

"While it's lovely, as always, to see you," Evelyn began.
"You didn't come over before nine a.m. to say hi."

"You've both been busy with the incident in Berlin and
the loss of your former CO," Norman replied. "I'm guessing you haven't been reading the newspaper cover to cover."

"No. Why?" Evelyn said.

"Joey Gallo never came home after he was picked up by
the police."

"Did he make it out of the station?" Nick asked.

"According to our lawyer, he was in decent shape when
they left around two a.m. I didn't hear from him in the
morning, which is unusual. Our guys are supposed to
check in, but Gallo's been known to go on a bender or two.
Yesterday morning, the police found his body dumped in
the LA River. He was badly beaten. Got one in the head,
two in the chest."

"I'm so sorry," Evelyn said.

"No one's taking responsibility for his death."

"Any issues within the organization?" Nick asked.

"Gallo could be a handful, but he didn't cheat people
and he didn't go after other guy's wives. Those are the usual
reasons someone wants revenge. Even then, it would re-
quire Mickey's approval."

"What about a rivalry? Someone outside looking to
start something?"

"Gallo's not high enough to make it worthwhile," Norman replied. "If you're looking to announce your presence, you go for a lieutenant, not a street thug. Besides, it's
been relatively quiet on that front."

"So, what can we do for you?" Nick inquired.

"You were looking into him for Helen Brecker."

"You don't think Nick had something to do with his
death?" Evelyn asked.

"Coroner seems to think it happened around six a.m., the morning he was released."

"When I was in jail myself," Nick said.

"So, if it wasn't Nick, and I'm assuming you're not here to accuse me . . ." Evelyn began.

Roth smiled slightly at the ridiculousness of that possibility.

"I need a private investigator. I doubt finding Gallo's killer is at the top of the LAPD's to-do list. I may not have liked the man, but he was one of our own. Can't let his murder go without a response."

Nick looked to Evelyn, whose eyes were wary. On one hand, refusing Mickey Cohen tended to be hazardous to one's health. On the other, turning over Gallo's killer was a death sentence for the perpetrator. It was a lot to have on their conscience.

"I'm in the middle of another investigation at the moment," Nick said carefully.

"I'd like you to rearrange your priorities," Roth replied. "I've known Helen since I was a child. She's like family. How do you put family aside?"

Roth's eyes narrowed. There was a white-hot anger just beneath the surface. For the first time, Evelyn understood why he was one of the most feared men in the city.

"Mickey believes you owe us a favor for information we've given you in the past."

"Something tells me these cases will overlap," Nick continued. "The police picking up Gallo and the raid on Helen's club feel too close to be coincidental."

"You think it's someone in the LAPD?" Roth asked.

"Maybe," Nick said. "We have reason to believe Julia's case is tied to the department."

Nick told Roth about their previous night's wild goose chase through the city.

"It's possible," Roth said, almost to himself.

"What is?" Evelyn asked.

"Gallo initially went to Helen for blackmail because his brother Bobby is awaiting trial. Gallo was desperate to find anything on the police, the prosecutor, and the judge. Especially seeing Bobby's about to be a dad. Gallo's a knucklehead, but the brothers are close."

"Did he say which cop he was going after?" Evelyn asked.

"All of them." Roth sighed. "Needless to say, Gallo was not a fan of the LAPD."

"Are any of you?" Evelyn wondered.

Roth gave her a wry smile. "I have my favorites."

Nick pulled out Julia's proof-of-life picture.

"You know anything about her?"

"Besides the fact that she's been missing for a few weeks and the kidnapper is trying to ransom her for Helen Brecker's cache of dirty pictures?"

"I don't know why I bother asking," Nick said. "You're better informed than the *Times*."

"They don't have my network," Roth replied. He pulled the photograph closer and pointed to where the white sheet behind Julia had slipped slightly. It was just possible to make out the corner of a picture frame. "Looks fairly thick, like a display case. I'm guessing it holds army medals. Seen a lot in our guys' homes. They're proud of their service."

"So, we're looking for someone who is a former soldier . . . or someone who lost a soldier," Evelyn said.

"That's over a thousand people just in the LAPD."

"What if Gallo was picked up because Caruso was trying to find Julia, but something he mentioned in interrogation got him killed?" Evelyn suggested.

"We tell our guys not to say anything until the lawyer shows up," Roth replied, "but Gallo was easily baited."

"Cops tend to protect one another," Nick said. "I could see Caruso currying favor with a warning to someone in the department."

"Or maybe someone overheard the questions," Evelyn added. "I wonder who was in the station that night."

Roth stood and looked to Nick and Evelyn.

"Perhaps our interests do align. Keep me informed."

He reached into his pocket for a card, wrote an address on it, then handed it to Evelyn.

"You may send Mickey's invitation there as well," Roth said.

Evelyn glanced down to see that he had given her a post office box number.

"How did you find out where I live?" Evelyn asked. "I'm not listed in the phone book."

"How does anyone find anything?" he said with a shrug. "Please give your delightful aunt my best."

With that, he showed himself out. Nick looked at the card and then to Evelyn.

"I'm sure Taffy can find room for a few more." Nick sighed.

"She has been encouraging us to expand our social circle," Evelyn replied.

They both started laughing and Evelyn tucked the card away somewhere safe.

# Chapter 45

Nick rang the doorbell of the Martinez house. It was answered by a nervous Camila.

"You shouldn't be here," she whispered.

Diego's voice boomed, "Who is it?" as he stepped out. His fists were clenched and he looked like he was about to throw a punch.

"I have good news," Nick said, withdrawing the proof-of-life photo of Julia from a manila envelope. "Your daughter's alive."

Diego did not look at the picture.

"My daughter is dead," he snapped, then shut the door.

Nick was horrified. He knocked repeatedly.

"Mr. Martinez! Mr. Martinez!!"

Diego opened the door again, glaring at Nick.

"Papa! Please, hear him out!" Camila pleaded.

Elizabeth, Julia's mother, stood in the background, wringing her hands.

"Yesterday morning, Julia was alive. What happened between then and now?" Nick asked.

"If you don't get off my property," Diego threatened, "I will throw you off myself."

Nick glanced to Camila and Elizabeth, both of whom

were silent in the face of Diego's rage. Realizing there was nothing more he could say, Nick stepped off the porch. Behind him, the door slammed so hard, it rattled the foundation of the house. Nick walked back to his car, confused and afraid. He thought they had done the right thing in blocking out people's faces from the photos, but now Nick worried the kidnapper had taken out his frustration on Julia. He was about to drive away when he saw Camila sneak out the back door.

"Come with me," she said. "My father can't see us talking."

They headed down the street, turned the corner, and walked a few more blocks before Camila felt comfortable slowing down.

"What happened to Julia?" Nick asked at the same time Camila said, "Let me see the picture."

Nick pulled it out and handed it to her. A small smile of relief crossed her face.

"She's really alive," Camila breathed, gazing down at her sister. "Thank God."

"But your father . . . ?"

"That cop. Caruso. He came to the house and told us Julia was a whore. He said you worked for her pimp."

Nick let out a long sigh. "Shit."

"Papa says she's dead to him. We're not allowed to mention her name. Every picture has been taken down and her belongings are packed away in the attic."

"Caruso shouldn't have done that," Nick stated with a quiet fury. "Your parents didn't need to know and moreover, it's not true. She was just a bartender."

"In a gentleman's club," Camila countered.

"Ironically, she only took the job to pay for your father's surgery."

"That just makes it worse. Papa's a proud man."

"Pride and stubbornness are often closely intertwined," Nick replied. "Neither will help your sister right now."

"My mother already lost two children," Camila said. "She can't give up on Julia, no matter what Papa says. It's why she sent me."

"Is there anything about this photo that stands out to you?" Nick asked.

"Well, her clothes. I've never seen that dress before, and it's not something she would choose," Camila said. "It's too frilly and she loathes high heels. Plus, it looks like there's a petticoat underneath the skirt, and that belt is too tight. Julia never understood why she should be uncomfortable just to impress a man."

"The dress looks new, or at least well cared for," Nick offered. "That's a good sign."

"It is?"

"If the kidnapper is providing her with clothes, he's probably also giving her food and water."

"That we should be grateful for the bare necessities—"

"Is there anything else you can tell me?"

Camila studied the photo again.

"Her necklace. She's still wearing it," Camila noted, pointing to the silver pendant. "Usually, she takes it off when she gets home from work and hides it in the back of a drawer. When she didn't come home, I looked for it, but it was missing. That means I was right. She was taken from outside our house."

"That helps establish the timeline," Nick said. "Is there anything else?"

"She really hates whoever is taking that picture," Camila replied. "See how it looks like she's almost smiling? When Julia likes someone, her whole face lights up. This is her pretending to be okay, but if you look at her eyes, they're hard. Angry."

"That's another good sign. It means she hasn't given up."

Camila nodded, then saw a family round the corner. "I have to go. Can I take this picture?"

"I made a few copies," Nick said. "Take this one instead."

He handed her a photo that had the corner of the frame cropped out. If the kidnapper was, in fact, a cop, the last thing Nick wanted to do was give Caruso any reason to tip him off. Camila tucked the photo into her pocket and ran back home.

Nick's next stop was the police station. The sergeant looked up in surprise. He was the same one on duty when Evelyn bailed Nick out of jail.

"Yep," Nick said. "Sometimes I come in through the front door, too."

Bypassing the sergeant's stuttered protests, Nick headed upstairs to the detectives' bullpen. Caruso was not at his desk and no one knew where to find him.

"I want to see that son of a bitch, now!" Nick roared loud enough to cause a commotion, which, of course, was the whole point.

"Stop being an asshole and get in my office," Wharton yelled across the room.

Nick complied. He waited until Wharton had slammed the door before ranting, "Do you have any idea what Caruso did?"

"No, and I don't care. You can't come in here raging like a wounded bear. If you think I won't toss you in a cell again, you're dead wrong."

"He told Julia Martinez's parents that she's a whore."

"Is she?" Wharton asked.

"No! And that's not the point. What good would that do, beyond ruining her life?"

"I don't presume to know the wonders of Detective Caruso's mind," Wharton snapped.

"Wait. Why would he do that?" Nick said, stopping to consider it for the first time. "Who's Caruso's partner on this case?"

"Detective Jordan," Wharton said with a sigh. "Dimmer than a five-watt bulb."

"He here?"

Wharton opened the door and bellowed the man's name. A medium-sized, medium-height man with brown hair stood up from his desk. He was so remarkably average, Nick would have sworn he had never seen him before, despite standing next to his desk less than three minutes before. Jordan shuffled into the office and looked at Wharton.

"Yeah, Cap?"

"What's going on with the Julia Martinez case?"

"The missing girl?" Detective Jordan asked.

"Yes," Nick said.

Jordan glanced between Nick and Wharton, uncertainly.

"Any leads?" Wharton prompted.

"Caruso thinks she might have had a boyfriend," Jordan said. "He says it's always the boyfriend who did it."

"Were you around for the interrogation of Joey Gallo?" Nick asked.

Jordan was thrown by the sudden change of topic.

"The gangster," Wharton reminded him. "Picked up by your partner a few weeks ago?"

"Oh, yeah. Yeah. Started in there, but Caruso told me to go get us dinner. Then, I dunno. Heard he got a lawyer and stopped talking."

"Anything strike you as funny about the conversation?" Nick asked.

"Brian doesn't really tell jokes," Jordan said.

"How about strange or noteworthy?" Wharton clarified.

"Dunno."

"Was there anyone else in the room?" Nick asked. "Or watching the interrogation from outside?"

Jordan glanced at Wharton, who stared back impatiently.

"At one point the DA went in with questions. A few of our guys were in the observation room. One had arrested his brother and made a joke about the whole family being in prison."

"Who was that?" Nick asked.

"McCauley. His partner, Anderson, was there, too."

"Did Gallo say anything that made them uncomfortable?" Nick prompted.

"He swore a lot, but I think they're used to hearing that kind of language," Jordan said.

Nick sighed in frustration. Again, Jordan looked up at his captain, hoping for a cheat sheet to get him through this interrogation.

"We're done," Wharton said. He opened the door, ushered the detective out, then closed it again. "It's like blood from a stone."

"Why do you keep him around?" Nick asked.

"Caruso likes the guy," Wharton said. "If I didn't know better, I'd guess it's because he doesn't ask too many questions when evidence falls into their laps."

Nick raised his eyebrows.

"Of course, I would never accuse one of my officers of being anything but honest," Wharton said.

"Of course not," Nick agreed.

"Why are you asking about Joey Gallo?" Wharton said. "You know anything about his unfortunate demise?"

"I know that he was looking for dirt on a few cops and DAs to get his brother out of jail. There wasn't a ton of time between Gallo's release and his death. Might be interesting to talk with McCauley and Anderson."

"You think it was one of my people?" Wharton asked.

"Is this where you go on a rant, telling me that while detectives might bend the rules, they'd never resort to outright murder?"

Wharton sat down behind his desk. He pulled out a bottle of whiskey and offered Nick some. Surprised, Nick agreed.

"I got into the LAPD because I believed I could make a difference. I wanted people to feel safe and improve their lives. Fuck, I wanted to be a hero. I dunno that heroes exist anymore. Maybe they never did," Wharton said as he tossed back his drink. "You can catch McCauley and Anderson before their shift tomorrow at eight a.m. Caruso took a few personal days. Something about a family emergency."

"Thanks," Nick said.

Wharton nodded, then tucked the bottle back into his desk. He didn't look up as Nick left the office.

# Chapter 46

"They're dead," Tom Rivers said to Evelyn.

He had shown up on her doorstep in the middle of the day looking six days' past haggard. His eyes were bloodshot and his skin sallow. Evelyn thought she could smell a faint trace of whiskey on his breath. They were sitting in the library, with Tom on the couch, clutching a cup of coffee. It seemed the only thing anchoring his hands still.

"How did you find out?" Evelyn asked.

"I, too, still have a few friends. They weren't really happy to hear from me. That last year of the war, I wouldn't describe myself as good company. An old buddy of mine from the OSS dug this up and sent it to me a few weeks ago. I couldn't bring myself to open it until yesterday."

Tom handed Evelyn a manila envelope. For a moment, he didn't want to let go, as if it was not real until another person confirmed its contents.

"Just remember you asked for it," he said, finally releasing them.

Evelyn opened the folder and found several photographs of Hannah and Sophie Vogel. They were both lying on the floor, dead. They had been brutally tortured before they were killed. Evelyn closed her eyes, knowing the images were now seared into her brain. They were among the worst she had ever seen. Evelyn slid the images back into their envelope.

"You wish you hadn't looked, don't you?" Tom asked.

"Yes."

"No one should die like that. Especially not a little girl."

"You didn't kill them," Evelyn said.

"They were on that farm for a year. That's plenty of time to go back for them. I could have saved their lives. I could have—"

"You could have done a lot of things, including trying to take them over the border and having your papers flagged. You could have fled through the mountains, with Sophie unable to survive the cold. You could have gotten into a terrible accident where everyone was killed," Evelyn said. "Or they could have lived on that farm for the rest of the war, safe and healthy."

"I was a coward."

"You seem determined to blame yourself," Evelyn said. "Why?"

"Don't you have regrets?"

"Of course I do," Evelyn replied. "You can't be a moral person in an impossible situation and not have regrets. If you feel nothing, that's when you should worry."

"So how do you do it? How do you get up every morning and make it through the day?"

"I remind myself that most things were beyond my control. I did the best I could in any given moment."

"I work so hard to stay calm, to be present," Tom said. "But it's just borrowed peace."

"Borrow anything long enough and it becomes yours," Evelyn replied.

Tom shook his head, not quite believing her.

"I'm also incredibly fortunate," Evelyn said. "I'm still surrounded by most of my team. We went through hell together. I could never try to explain what it was like behind enemy lines. With them, I don't have to try. They help me through the bad days and make me feel like I'm not alone. Why don't you spend some time with us? I know we weren't on the same missions, but we do understand what you've been through."

"I'm not ready," Tom said.

"When you are," Evelyn offered.

"What are you going to do with those pictures?" Tom asked.

"Burn them. I'll tell Kurt Vogel I found proof his family is gone. He doesn't need to know the details."

"I don't understand." Tom frowned. "He's already seen them."

"What?" Evelyn asked.

"During the war, Vogel went on strike. These photos were in a cache smuggled out by another team. General Anders, who was in charge of research and development, showed them to him as motivation to get back to work."

"That wasn't in his file," Evelyn said, confused.

"The army isn't known for advertising their mistakes. My friend who found the pictures said they were labeled top secret."

"But Kurt called General Gibson about the postcard. Why would he do that if he knew his family was dead?"

"Probably grabbed onto any hope they were alive. Maybe he thought the pictures were faked, or maybe he just wanted to believe they were still out there. Wouldn't you?"

That question stayed with Evelyn long after Tom left. She sat down to work but was distracted. Finally, she gave in and hobbled upstairs to Matthew's room. Taffy found her there an hour later, wearing one of Matthew's old sweaters, surrounded by letters and photographs.

"I miss him," Evelyn said by way of explanation.

"I still miss your mother," Taffy replied. "Doesn't mean we should hold a shrine to them."

Evelyn looked around the room with a sad smile.

"Sometimes when I'm here, it's like I'm fourteen again and he's going to walk through that door any minute."

"What about when you have to come back to the real world?" Taffy asked.

"Agony," Evelyn admitted. "I know I should pack all this away, but it's so hard. It makes his death seem final."

"I think your father felt the same way about your mother. Did you know he kept all her clothes?"

"Even after all this time?"

"I have something to show you."

Taffy led Evelyn into her parents' room. She went to the closet, opened the doors and found a large white cardboard box on the top shelf of Anna's closet. The edges were yellowed with age. Taffy pulled it down and set it on the bed.

"Open it."

Wrapped in tissue paper, Evelyn found long folds of white silk. Holding it up, she discovered a beautiful dress with delicate beading. It had a square neckline and a skirt that flared out into a small train.

"My mother's wedding dress," Evelyn said in surprise.

"First it was her debutante dress," Taffy replied.

"I didn't even know it was here."

"Try it on."

Taffy helped Evelyn into the dress, sliding it gently over her head. She did up the buttons in the back. Evelyn didn't recognize herself. Until that moment, she always thought she took after her father, but now she finally saw parts of her mother.

"We can take it to your friend Lily and have a few alterations done—"

"It's perfect," Evelyn exclaimed. She turned to Taffy and gave her a huge hug. "Thank you."

Taffy blushed and shrugged. "It's nothing."

"Not just for the dress," Evelyn said. "But for the planning and all the hard work. And understanding me well enough to know that this is exactly what I want."

"I love you, sweetheart," Taffy replied.

"I love you, too."

Evelyn looked at herself in the mirror, and for the first time, she could imagine her wedding. A bouquet of roses from the garden. Nick standing at the end of the aisle, a broad smile across his face. She felt the excitement of joining their lives together. Then she looked to the woman beside her who had done everything she could to be there for a girl who would always long for her mother.

"You should walk me down the aisle," Evelyn said.

Taffy looked at her in surprise. "Oh, no. I can't. It's not traditional."

"In case you hadn't noticed, neither am I. You said it's my wedding and I should have what I want."

"You really mean it?" Taffy asked.

Evelyn nodded.

"In that case, it would be my honor," Taffy said with a proud smile.

# Chapter 47

"You actually found a dress?" Nick asked.
"Out of everything I told you, that's your focus?"
Evelyn laughed.

"It's huge!"

"Taffy was so excited she made me go straight to Lily's to have it fitted. Leg brace and all."

They were lying in Nick's bed in the pool house. Evelyn snuggled close to him, resting her head on his chest. He ran his fingers through her hair, with the dark waves catching the low light. He loved these quiet moments. Having her beside him was all he needed to find peace. They were both drifting off when they heard the sound of a motor roar up the driveway.

"What the hell?" Evelyn asked, alarmed.

Nick sprang up and grabbed his gun. He threw on pants and ran outside, just in time to hear a car smash through the front door. In the distance, a man's figure, dressed in black, fled across the lawn. Nick chased him. Evelyn wrapped herself in a silk robe and limped toward the house to investigate. Before she got there, however, a huge explosion threw her backward. Flames raced through the ground floor and leaped out of the second-story windows.

"Taffy!" Evelyn screamed, rushing forward on her bad leg.

"Evie! No. I've got this," Nick yelled as he ran past her and threw open the kitchen door. The fire pushed him back. Evelyn hobbled around, looking for another way in. Then she heard a banging from the inside of the library. Taffy, looking panicked, struggled to get the window open. It wouldn't budge.

"Nick!" Evelyn yelled.

There was a sharp crack as half of the ceiling fell. They could no longer see Taffy. Nick searched for anything to break the glass.

"Here!" Evelyn yelled, tossing him an edging stone from one of the flower beds. Nick smashed the glass, then climbed through. It was an agonizing minute before he emerged with Taffy's inert body. He carried her across the lawn to fresh air. They knelt beside her, Evelyn's ear on her chest. Nick had her wrist and was checking for her pulse. Finally, Taffy began to cough.

Several hours later, the blaze was just starting to die down. Evelyn stood beside Nick, watching the only home she had ever known turn to embers. The roof had caved in, as had most of the second story. Every time something more collapsed, Evelyn shuddered as if it were a physical blow. Her eyes were dry, and Nick held her close. There was nothing he could do to alleviate her pain.

Finally, Taffy turned to Evelyn and said, "This isn't doing any good. We should find somewhere to go for the night."

Evelyn nodded without moving. Nick looked to their cars, but they were partially melted from the heat of the fire.

"I'll get one of the cops to call a taxi for us," he said, stepping away.

Taffy took his place, supporting Evelyn.

"Well," Evelyn said eventually. "You said I should clean out the house."

"I was thinking of a more subtle approach," Taffy replied.

Evelyn began to laugh and Taffy joined in. It wasn't a happy sound.

"You've survived worse," Taffy said sternly. "You'll survive this."

"I know," Evelyn replied quietly. "But it still hurts."

"Of course it does, sweetheart."

Taffy led Evelyn away from the remains of the Bishop mansion. "Thank God you and Nick were sleeping in the pool house instead of your room."

"You knew?" Evelyn asked.

"Of course."

"I thought you'd give me a lecture about propriety."

Taffy snorted. "I have better things to do."

At the foot of the driveway, they found Nick talking to Captain Wharton.

"We're gonna need a statement after you've had a chance to pull yourselves together," Wharton said. "Where can I reach you?"

Nick glanced to Evelyn.

"I . . . I haven't thought that far ahead," Evelyn replied uncertainly.

"How about the Chateau Marmont?" Taffy suggested. "We can stay in one of their cottages while we sort everything out."

Evelyn nodded her agreement, grateful she didn't have to make the decision, but Wharton put his foot down.

"Absolutely not. Usually, Gallagher's the one pissing people off, but between this and Berlin . . . ? Someone's trying to kill you. Five-star hotels are the first place they'll look."

"He has a point, Evie," Nick said. "We thought that bomb

was meant for General Gibson, but you didn't exactly come out unscathed. Now this?"

"You need somewhere completely unconnected to your life," Wharton insisted.

"I know a place," Nick assured him.

Rather than trusting a taxi, Wharton had a patrolman drive them. When they reached the address, Nick helped Evelyn and Taffy out of the car and up the front walk. The lights were off and the house was dark. Nick rang the bell. Silence. After a minute or two, he rang it again. Finally, Helen opened the door, looking as if she had just gone to bed.

"It's five in the morning," Helen said. Then she really looked at them, and her eyes widened. "What the hell happened to you?"

# Chapter 48

Evelyn woke in agony. More than just her injured leg, her lungs were scorched and she felt beyond exhausted. Every muscle ached from the tension of being powerless while her house went up in smoke. It was not the objects she mourned; it was the memories associated with them. No longer would she pass the doorframe where Matthew and her heights were measured every year. No longer could she drink tea from her father's favorite chipped mug or hold the baby blanket her mother knit for her. There was a new finality to the loss of her family.

The door opened, and Nick entered with a cup of coffee. He set it down on the nightstand and sat down beside Evelyn on the bed. She tried for a smile, but it never reached her lips. Nick put his arm around her and she wept all the tears that had not come the night before. She did not know how long she cried, only that when she finally pulled away, there was a large wet patch across Nick's shoulder.

"Your shirt," she said, for lack of anything better.

"I have others."

"Unlike me," she replied with gallows humor. Nick took it as a good sign.

"Hope you don't mind," he said, motioning to a chair in the corner, "but I took the liberty of calling Lily. She went shopping early this morning and brought over a few things."

Stacked in a neat pile were two pairs of slacks, two shirts, two sweaters, a simple dress, some shoes, and several changes of undergarments.

"She told me this should get you through the next few days, but she'll come by with more."

"God, I love her," Evelyn replied.

"Why don't you shower and we can discuss everything over breakfast? I have a doctor coming in an hour to look at your leg. You didn't do yourself any favors last night."

"Maybe not, but we're all here. We're all safe. I need to focus on that."

Nick tried to help her up, but she realized that she could not stand. He carried her to the bathroom and they cleaned off the previous night's ash together. Afterwards, they entered the kitchen to find Taffy sitting with two of Helen's employees, who were relaxing before the club opened at noon. The young women were dressed in short skirts and bustiers. One had a cardigan over her clothes, with reading glasses propped up on her head and a history textbook in front of her.

"I swear by it," Taffy was saying. "Pond's Cold Cream every night. Takes your makeup right off."

"My mom uses it," one of the women replied.

"Don't fuss with all that newfangled stuff," Taffy insisted. "They're just trying to get you to spend more money."

"Thanks," said the other woman as she adjusted her bustier. "And thanks for helping me make this thing more comfortable."

"Get to my age and you learn a couple of tricks."

"Care to share any others?" the first woman asked with a sly, joking smile.

"Some things are better to learn on your own," Taffy answered. "Though thirty years of a happy marriage teaches you a lot."

The two women were howling with laughter as Helen entered. They each gave Taffy a quick hug, then headed toward the front of the house.

"How are you feeling?" Helen asked Evelyn.

"Horrific," Evelyn replied. "But also, very grateful. Thank you for taking us in."

"Of course. I'm . . . I'm really sorry this happened to you."

Evelyn reached out and took Helen's hand. For a moment, Helen looked stunned, then she squeezed Evelyn's fingers in response. They turned as Gregory entered. Most of his bruises had faded, but the cut above his eye was still stitching itself back together.

"There's a gentleman here to see you," he informed Nick and Evelyn. "Carl Santos."

"I asked him to come by," Nick said.

"I'm afraid we're turning your house into Grand Central Station," Evelyn apologized to Helen.

"Just your average Wednesday," Helen replied as Earl entered.

"Did you find anything?" Nick asked, knowing that he had come from the ruins of Evelyn's house.

"It's still too hot to get close," Carl said. "Based on what you reported and the burn pattern, the fire marshal thinks that the car had an initial incendiary device."

"You mean a bomb," Evelyn clarified.

"Yep. The car was also filled with tanks of 'high-quality accelerant.'"

"In English?" Nick asked.

"Jet fuel," Carl said. "Which is rather ironic, all things considered."

"At least David can rest assured that someone is after me personally, rather than trying to derail the peace in Berlin."

"I wouldn't think jet fuel is easy to get a hold of," Taffy said.

"It's not," Nick agreed.

"I know one person who has plenty of it," Evelyn noted. "His job is to make it more efficient, so there's probably a lot laying around for experiments."

"Kurt Vogel," Nick replied.

"He blames you, me, and General Gibson for being separated from his family," Evelyn said. "I think he feels like if he had stayed in Berlin, he could have saved his wife and daughter. When we met at JPL, he called me Anna Schmidt, my old code name, but on a telegram to General Gibson, he asked for Evelyn Bishop. He must have seen the announcement in the *Los Angeles Times* when I took over as president of the company. That's how he knew to find me."

"You think he set the whole thing up with the postcard from Berlin?" Nick asked.

"Not alone, but yeah, I do. Perhaps we were supposed to get killed when I was first there, but he couldn't make it happen."

"Or he needed a way to get to Gibson, too," Nick suggested. "Didn't you mention that Kurt specifically asked the general to come to the meeting with the woman pretending to be his wife?"

"She wanted to have it at the professor's house instead of American HQ to make it easier on her daughter," Evelyn said. "When they met, I thought it was real. It's hard to fake that kind of emotion. Maybe there was a moment when he wanted to believe it was his wife. The whole trip there, he acted strangely. Just worked in this little notebook. Now that I think of it, we should check with David to see if it was in his pocket when they collected his clothes at the hospital."

"I'll bet that information was payment to the Russians for setting everything up," Carl replied. "The bureau's been going after Frank Malina at JPL, but they might be on the wrong path to find Russian spies."

"We don't have enough proof to arrest Kurt," Evelyn said. "Right now, it's all speculation."

"Give me a day or two," Carl said. "Let me see what I can dig up now that I know where to look."

"I'll call David and have him bring in Ilsa again for questioning," Evelyn replied. "And then there's Alexei . . ."

"You really think he's going to tell you the truth?" Nick asked.

"Maybe not, but I still have to ask the question," Evelyn said.

With their plans in place, Nick walked Carl out to his car.

"I need your thoughts on a few of your former coworkers. What do you know about McCauley and Anderson? I was supposed to have a chat with them this morning, but with everything going on . . ."

"I know them," Carl said in a voice that left no doubt as to his dislike.

"Think they would kill a suspect?"

"They're not known for their restraint. I could see them trying to arrest a person and getting a bit overzealous."

"Enough to put three bullets in him?"

"They couldn't hit the broad side of a barn." Carl snorted.

"What about these guys? Any thoughts on them?"

Nick handed Carl a list of Helen's clients who were members of the LAPD, with the veterans' names circled. Carl looked them over and pointed to three names.

"They work for Mickey Cohen. He wants a place taken out, Cohen tips off the cops and they raid it. Works out well for everyone. They get collars and Cohen handicaps a rival," Carl said.

"Anyone else?"

Carl pointed at another name.

"Russo always struck me as a stand-up guy. Might never set the world on fire, but honest. Got some family money, so I could see him coming to a place like this. He'd consider it getting an itch scratched, nothing more. These other guys I don't know anything about. Never really worked with them."

"Thanks," Nick said.

Carl looked down the page and stopped at Brian Caruso's name.

"You forgot him."

Nick frowned. "Didn't know he served."

"He banged up his knee getting off a boat in Italy and somehow managed to get an honorable discharge for medical reasons," Carl said. "Think they even gave him a Purple Heart."

"Really?" Nick asked. "You have any other insights into Caruso?"

"Beyond the obvious? He's a smug son of a bitch who's used to getting everything he wants and isn't great at accepting the word 'no.' I pulled a high-profile case last year and he told the whole station I wasn't a 'real' American. Went downhill from there. He's not the only reason I left, but he certainly didn't help matters."

"You know where to find him? Wharton says he's off until tomorrow."

"He once told me to pick up his dry cleaning," Carl said. "Said I could find his address in the phone book."

"Should I ask what happened to his clothes?"

"Let's just say there is a young man at my church who went to college in an extremely nice suit."

# Chapter 49

Caruso's house was red brick with white shutters. It had a neat lawn and a late-model Cadillac in the driveway. Located on Crescent Drive, north of Santa Monica Boulevard, it was squarely in the middle of Beverly Hills. Though not as large as the neighbors' homes, it was definitely outside an LAPD detective's salary.

Nick knocked on the door, but there was no answer. He rang the bell and knocked again. Still nothing. After the third unanswered knock, Nick stepped off the porch to look around. He found a gate to the backyard. A neatly trimmed green lawn was bordered by a few shade trees. There was nothing out there—not even a hammock, a patio chair or a grill for cooking. It was a strange place for a single man, especially one so intent on rising through the ranks. This kind of family home required a lot of upkeep. Nick looked towards the back windows, but all of them had their shades drawn. Then he made his way back to the front, where he knocked once again. This time he heard movement from inside. It was another long minute before a flustered Caruso opened the door.

"Gallagher. What are you doing here?"

"I tried you at the station, but Wharton said you were out on a personal matter."

"So you decided to bother me at home?"

"We got proof of life for Julia Martinez," Nick said. "Can I come in?"

"Now's not really a good time."

"I know you were one of Helen Brecker's clients. If you want to talk about visiting prostitutes on your front stoop, that's fine by me."

"Jesus, Gallagher, I got neighbors," Caruso said, ushering him inside.

The interior looked as though it came straight out of the Sears, Roebuck catalogue. Everything was a little too neat and a little too new, as though the plastic had just been pulled off after it was delivered. The carpet was pristine and the table did not have a scratch or a scuff. The couch cushions were perfectly flat as if no one had ever sat on them. There were no personal objects, just mass-produced art that looked like it came as part of a set. The whole place felt sterile and slightly creepy.

"Make it quick," Caruso snapped. "I'm kind of in the middle of things."

Nick handed him the doctored proof-of-life photo of Julia Martinez.

"She's alive," Caruso said.

"At least for now," Nick replied. "Why are you pretending not to recognize her?"

"The hell are you talking about?"

"You were at the club when Julia was working."

"Listen, I'm not proud of visiting a whorehouse, but sometimes a man has certain needs. The girls are clean and the place is discreet."

"Wow," Nick said. "Don't get too effusive."

"What do you want from me? Half the guys on the force visit hookers. More than a few have been to Brecker's club."

"I know, I have a list."

"And you're what? Blackmailing me?" Caruso demanded.

"If this was blackmail, you'd know," Nick replied. "I'm trying to get Julia Martinez home safely and you've been lying to me this whole time. Makes me wonder why."

"I genuinely don't have a clue who this girl is. All I know is that I didn't fuck her. Hell, she's not even my type. Why are you so obsessed with this case? These girls disappear all the time. No one misses them."

"Her family does," Nick said. "Despite the fact that you've done everything in your power to turn them against her. Why did you tell them she was a prostitute?"

"First you're on my ass because I'm not doing enough. Now you're giving me shit for doing too much. Which is it?"

Nick's hands curled into fists. He wasn't going to hit Caruso, but for a brief moment, he enjoyed the fantasy. Taking a few deep breaths, he looked around.

"You've done this place up nice," Nick said, stepping into the living room. He sat down on the couch and bounced a few times on the stiff cushions. Lying back, he put up his feet.

"Comfy," Nick said.

Caruso swatted his shoes off the furniture, then brushed away the specks of dirt Nick had transferred onto the fabric.

"What are you doing?"

Nick ignored the question, as he stood up and walked around the room. He ran his finger over the empty bookshelf. No dust.

"Must have a great cleaning woman," Nick observed.

"Get the hell out of my house," Caruso said.

Nick continued looking around, noticing a small indent

in the carpet. A chair had been moved and put back just slightly askew. Nick ran his hand along the wall behind it.

"This is nice wallpaper. Did you install it yourself?"

"Do I need to have a couple of buddies come over and arrest you?"

Nick's fingers felt a slight hole, where a screw had been drilled into the wall, probably holding a picture frame . . . or perhaps a medal case. Nick bent down, pretending to tie his shoe and there, under the chair that was moved, he saw something shiny. He scooped it up.

"I'm going to find Julia," Nick promised, straightening up to look Caruso in the eye. "When I do, I'll make sure her kidnapper will never hurt her, or anyone else, ever again."

"Out," Caruso growled.

Nick left. He drove a few blocks before looking at what he had found on the carpet. It was Julia's necklace.

Nick's next stop was the police station. Once again, the duty sergeant tried to stop him, and once again, Nick made it to Wharton's office.

"You need a better guard out front," Nick chided.

"And you need to start listening when someone tells you no," Wharton replied.

"If he really meant it, he would've tried harder."

"I'm not talking about him. Got a call from Brian Caruso saying you were over at his house. Said you harassed him and refused to leave. How much of that is true?"

"About eighty-five percent. I was definitely there and I definitely overstayed my welcome. If that's harassment . . . ?"

"He's filing a complaint. Wants your license revoked and to see you tossed in a cell."

"Already been there," Nick replied. "Recently. Besides, I don't give a shit what Caruso wants. He kidnapped Julia Martinez."

"You start throwing accusations like that around, you'll find yourself in even deeper shit," Wharton warned. "Those cops out there are tight. If you pick this battle, you'd better be certain."

Nick pulled out Julia's proof-of-life photo.

"Look at her necklace."

Wharton took the picture and glanced at it. When he looked up at Nick, it was dangling from his fingertips.

"Found this in Caruso's living room."

"You know he'll say you planted it."

"But you believe me?" Nick asked.

Wharton was silent for a long while.

"Doesn't matter," Wharton said eventually. "There's no way I can get a search warrant. Every single judge in this city thinks the sun shines out of Caruso's ass."

"She's in there, Captain," Nick insisted. "I know she is."

"What reason could he possibly have for taking her?"

"I'll bet if I showed his picture around campus, all her friends will point him out as her stalker. It explains why she told her friends to just ignore it. She knew there was nothing she could do because he was a cop. He's got a screw loose and became obsessed with her. She wasn't interested. He refused to take no for an answer."

"You don't know this guy," Wharton said. "He can talk his way out of anything. There won't be prison in his future. Instead, the mayor will give him a medal for finding her and reward his 'dedication to the service.' The guy's untouchable."

"What if there's a murder charge?" Nick asked. "Joey Gallo was looking for dirt on a cop he thought planted a gun on his brother Bobby. You said it yourself. These guys worship Caruso. If he had a run-in with Bobby a few weeks before, how hard would it be for Caruso to suggest McCauley find a gun in his car? Gallo's been on a mission and I'd guess he discovered a few more things beyond his brother's frame-up. Probably how he ended up in the LA River."

"Even if you could prove it, no jury's going to convict him. Caruso will claim self-defense and most people will probably think it's a public service. Gallo was a mobster."

"So, you're telling me this guy's just going to walk free," Nick said with disgust. "What's to stop him from taking someone else?"

"I'm telling you there's nothing *I* can do," Wharton replied.

The two men stared at each other for a long moment. Finally, Nick nodded.

"Understood."

# Chapter 50

Nick walked out of the police station and made a few calls. Carl got a friend in vice to let Caruso know they had a lead on Helen's photographs. If anything could lure him out at Caruso's house, it was that. When Nick arrived, the detective's car was still in the driveway. After twenty minutes, the front door opened. Caruso stepped out looking slightly harried in wrinkled khakis. Glancing over his shoulder, he got in his car and peeled out of the driveway. Nick waited a minute more to make sure he was really gone, then broke into the house. Trying every door, Nick finally reached a closed one in back and picked the lock. He opened it to find Julia Martinez, standing alert. She was chained to a bolt in the floor.

"Who are you?" she asked, alarmed. Then, looking closer, "Nick Gallagher?"

"And this from a woman who can't remember names," Nick said, recalling their first conversation. "Helen Brecker sent me to bring you home. I found your necklace when I was here earlier today. I know your boyfriend Gabe gave it to you a few months ago."

Nick held it out to her. Julia smiled at it briefly before slipping it into her pocket.

"I'm going to unshackle you," Nick said. "You don't have to come with me. It's your choice, but if you want to leave, I'll take you anywhere you want to go."

Julia sat down on the bed and extended her leg. Nick pulled out his tools and sprang the lock holding the chain together. Julia's ankle had red angry sores from where the metal rubbed her skin. Just then, they heard the sound of a car horn warning them from outside.

"He's back," Nick whispered as he quietly shut the bedroom door. Pulling his gun, he stepped in front of Julia as they heard Caruso enter the house. "Stay behind me. If you get a chance to run, take it."

Footsteps came down the hall and turned into another room. Nick and Julia held their breath. Then the footsteps returned, stopped for a moment. The door flew inward. Caruso entered, his gun drawn.

"I knew you were getting a bit too suspicious," Caruso said to Nick. "Julia, come here."

"No." The strength in her voice impressed Nick.

"Julia!" Caruso commanded. "Come here right now or I will be forced to punish you later."

She didn't move.

"I'm just trying to protect you," Caruso said. "This man has broken into our house. He'll be shot as an intruder."

"Our house?" Nick asked. "What exactly do you think is going on here? Somehow this isn't a kidnapping?"

Caruso's finger tightened on the trigger. Nick pulled Julia to the ground as Caruso fired his gun. Nick rolled to his feet and charged at Caruso. They tumbled out into the hall and smashed against the wall, sending a few pieces of catalogue art crashing to the ground. They fought for the gun and Caruso fired again. The bullet lodged in the ceiling, raining down bits of plaster. Nick broke Caruso's grip on the gun. It clattered to the floor, then Nick grabbed him and dragged him into the living room.

"Julia, go!" Nick said.

She didn't have to be told twice. Without a backward glance, she rushed outside. Caruso struggled against Nick, elbowing him in the ribs. Nick let out a soft grunt of pain but did not slacken his grip. Caruso twisted and drove the side of his hand into Nick's neck, breaking free. He dove for the sofa, grabbing a gun from underneath. Standing up, he found Nick with his gun out, waiting for him.

"What's the play?" Nick asked. "Wharton knows you kidnapped Julia."

"Then why isn't he here?" Caruso taunted. "Maybe 'cause he can't touch me."

"Then there's the question of Julia. Were you going to keep her here forever?"

"Don't fucking say her name!" Caruso yelled. "She's mine."

"Is she?" Nick intoned. "Seems pretty eager to get away."

"Shut up! Shut up! I just need a minute to think. Julia . . . Julia will be fine. I saved her from you. Yeah, that's it," Caruso said. "No one's going to believe a whore."

"Saved her from me?" Nick asked, incredulously.

"You're in my house because you're trying to frame me for Julia's kidnapping," Caruso mumbled to himself. "You brought her here."

"Why would I do that?"

"Because I have dirt on you!"

"There are exactly three people in this world whose opinions I care about and they already know everything about me," Nick said. "Do your worst."

"What if it's not you I have information about? How well do you really know Carl Santos?"

Nick did not respond.

"I could tell you things about him—"

Nick tackled Caruso knocking the gun from his hand once again. This time he drove Caruso out the door and onto the lawn. They wrestled across the grass, trading punches.

"Enough!"

Caruso looked up to see Evelyn, leaning against his car, with her gun pointing at him. Julia was beside her.

"It's over," Evelyn said to Caruso, who slowly found his feet.

"How did you know he'd turn back?" Nick asked Evelyn.

"Seemed wise to prepare for any eventuality. Did you genuinely forget something?" Evelyn asked Caruso. "Or did finding the photographs seem too convenient?"

"Fuck you," Caruso said.

"Then answer this question, just for my own piece of mind," Nick said. "Why did you kill Joey Gallo?"

"He was a piece of shit, like his brother."

"Must have found something really juicy," Evelyn guessed.

"Doesn't matter," Caruso said. "There's no judge in this whole state who'll convict me."

"I know." Nick sighed. Then he called out, "He's all yours."

Norman Roth stepped out of a car parked on the street. Three large men got out, as well. For the first time, Caruso looked afraid.

"Joey Gallo was one of our own," Roth said. "An example must be made."

"You won't get away with this!" Caruso insisted.

Roth's men grabbed Caruso's arms and he struggled against them.

"Let me go!" Caruso yelled. "I'm a cop! I'm a cop!"

The other man lifted his legs so he was strung between them, absolutely helpless. Realizing there was no way out,

Caruso began to cry. He looked around to Nick, Evelyn, and, eventually, to Julia. "Please. Please don't let them take me."

Julia walked up to Caruso. For a moment, he looked hopeful, a slight smile playing across his lips. She got very close to him and said, "You will never hurt me or my family again."

Then she stepped back to stand beside Evelyn, her expression hard. The men dragged a screaming, crying Caruso and threw him in the trunk of a car. Roth held out his hand to Nick and Evelyn in turn.

"Glad we could help one another," Roth said.

"And I'm glad we're even," Evelyn replied.

Roth studied her for a long minute, nodded once, walked back to his car, and drove away.

"It's really over?" Julia asked Nick.

He nodded. Her knees buckled and she slid down the side of the car until she was sitting in a heap. Great sobs wracked her body, and for a long time, all she could do was cry.

Helen's club was the most convenient place to take Julia. For the first time in years, Helen closed for the night, wanting to give Julia as much peace and privacy as possible. After she had showered and changed into fresh clothes, she was ready to tell them the story. Caruso first saw Julia when she was tending bar. He tried to get her to go upstairs with him, but when he found out she only poured drinks, his interest spiked. He came in a few more times to ask her out, but she refused, telling him she was not allowed to date. She had no idea how he learned where she went to school, but he started showing up on campus. Then one night he followed her home. That was when she got really scared. It wasn't like she could go to the cops, and she did not know how to make him go away.

"Why didn't you tell me?" Helen asked.

"You didn't need that kind of trouble," Julia said. "Besides, he stopped coming around here. He wasn't your problem."

"My protection doesn't end at the door," Helen insisted.

"When Caruso heard about Rosa landing in the hospital, he got there first," Julia said. "She thought he was the cop assigned to her case and told him about Gallo asking for the photos. When he took me, he claimed it was for my own protection. Then he chained me up and said I'd be free as soon as I loved him like he loved me. Told me he bought the house right after we met because he knew we were soulmates. One day soon I would come around and we needed room for our children. He actually expected me to marry him."

For a moment, no one knew how to respond.

"So, he was crazy?" Evelyn asked eventually.

"As a cat in a brick shit house on the Fourth of July," Julia concurred.

Just then, there was a knock at the door. Nick opened it to reveal Gabe. He looked anxious, but when he saw Julia, a broad, relieved smile crossed his face. He rushed to her but stopped before embracing her.

"What's wrong?" she asked.

"I want to hug you, but you might not be ready, and that's okay," Gabe began. "These past weeks everything was out of your control. I don't know if he . . . how he . . . what happened, but you never got the chance to say no. I'm here for you, however you need. I just want you to feel safe with me."

Julia wrapped her arms around him.

"I worried you thought I was broken," she said.

"You're perfect," Gabe replied. "No matter what, you'll always be perfect to me."

Julia buried her face in his chest and he held her close. This was how her mother and Camila found her when they arrived a few minutes later.

"Julia!" Camila cried, throwing her arms around her sister and Gabe. For a moment, Elizabeth stood uncertainly. Carefully, Julia stepped out of Gabe's arms.

"Mama?" Julia started. "I know what that man told you and Papa. It wasn't true. I've never slept with men for money. I have the morals that you instilled in me. But I also have Gabe. He's a good man. I know this is not how you and Papa expected things to go, but I love him. You have to be okay with that. You have to be okay with me."

Elizabeth nodded, tears streaming down her face. "I couldn't lose you, too, *mija*. Nothing else matters besides you being safe."

Julia hugged her mother, then opened her arms for Camila. They held each other for several minutes before Julia asked the question she had been dreading.

"Y Papa?"

Camila let out a long string of expletives, cursing her father's stubbornness. Elizabeth just shook her head.

# Chapter 51

Evelyn was sitting at Helen's kitchen table with piles of reports covering every inch of it. Nick had left early in the morning to see Captain Wharton, Taffy was shopping for new clothes, and Helen was in her office doing work. Julia came downstairs, wearing oversize pajamas with the sleeves rolled back. Not being welcome at home, Helen offered her a room for as long as she wanted to stay.

"Morning," Evelyn said. "Coffee's on the stove."

"Thanks," Julia said, pouring herself a cup. "Want any?"

Evelyn shook her head and cleared space for Julia to sit.

"How are you?" Evelyn asked. "Sorry, that's a stupid question."

"No one really knows what to say to someone who's been kidnapped by a cop and held hostage for weeks. Somehow, Emily Post forgot to include that chapter."

Evelyn laughed.

"Why are you staying here, again?" Julia asked. "I wasn't paying attention last night."

"Someone's trying to kill me," Evelyn said.

"Oh, is that all?"

"Happens more often than you'd think."

"Well, no one's life is perfect," Julia replied. She turned back to her coffee, then glanced at the pages in front of Evelyn. "What are you working on?"

"I'm trying to expand my factory and need to make sure I have the money for construction."

"May I?" Julia asked.

Amused, Evelyn handed over the pages.

"Please tell me you can find a magic account hidden somewhere."

"If only," Julia replied. "I have no idea about the money, but it's going to be a lot easier to figure out if you rearrange your data. You need a summary page, rather than glancing back and forth and trying to keep all these numbers in your head."

Julia grabbed a sheet of paper and flipped it over to the blank side. She glanced at Evelyn, who nodded. Then she sketched a new table, inputting information from all the different sources.

"Here. Should make a lot more sense," Julia said, showing Evelyn her work.

"You're brilliant," Evelyn marveled.

"I have to do it for my accounting classes. The way most people organize things makes no sense whatsoever."

"You're at UCLA?"

Julia nodded. "Initially, I wanted to go to Cal Tech, but . . ."

"Heaven forbid we sully their hallowed halls with our delicate lady brains," Evelyn said.

"I like you," Julia said with a smile.

"The feeling's mutual," Evelyn assured her.

Just then, Helen walked into the kitchen.

"At this rate, I'm going to need to get a new phone line installed just for you," she grumbled. "Do you know how many people call here for you? I thought you were supposed to be in hiding."

"Apologies," Evelyn replied, chagrinned. "Can I take it in your office?"

Helen nodded. Evelyn could not blame her annoyance. Ruth called several times a day with updates from the office, as well as David, giving her news from Germany. Last they spoke, David went to question Ilsa, but she had disappeared without a trace. Evelyn made her way to Helen's office and picked up the phone.

"Hello?" she said into the receiver. It was Carl.

"We have proof," he said. "Kurt Vogel is spying for the Russians."

"You going to pick him up?" Evelyn asked.

"Arranging a team now. Thought you might want a word before we brought him in."

"I'll meet you there in an hour."

Evelyn hung up the phone, thought for a minute, then dialed a number in Berlin. It was one she was not supposed to have. Getting a call from America would do him no favors, yet she didn't bother hiding her accent. A soldier answered the phone and she asked for Alexei Antonov.

"You trying to get me killed?" he asked when he finally came on the line.

"Could ask you the same question," Evelyn countered. "Did you set the bomb?"

There was a long moment of silence, broken only by the static of the long-distance call.

"No."

"Tell me how much I have right," Evelyn said. "Just between old friends. An American scientist comes to you and offers not only his research but also to sabotage America's development of rocket fuel. In exchange, he needs your help getting revenge for his family. He doesn't know who left them behind and he can't get to the people who actually killed his wife and child, so he'll settle for the ones who took him out of Berlin. One of whom is still in the army. Another he can't find, but the last was just featured in the newspaper. He needs you to arrange a way to lure them to Berlin. Am I getting close?"

"I didn't know it was going to be you," Alexei said eventually.

"You must have realized when I looked you up," Evelyn replied.

"Things were already in motion. It was out of my hands. I did try to warn you."

"Not strongly enough," Evelyn said. "I saved your life."

"That was then and this is now. The world has changed."

"I didn't think *you* would change."

"Then perhaps you never knew me. Don't call again."

Alexei hung up the phone, leaving Evelyn with nothing more than a severed connection.

Evelyn pulled up outside Kurt's building at JPL. Nervous energy thrummed through her. Alexei's betrayal cut deep. Evelyn believed the bonds she formed during the war were unbreakable. Maybe she was naïve to believe that trumped nationalism. Or perhaps the Soviet Union could grind that instinct out of a person. After all, survival was paramount.

Carl pulled up and got out of his car.

"The building's circled. We just have to bring him out," he said.

Evelyn opened her glove box and reached for the gun she kept in there.

"Sorry, Evie, bureau rules. No armed civilians," Carl

said. "No one wants a trigger-happy agent shooting you by accident."

"You know, I hate it when you're logical," Evelyn replied, setting the gun back down.

Together, they walked up the stairs to the second floor. Evelyn stepped up to the door of the office and knocked.

"Enter!" a voice barked.

They found Kurt standing at his chalkboard, writing an equation. He didn't turn around, seemingly oblivious to their presence. After a minute of being ignored, Evelyn went to the board and erased the number three next to the symbol for oxygen, replacing it with the number two. Finally, Kurt looked at her.

"Those weren't the equations you wrote in your little book on the way to Berlin," Evelyn said.

"What the hell do you think you're doing?"

"Triatomic oxygen is highly unstable. Likely to explode under practical conditions in an engine, or perhaps when driven through a person's house."

Kurt set down the chalk and turned to look at her.

"So, you figured it out."

"It was your choice to flee Germany," Evelyn said. "I didn't make the decision to split up your family. I wasn't responsible for getting them out of Berlin. I didn't turn them into the Nazis and I didn't kill them. The only thing I did was keep you safe."

"And alive," Kurt said.

"And alive," Evelyn agreed.

"That's what I can't forgive. Do you have any idea what it was like seeing the pictures of their deaths? Knowing how much they suffered? If I had been there, the Nazis would have just taken me. I could have protected them."

"You don't know that," Carl replied. "The SS was filled

with madmen who killed Jews for sport. How were you supposed to fight against that?"

"Germany needed me," Kurt insisted.

"They needed a lot of people they killed," Evelyn said. "There were brilliant minds in Auschwitz and Dachau and Bergen-Belson and Ravensbrück and—"

"Stop!" Kurt cried. "Just stop."

"You weren't the only one who suffered," Carl added. "You weren't the only one who lost someone they loved."

"While looking for Hannah and Sophie, I talked to a lot of people who knew them," Evelyn said. "Each and every one mentioned Hannah's kindness. How do you think she'd feel about what you've done? Do you really think she'd want you to seek revenge?"

"You didn't know her," Kurt snapped. "You don't know anything about her."

"Would she recognize the person you've become?"

Kurt's shoulders slumped. He walked back to his desk and sat behind it, collapsing into his chair.

"Sometimes I see young girls, twelve, thirteen, and think that could be Sophie," Kurt began. "I wonder what she'd be learning in school or if she might have her first crush. Sometimes I'm at a party and I turn to tell my wife something, only to realize she's not there. She'll never be there. Every morning there's that instant between sleeping and wake, where I imagine my life has meaning again. That I am whole. Then I open my eyes to reality. I am haunted by them."

Kurt withdrew a gun from his drawer and pointed it at Evelyn. Carl was equally fast.

"Put it down," Carl warned, his gun level.

Kurt began to squeeze the trigger. There was a loud bang, and Kurt's head snapped backward, a single bullet between his eyes. The gun slid from his lifeless hands. Carl kicked it away, then moved to the body and felt for a pulse.

Looking at Evelyn, he shook his head. From the hallway came the footsteps of a dozen FBI agents running toward them. Carefully, Carl holstered his weapon as the door burst open. Men in suits flooded in. From across the chaos, Evelyn looked to Carl.

"Thank you."

It felt inadequate, but she did not know what else to say. Perhaps, in time, she would find the words.

# Chapter 52

Nick and Evelyn surveyed the remains of her home. Two blackened chimneys stood tall against the sky, with burned bricks crumbled among the ashes. The pool was cracked and filled with broken rafters that fell when their underpinnings collapsed. The rosebushes next to the house were gone, and even the driveway was a charred wreck. Carefully, Evelyn walked over the ruins, kicking through the little that survived with the toe of her boot. A few things she crouched down to look at, checking to see if they were anything she recognized. Anything she could salvage. She picked up a few shapes and brushed them off. After a minute, she tossed them back into the heap. Nick was there to support her, both emotionally and physically, as she was still limping on her unhealed leg. Finally, Evelyn hobbled out of the rubble and stood on the singed lawn. The only building still standing was the smoke-stained pool house that had somehow survived the worst of the fire.

"We're safe. Taffy's safe. Our friends are safe," she said, reciting a litany of blessings.

"And we have each other," Nick added.

She slid her arms around him and leaned her head against his shoulder.

"I'm pretty sure our wedding invitations were in the house," Evelyn said.

"At least they didn't go out yet. We may need to change the venue."

"The background isn't quite as picturesque as we hoped."

"Though it's definitely dramatic," Nick offered.

"You once told me you wanted a little house on the beach," Evelyn said.

"With a room for just books?" Nick asked, remembering a conversation they had during the war.

"I think we could make it more than two weeks without killing each other," Evelyn said. "I found a place for us to rent while we figure out what we want to do next."

"Won't we rebuild?" Nick asked.

"Maybe," Evelyn said. "Or maybe we'll find somewhere else. I know this never felt like your home, but our next place will."

"Thank you," he said, grateful she had given voice to something he would never admit.

They drove out to Santa Monica to see the house. It was three bedrooms, with a front lawn that opened onto the beach. To Nick, it was like a dream. They signed the lease and made plans to move in immediately.

"I was thinking we could get married here," Evelyn said, looking at the expansive view. "Rather than having giant centerpieces of hothouse flowers, we could get wildflowers and dune grass. Lunch, rather than a five-course meal. Something simple, with our closest friends and family."

"That sounds perfect," Nick said. "At the end of the day, the only thing that matters is that I get to be your husband."

Evelyn leaned over and kissed him. After all the stress of trying to plan a giant event, she felt the relief of getting exactly what she wanted.

Later that night, Evelyn and Nick sat at the bar in Helen's club with Taffy beside them. They made a strange sight in the room full of men, but they were celebrating their final evening as Helen's guests.

"I'll bet you're glad to see the last of us," Evelyn said to Helen.

"It's been good getting to know the woman who makes Nick so happy. I admit, I was skeptical at first."

"Because I'm not his type?" Evelyn asked.

"Because the Nick I knew was a survivor. Our happy endings rarely come without strings, but you two really love each other," Helen said. "Plus, for being a rich, spoiled socialite, you're not that bad."

"Stop with the effusive praise." Evelyn laughed. "You're going to make me blush."

Carl entered, looking tired in the way of a person who's spent too many hours sitting behind a desk. There was a slight restlessness to him and his eyes were blurry.

"Still in paperwork hell?" Evelyn asked as he took a seat beside her.

"Should've just let you carry a gun," he said. "Every form needs to be typed in triplicate. Plus, the official interviews and after-action reports."

"I'm happy to tell them how grateful I am to you for saving my life," she offered.

"Any chance you could tell them all about Vogel's spy ring?" Carl asked. "My bosses are torn between being glad I found a spy at JPL and angry he can't implicate others."

"He was probably acting alone," Nick said. "I don't think he was idealistic about Communism."

"Russia was just the means to an end," Evelyn agreed.

Julia approached with a fresh round of drinks. She was back to work, efficient as ever, but her smile was slightly dimmed.

"Three Old Fashioneds, a vodka martini, and a glass of champagne," she said, setting the drinks in front of Evelyn, Nick, Carl, Helen, and Taffy. "Cheers!"

They raised their glasses to one another and drank.

"This is incredible," Evelyn said to Julia. "Is there anything you can't do?"

"Fly," Julia joked.

"Would you like to learn?" Evelyn asked.

"Sure. You're gonna help me to grow wings?"

"I was thinking of a plane, but either way. I'm offering you a job," Evelyn said.

"I don't understand."

"I know you've been working here a while and if you want to stay, I respect that," Evelyn said. "But I'm looking for a new assistant. It needs to be someone who's whip-smart, brilliantly organized, and really, really good at handling people. Plus, I think we could learn a lot from each other."

"I . . . I don't know," Julia said.

"What are you making here?" Evelyn asked. Julia told her the number. "I'll double it."

Julia's eyes widened. Evelyn shrugged.

"It's more than the typical starting salary, but it's an incredibly difficult job. You're the only person I've met who I think could do it."

A slight smile played across Julia's face and there was tempered excitement in her eyes.

"I have another semester of school," she said. "I'll be the first person in my family to graduate college. I want to be an example for my sister."

"How about you start part-time? My current assistant knows everything under the sun. Once there's an end in sight, she might be willing to stay on a bit longer to help you get acclimated and finish your degree. Then you'd come on full-time."

"I, uh . . ." Julia began, glancing toward Helen.

"After everything that's happened, you're not yourself," Helen said. "You're not as comfortable. You'll always be welcome here, but I think Evelyn's offering you something better. You can grow and have a real career. You can tell your parents about it."

Carl, in his capacity as an FBI agent, had gone over to the Martinez house to explain Julia's kidnapping to her parents. His badge meant that Diego was willing to hear the whole story, but his resolve did not soften. He still refused to allow her to come home.

"Plus, if you like, you can move into my pool house," Evelyn offered. "It's a bit smoke-stained, but we can get it into shape."

"You have all the answers," Julia said. "I don't want you to do this because you feel sorry for me."

"Everything I'm offering is because I'm selfish," Evelyn said. "I wish we had met under better circumstances, but I'm offering you this job because I genuinely think you'll make my life easier. I also like the idea of someone staying at my old house. You can tell me if something else falls apart."

"Everything's happening so quickly," Julia said.

"There's no pressure. Why don't you come to the office tomorrow. You can look around, meet Ruth, and see if it's a good fit."

"Okay." Julia nodded.

"Plus, I'll teach you to fly."

That got a bright smile out of Julia.

"It feels like freedom," Evelyn promised.

# Chapter 53

It was a crisp, sunny day in early January when Nick and Evelyn got married. Julia, who now lived in the pool house, informed Evelyn her mother's roses had returned. Not even the flames could kill them. Work was back to usual and Ruth adored Julia. They grew thick as thieves. Evelyn often walked in to see them laughing together over a private joke. Carl earned a commendation for his investigation of Kurt Vogel. Despite all the paperwork, it was a nice validation in a job Carl had yet to find truly fulfilling. Nick and Evelyn, meanwhile, turned the beach house into a home. Though it came furnished, Evelyn bought blankets and pillows to make it comfortable. Nick found books at the local shop to fill their shelves and give them something to do during restless nights when the past intruded on the present. Though those times would never fully go away, he and Evelyn often fell asleep with the windows open, listening to the sound of the crashing waves.

They offered Taffy a place with them, but she felt they cramped her style. She had grown to love the weather in Los Angeles and she knew Evelyn needed her more than she was willing to admit. Continuing to do philanthropic work, Taffy's social calendar was always full. She bought a house in Beverly Hills and decorated it with her personal flare. On the walls, she hung modern artists like Picasso, Chagall and Mondrian that she collected during her travels. Evelyn had to admit, the woman had style.

Rather than mail out invitations to their wedding, Evelyn and Nick called their close friends to tell them the date and time. The morning of their marriage, a new Packard arrived in the driveway. It was a gift from Norman Roth, with regrets that he could not attend the festivities.

"Can we keep it?" Nick asked.

"I think he'd be insulted if we sent it back," Evelyn replied, tossing Nick the keys. "It's more your style than mine."

While Nick looked over the last-minute arrangements and helped the caterers find their way in the small kitchen, Evelyn got ready in the upstairs bedroom. Her wedding dress was spared the fire by virtue of being at Lily's salon for alterations. It fit beautifully, and somehow, despite the years, it felt modern and fresh. Julia brought fresh roses from the house and Colette wove them through Evelyn's hair. For the first time in a year, Colette wore something other than black. Her cobalt-blue dress set off the color of her eyes.

"George would've been so happy to see this day," she said. "He'd never forgive me for wearing mourning during this wonderful occasion."

"I wish he could've been here, too," Evelyn replied.

"I have something for you," Colette announced, handing over a large envelope.

Evelyn opened it to find the final approval for her factory expansion.

"What? How?"

"I had a chat with Alan Hunsaker in his office. He brought these over yesterday."

"Wait," Lily asked, "he brought them to your house?"

"This might have less to do with Bishop Aeronautics," Evelyn said. "And more to do with someone having a crush on you."

Colette blushed and shook her head.

Whichever it was, this was another step towards fulfilling Logan's dream. Evelyn always missed her father, but today more than most. The night before, she slipped out to a pay phone a few blocks away. Armed with a mountain of quarters, she called a small house in Cuba where her father lived. They talked about everything and nothing. Hearing his voice was the present she gave herself when she needed it most. She told him all the details about the ceremony.

"Not that you need it," Logan began. "But you and Nick have my blessing."

"Thank you," she said.

"Any last-minute jitters?" he asked with fatherly concern.

"No," she replied. "Of all the things I question, whether to spend the rest of my life with Nick is not one of them."

"I hope, one day, to get to know him better."

"You'll like him," Evelyn promised.

"Of course I will," Logan replied. "You chose him."

When she was dressed, Evelyn went downstairs with Colette, Lily, and Taffy beside her. Evelyn thought the idea of bridesmaids was silly, but she also knew it was a nice way to honor the women who had become her closest friends. They walked ahead of her down the grassy aisle. Nick's face glowed with happiness. Beside him, Carl acted as best man, with the rings tucked into his jacket pocket. Evelyn slid her arm through Taffy's.

"I know this isn't the wedding you dreamed of . . ." Evelyn began.

"This is even better because it's yours. My mother planned

mine and I resented the hell out of her for it. Somehow, I forgot that."

"You were just trying to help," Evelyn replied. "And to be honest, I think we needed the kick in the pants."

Taffy laughed, and together they headed toward the makeshift altar. Evelyn's eyes found Nick's. In that instant, they were the only two people in the world. Then she looked around at those in attendance.

David flew in from Germany, and though jet-lagged beyond belief, his smile betrayed his excitement. Ruth stood beside Julia, who brought Gabe. Helen and Gregory stood in the third row. To Evelyn's surprise, Helen looked almost emotional. Theresa, General Gibson's widow, had driven down for the day, knowing how much this would have delighted her husband. In the very back stood Tom Rivers. Evelyn had invited him on impulse and was pleasantly surprised to see he came.

Not being religious, Evelyn and Nick had a judge perform the ceremony, with the promise to obey conveniently left out. It didn't seem like something either of them could manage for a lifetime. Evelyn never thought she would feel sentimental about her wedding, but Nick was right. Proclaiming their love in front of the most important people in their lives held deep meaning. She always felt committed to Nick, but now it was something more. In the eyes of the world, they were family.

# Author's Note

Years ago, I got a master's degree in "Interdisciplinary Studies and Social Thought." It's the kind of thing a person does when they know they want to write, have no idea how to turn that desire into a career and conveniently forget they'll have to repay student loans.

At the time, America was gearing up to invade Iraq. While visiting a neighbor, I saw a graphic on her TV that read "America vs. Iraq". Whatever else war is, it should not be advertised like a boxing match. This image stuck with me as I designed my own course of study, looking at the way war is reflected in art and literature. This was the start of my life-long interest in what happens to people after a conflict ends. How does an individual and a society make sense of the carnage? How do they move forward?

The Berlin airlift has all these questions wrapped up into a particularly complex moment in time. On a global scale, two major countries, the United States and Russia went from allies to enemies in less than three years. On a personal level, Germans, who committed horrible crimes against humanity, struggled to find basic necessities while keeping themselves and their families safe. American soldiers, who lost many friends in the quest to defeat Germany, risked their lives to ensure West Berlin had enough food and coal to keep its citizens alive. I found a few books incredibly helpful while researching this period. They include, but are not limited to: *Candy Bombers* by Andrei Cherny; *The German War* by Nicholas Stargardt; *Aftermath: Life in the Fallout of the Third Reich, 1945–1955* by Harald Jähner; and *Postwar: A History of Europe Since 1945* by Tony Judt.

Additionally, one of the central elements of the noir genre is the corruption of authority, most often the police. The assumption of good and evil is turned upside down. It's hard to feel safe when you don't know who you can trust. A great book dealing with the complex relationship between the police and the Mafia is *L.A. Noir* by John Buntin.

I am indebted to Michelle Teodo, an archivist at the Jet Propulsion Laboratory. She gave me documents and photographs from the late 1940s that really made that era come alive. JPL is one of my favorite places. They send robots into space, while exploring other planets and their moons. They study our climate while also searching for the origins of the universe. I have visited many times, both for lectures and tours and I am always amazed by their work.

In the late 1940s, America was at the beginning of the Red Scare. The FBI accused Frank Malina, one of the founders of JPL, of being a communist. While there was a great deal of Russian espionage during the Cold War, there were also many lives ruined by unfair accusations. The House Un-American Activities Committee and Senator Joseph McCarthy targeted people from businessmen, to housewives, to those in the entertainment industry . . . and many others.

# Acknowledgments

A huge thank you to my agent, Kathy Green. I am so grateful for your kindness, encouragement, and for believing in me and these books. John Scognamiglio you are an incredible editor, who gives the best notes. Thank you for your patience, understanding and support. To the amazing team at Kensington, you have done such a brilliant job making these books better and getting them out into the world.

Dave Ihlenfeld, thank you for your time and your utter brilliance. Leif Lillehaugen, sometimes I need you to tell me to just go write the thing. Tracey Nyberg West, I so appreciate you standing up beside me and making me look good.

As I was finishing this book, my life fell apart. I am deeply indebted to those who held me together and made the impossible, manageable: Neda Laiteerapong, Missy Stamler, Ken and Judy Freedman, Marcia Adelman, Madeline Woodward, Richard Fischoff, Carol Anne Been, Lois Glick and Pat Benenson. I don't know how I would have gotten through this year without your help. You will forever be in my heart.

To CeCe Pleasants Adams, Jessica Yarkin, Ezra Siegel, Jessica Stebbins Bina, Alex Dueben, Tucker Hughes, and Danielle Lindemann. You are there through the good, the bad, and the ugly. I am so lucky to have you in my life.

To my son's teachers, my work is only possible because I know Akiva is safe, loved, and learning so much that it's hard to keep up with him. I am fortunate to have such incredible partners in helping him grow into a kind person. You have no idea how much I appreciate and admire you.

And to Jason and Akiva. You are my home and my heart. I love you more than all the stars. . . .

# AN UNQUIET PEACE

## ABOUT THIS GUIDE

The suggested questions are included to enhance your
group's reading of Shaina Steinberg's
*An Unquiet Peace*!

1. What made you want to read this book? Did it live up to your expectations? *An Unquiet Peace* fits into a lot of different genres such as historical fiction, mystery and noir. Do any of those specifically appeal to you and why?

2. If you read *Under The Paper Moon*, the first book in the series, how does this compare? Which themes continued and which changed? Do you have a favorite part of either book?

3. Helen, one of Nick's long-lost friends, reappears asking for his help. Do you think they would be friends if they met for the first time as adults? Have you ever reconnected with an old friend? Was it a good experience?

4. One of the themes throughout this book is friendship—specifically between Evelyn, Colette, and Lily. Also, between Nick, Evelyn, and Carl. How do you think they support each other? What do you think Tom Rivers misses out on by not having a close group of friends? How do your friends support you?

5. While Evelyn loves Nick, she is nervous about marriage, for fear of losing her independence. What do you think this says about Evelyn and Nick's relationship? Is true love an absence of doubt?

6. Evelyn's Aunt Taffy shows up to help plan Evelyn's wedding. She can be overwhelming at times. How are she and Evelyn different? How are they alike? Is there anyone in your family who can be a bit much? If so, how do you deal with them?

7. Wealth and class are a theme throughout the book. Nick and Helen grew up with very little. Evelyn and

Taffy always had more than they needed. How are each of their characters shaped by their economic background? What other factors shape someone's personality? What do you think most influences children as they grow into adults?

8. Unlike her previous life, Evelyn finds herself in the newspapers a lot. Do you think she enjoys it? What are the advantages and the drawbacks of being a media figure? If you could be famous, would you want that? Why or why not?

9. As a child, Nick committed a variety of crimes. Do you think his stealing is understandable? Are there times when committing a crime is justifiable? If so, which crimes and under what circumstances?

10. The Berlin airlift was an incredibly tense time in American-Soviet relations. Back in the States, opinions were divided, with some people thinking that America should not help their former enemies. Other people specifically made parachutes for the candy pilots would throw to children. Are there any world events you feel strongly about? Do you discuss them with friends, family, or strangers? Why or why not?

11. Towards the end of the book, Evelyn loses something precious to her. How do you think that will change her? Have you ever lost something very meaningful?

12. In the *Under The Paper Moon*, Nick and Evelyn worked on a single case together. In *An Unquiet Peace* they each have their own case. How much do they help each other? Do you think they're more effective as a team or as individuals?

13. How much do you think the title and cover of this book represents the story?

14. If you were casting this movie, who would be your dream actor for each role?

15. Where do you want to see Evelyn and Nick go from here?